Praise for Nicole C

"A dizzying story about one individual's confrontation with the transient nature of reality, and what this encounter strips away within her. A sharp, quirky adventure that overlaps alien abduction, horror, conspiracy, cryptids and existential dread in a way that only Nicole Cushing could manage to pull off."

—Brian Evenson, author of
Song for the Unraveling of the World

Praise for Nicole Cushing's *A Sick Gray Laugh*

"Noelle Cashman—I mean Nicole Cushing—has delivered a shocking and satirical survey of the failed American experiment and its many horrifying discontents. *A Sick Gray Laugh*'s warts-and-all metanarrative is reminiscent of such recent genre touch-stones as Caitlin R. Kiernan's *The Red Tree* and Gemma Files's *Experimental Film*, but told in a brutal and uncompromising style that is all Cushing's own."

—Robert Levy, author of *The Glittering World*

Praise for Nicole Cushing's *Mr. Suicide*

"…a work of brutal and extreme horror… disturbingly graphic content…"

—*Publishers Weekly*

"This tale of a damaged and murderous child is the most original horror novel I've read in years. Cushing's prose is rapid-fire, grisly, and passionate."

—Poppy Z. Brite, author of *Exquisite Corpse* and *Lost Souls*

Praise for Nicole Cushing's *Mr. Suicide* (continued)

"Novels don't come much more transgressive than this one, folks. Got a taboo? Watch Nicole Cushing grin while she dances all over it. In other hands that might be reason enough for the witty *Mr. Suicide* to exist. But this is more and better than that—a truly nightmare world, richly imagined, told to us in a canny, subversive second-person voice that makes you, the reader, the hero of this tale, like it or not. That it also manages to be ultimately life-affirming is yet another wonder."

—Jack Ketchum, award-winning author of
Off Season and *The Girl Next Door*

"Nicole Cushing uses her sharp and confident prose like a surgical instrument to dissect both her characters and our emotions. *Mr. Suicide* is horrifying and harrowing, but just as much for the emotional devastation it causes in the reader as for the violence and depravity—as well as the twisted humor—it portrays. This is horror fiction that leaves marks."

—Ray Garton, author of
Live Girls and *Sex and Violence in Hollywood*

Praise for Nicole Cushing's *Children of No One*

"The confidence and expertise so blatantly evident in Nicole Cushing's writing is astonishing."

—Thomas Ligotti

MOTHWOMAN

MOTHWOMAN

Nicole Cushing

WORD HORDE
PETALUMA, CA

First Edition

ISBN 978-1-956252-04-0

A Word Horde Book

To Arachne, Spinner of Truths

Part One: Home

1

The alien in the illustration has chalk-white skin and pouty lips. The eyes seem glassy, unfocused. A gray helmet (or helmet-shaped turban) adorns the head; a wolf-like ear emerges from one side.

The alien wears a gray uniform with a question mark emblazoned on the chest. He's embracing a chalk-white, fox-like creature that has a single horn emerging from its forehead.

Of course, this may not be an alien at all. It's impossible to say exactly what the artist had in mind. She may have wanted to depict a demigod, or some demented superhero. For that matter, I'm not even certain about the identity of the artist. Pat Steir is credited with "cover design". Does that mean she drew the image? Or does it only mean that she selected it, and the title font, and the byline font, and figured out the ideal spatial relations between the three?

What can I say, for certain, about this illustration? Only that the publishing firm of Harper & Row found it suitable for the cover of its 1968 paperback edition of *Myth and Reality*. The book's genre? Scholarly nonfiction—an examination of mythological themes that have recurred throughout history.

The author? A Romanian named Mircea Eliade.

I'm reading it now.

Well, I'm not reading it *right now*.

Right now, I'm taking a break from reading the book so I can admire that cover art. I have a hunch that if I keep staring at it I'll discover some fascinating, previously unnoticed detail. Throughout my life, in many different contexts, I've found staring to be a useful tactic.

When I'm not staring at the cover I'm compulsively smelling the pages. They're humid.

Well, that's not quite accurate. If I tell you: "they're humid", you'll assume they're slightly damp to the touch. You may think they smell of mildew. That's not what I mean. It's more subtle than that. What I mean is, they may have been *exposed to humidity* sometime in the past. They're *half*-humid. Haunted by the *ghost* of humidity.

I bought this edition of *Myth and Reality* from a used book store. That said, I'm not certain this book was ever really *used*. It looks like the kind of book someone bought for a college class, but never read.

Such a sad-looking book. I imagine that it languished for years on the bookshelf of the student who never read it. Long after she graduated, she kept it around as a trophy of her education. (She needed something "deep" on her shelves to counterbalance all the knick-knacks and stuffed animals.)

Maybe the plan worked, and visitors to the student's apartment noticed her bookshelves. Maybe, after scanning a shelf and coming across the title *Myth and Reality*, the visitors decided she could be taken seriously (but, as the stuffed Snoopy doll right next to the book testified, *not too seriously*).

On the other hand, maybe the student never had any visitors to her apartment. Maybe she suffered from insomnia. Maybe she had no coping skills with which to navigate the post-college world. Everything had been so structured, in college. There were clubs and classes and parties. Even if you didn't attract boys, you could pretend they noticed you. Even if you didn't care about the classes, they gave you something to do. Even if you didn't have friends, you could find drinking buddies. You could forge pseudo-friendships. You could become some more popular girl's hanger on.

Okay, maybe you couldn't be *the* most popular girl's hanger on, but you could be a hanger on for a third-tier girl. Even if you weren't the queen bee (or a lady-in-waiting for the queen bee) you could still feel the buzz of the hive.

But I digress. The important thing is that, at some point (years later), the student died. Granted, I don't know if that's true. Nonetheless, I'm including it because these daydreams of mine, these little stories I invent, benefit from a dollop of pathos.

And let's say that after the student died, her aunt went through her apartment. And maybe that aunt held no real sentiment for the student. So, the aunt threw almost everything into the trash. In fact, only two objects survived the cull: the stuffed Snoopy and the unread 1968 edition of *Myth and Reality*.

The aunt imagined an *Antiques Roadshow* sort of moment. She'd take both objects to a secondhand store, where they'd be appraised and found to be Valuable Collector's Items.

This did not happen. The dude behind the counter refused to take the Snoopy doll, as one of the seams on its right ear had torn open. He did give the aunt forty-nine cents for *Myth and Reality*. Of course, he later priced it at $4.99. He had to make his profit.

To be clear: that last part, in which I related the price of the book, is the only part of this little story that's demonstrably true. I know that part because I bought the book from that exact dude, behind that exact counter, for that exact price, five years ago. Yes, I bought it five years ago. I'm only now getting around to reading it.

I probably shouldn't invest so much time in making up little stories. But that's the kind of person I am: I enjoy making up little stories about the previous owners of the books I find at secondhand shops.

I enjoy making up little stories about lots of things. It kills time.

I used to think time was too precious to kill. Now that I'm unemployed, I know better. Work is toil, yes. I hate work. But the only thing I hate more than work is the absence of work. Work means money. Even more importantly, work is Something to Do.

Without work, I find myself staying in bed for too long, inhaling the sour odor of unwashed socks and gazing up at the mountain range of dust growing atop the ceiling fan. Sometimes I get tired of the view. Women aren't supposed to live in such conditions. Not even single, middle-aged women. We can be hoarders, I suppose. Crazy cat ladies. We're given that freedom. But we're not supposed to have mountains of dust on our ceiling fans. Nor are we supposed to have disgusting bathrooms.

I have both, and live completely alone. I have no man to blame. Nor am I a cat owner. I am the sole architect of my squalor.

Sometimes, I have to stop looking at the mess. So, I turn the fan on. When the blades whirl around, the motion makes them blurry. That way, I don't have to look at the dust. I can lie in bed, stare at the ceiling, and pretend everything's normal.

I know I should clean the ceiling fan. It would not only improve my view, it would provide a sense of accomplishment. For that matter, why stop at the ceiling fan? I could make a list of five things to clean every day, make checkmarks next to the tasks as I complete them, and feel an even greater sense of accomplishment.

That would be a reasonable approach. It would make sense. I'd feel so much lighter, so much freer as a result.

But I can't be reasonable. Something irrational, heavy, and intrusive has taken over my brain. It weighs my head down. Yes, my skull is every bit as heavy as a cinderblock. My neck would break if it had to support such a burden on its own! So, I must always lie down.

No, that's not the case. I exaggerate.

I can get up to turn the ceiling fan on. I can get up to piss and shit and check the mail and go to the grocery store.

The truth: I *can* move, but have decided the rewards of cleanliness aren't worth the effort required to obtain them. My mother would say I'm lazy. If I were to confide in her about the irrational, heavy, intrusion she would say I was being gratuitously weird. Only, she wouldn't use the word "gratuitously". Such words are beyond her. She would simply scowl and say "You're *weird*!" My weirdness has always exasperated and disgusted her. Her ignorance has always exasperated and disappointed me. She and I do not think alike. Not even remotely alike. My thinking is a foreign language to her, and vice-versa. We look exactly alike, facially. We have the same dishwater blond hair too. It's even styled the same. But we're nothing alike, in our souls.

Bottom line: I know I'm not lazy. I know the irrational, heavy intrusion is real. I can't see it, but it's there.

I know it has a name. I know that name rhymes with "recession". I know our society has said it's a disease. I know there are doctors who could, for a price, provide a cure. A pill, a potion, an incantation, a validation. Pharmaceutical corporations make a fortune off such magic. They're always advertising on TV.

I don't trust anything advertised on TV.

I fear I'm coming across as cynical (or even paranoid). I don't want to come across as cynical (let alone paranoid). I'd love for this irrational, heavy intrusion to be lifted from me. I'm just not convinced the helpers offer anything better.

I have an earnest heart. I would like, more than anything, to believe in the goodness of doctors. However, I can't trust them. I've crossed paths with a few of them. They never seem like real people.

2

So, I stay in bed. I read. Or, at least, I admire the cover of the book I'm reading. I think about its previous owner(s). I get up to turn the ceiling fan on. I perform the various and sundry movements necessary to piss and shit. I check the mail. Go to the grocery store.

That's how I spend my days.

But what about my nights?

Well, it's the funniest thing. The irrational, heavy, intrusion lifts after dark. What I mean is, it doesn't lift completely. Darkness isn't *a cure*. It is, however, *a treatment*. It gives me enough energy to walk (or at least shamble) through my neighborhood.

It's puzzling. Why should depression lift, just a little, at nightfall? I can think of no physiological reason for this to be the case. So, to find the answer, we have to look beyond mere physiology. We must look to axiology (the study of value), perhaps even to ontology (the study of being). At least, I *believe* it's in these realms that I discovered a possible answer; that is, a theory that might explain this strange alleviation of my suffering.

I call it The Theory of Nocturnal Purgation. In plain English, I believe my depression lifts after dark because daytime is cluttered and nighttime is clean.

I mean, just think about it. Daylight allows us to see all sorts of objects. Too many objects. The world is now surfeit with objects. Little plastic things. Big plastic things. Ironic things. Action figures. Cute little collectible Funko Pops! Candy. Pills. Rusted-out sheet metal. Plastic grocery bags. Squirrels. Broken glass. Dogs with only three legs. Dogs cross-bred with coyotes. Ridiculous small dogs. Cats with debilitating mutations. Televisions infected with talking heads. Screaming heads. Doll heads. Shrunken heads. Secondhand books with strange cover art. Store brand soda cans. Store brand cereal boxes. Obsolete electronics. Phones and stop lights and microwaves and refrigerators.

Homo sapiens was never meant to look at so many objects. They rush, en masse, at our eyeballs. They clog up our pupils the way leaves clog up gutters.

Oh, and speaking of eyes, they're objects too—just like tongues, breasts, and armpit hairs. Objects are all over the place. We're enclosed within certain objects (e.g., houses) and *we enclose other objects within us* (apples, hot dogs, Twinkies). We are like those nested Russian matryoshka dolls, simultaneously surrounded by objects and surround*ing* objects.

No doubt, the number of objects has proliferated exponentially since the dawn of mass production and the invention of molded plastic. Surely, more objects exist on Earth than have ever existed here before. (Cavemen knew nothing of venetian blinds and phone chargers, step ladders and stuffed animals. Theirs was a simpler, purer world. Earth, wind, fire, watering holes, animals—that was all they had to worry about. Sturdy objects, all of them.)

Our modern objects are anything but sturdy. The increase in the quantity has necessitated a decrease in quality. Objects are flimsier than they used to be. Uglier than they used to be. Mutable, meltable, disposable.

During the daylight hours I'm forced to look at all the crap in my house. I become aware that I'm surrounded by layers of junk. I ruminate on how *everyone* is surrounded by layers of junk. (Even people with uncluttered houses. Their junk might be better organized, but it's still junk.)

We are all shrouded and suffocated *under* junk.

We, ourselves, *are* junk. (No exceptions.)

We shroud and suffocate other bits of junk *within us*.

Nighttime purges this Hell from my sight. I'm still shrouded and suffocated by junk, but I'm less aware of it.

I sense an objection. (Ha! "*Object*ion".) Is "junk" the right word? Isn't that too dismissive? Are newborn babies and mighty sequoias merely "objects"? How can I possibly dismiss them as such? If we consider each of them one at a time, as abstract mental images, taken alone, they seem to transcend such classification. They seem magnificent.

But that takes us to the crux of the issue: in *real life*, they're never isolated. Never alone. Thus, never untainted. When it emerges from the womb, the newborn is slathered in all sorts of unpleasant gunk (a casserole of blood, amniotic fluid, waxy vernix, etc.). Yes, of course, the casserole is soon washed off. But other objects soon take its place.

When *gunk* disappears, *junk* fills the void. For example, the mewing goblin finds itself wrapped in a plastic diaper, under a Walmart onesie. It finds itself placed within the confines of a hand-me-down crib, forced to stare up at a cracked ceiling. To be born is to be smothered in junk.

I've discussed the objects *surrounding* the baby. But what objects does *the baby surround*? Urine in the bladder. Feces in the intestines. Tears holed up in ducts, waiting for an excuse to escape.

As for the sequoias, they're also better considered in a vacuum. Taken alone, out of context, they ooze grandeur. But Nature abhors a vacuum. It sadistically insists on prohibiting solitude. Thus, the sequoias suffer under the footfalls of squirrels. Birdshit stains their leaves. Even worse, some have been partially hollowed out to allow cars to pass through them. Behold the obscenity: turds tucked inside humans, humans tucked inside cars, cars tucked inside sequoias, sequoias covered in birdshit. Junk nested within junk, shit nested within shit, ad infinitum.

Thus, darkness is a blessing. Night hides things. When one takes a walk down a suburban street at midnight, one is troubled by relatively few objects.

Now you may be thinking to yourself: *But what about the stars?* The existence of stars complicates matters. There are hundreds of them visible in the night sky, right? And therefore, nighttime is even more glutted with objects than day!

Perhaps.

But when was the last time you saw hundreds of stars in the night sky? I live in a little working class subdivision. Lights from a nearby city shine brightly enough to keep most stars at bay. Besides, there's an easy way to protect oneself from the nuisance of stars: never look up.

3

Anyway, where was I? Ah yes, energy.

I should clarify: the energy required to shamble isn't a *great deal* of energy. However, it's far more energy than I can summon by day. (A clarification: although I just described a nocturnal surge of energy, I am not a vampire. Vampires aren't the only ones energized by night, you know! Also, don't pay too much attention to the verb "shamble". I'm not a zombie. Zombies aren't the only ones who shamble!)

I leave my house around ten p.m. I turn and twist through a half-dozen Drives, Courts, and Circles; cul de sacs, intersections, side streets, and main thoroughfares.

I encounter no vehicular traffic.

I'm the only pedestrian.

If you could stretch all the streets out, end to end, they would run twenty miles. But they're squished together, claustrophobically, into a square mile. In this way, my neighborhood is like an abdomen. Its streets are like intestines. I'm a rebellious chunk of meat that swims against the tide of gastric acids. I refuse to be digested into a good night's sleep.

Even though I'm not very pretty, I carry a little tube of pepper spray with me. Not just on these walks, but everywhere. My mother always warned me that a woman doesn't have to be beautiful to get raped. I know this to be true.

And speaking of precautions, it's best to wear a jacket outside at this time of year. That way, you don't catch a cold. I realize it's silly to worry about a cold. A far nastier virus is hacking its way through America. In all honesty, I don't worry about catching a cold. But *children* should worry about catching colds. I think we all agree on that point.

Last night was Halloween. Indiana is full of Covid deniers, so trick-or-treating flourished per usual. The temperature dipped under fifty degrees. I turned on the heat for the first time since April. I turned on the heat and I turned out the lights. (Lights encourage trick-or-treaters and I didn't buy candy to hand out to them.)

Actually, that's a lie.

I *had* bought some candy to give out to the youngsters, but I ate it all. Tootsie Rolls. Tootsie Fruit Chews. Tootsie Pops. Fifty pieces. I was running low on actual food and wasn't in the mood to go shopping. So, I ate all the candy instead. Breakfast: Tootsie Rolls. Lunch: Tootsie Fruit Chews. Dinner: Tootsie Pops.

I finished off the candy and I hid in my shabby dark house, listening to the sound of little feet scuffling across sidewalks. Little yips and little laughs. Mothers forcing their children to act polite ("Say 'Thank you!'"). Kids doing what they're told, playing the role of sullen ventriloquist's dummies, mumbling unconvincing expressions of gratitude to their benefactors.

I thought the cold might keep them away, but I looked out the window and saw little dark shapes leaping in the lamplight. Leaping and laughing, bragging and bullying. It was hard to tell if they were wearing coats. They should have been wearing coats, but I'm not certain they were.

I would be a terrible parent. I'd make my child wear a jacket, but I would go without one. "Do as I say, not as I do."

I always carry pepper spray when I leave the house, but I seldom wear a jacket. One is a matter of safety, the other a matter of comfort. That said, I would not allow a child to carry pepper spray. No matter how much they begged, I'd refuse. Because I would be a good parent.

"But *you* carry it, Mom!"

"Do as I say, not as I do."

This is all a daydream. I have no children and I'm afraid of men, so I'll drop the subject.

I leave the house without a jacket, without so much as a long-sleeved shirt. I'm wearing a T-shirt, sneakers, and jeans. My little tube of pepper spray dangles from my keychain. Or, more accurately, my keys dangle under my little tube of pepper spray. I say "more accurately" because I'm holding the pepper spray in my hand, at the ready, and letting the keys dangle underneath.

The keys jingle in the otherwise-noiseless night. *Ke-she, ke-sha, ke-she, ke-sha.* I wonder if this noise puts me at risk. I'm announcing my presence to any assailant poised in the shadows.

The street lamps look like strange, branchless trees. Blobs of light grow out from the tops, like mutant fruit. But enough about pseudo-trees. I need to tell you about my neighborhood's *actual trees*. There's something wrong with them. They're acting up.

What I mean is, they're violently swaying and rustling. Violently rustling and swaying. They're moving the way normal trees move in response to a thirty mile per hour gale.

Only, there is no thirty mile per hour gale. There doesn't seem to be any wind *at all*. At least, I don't *feel* any wind on my face. My hair isn't getting blown over my glasses, the way it ordinarily does in a windstorm. Nor do I hear empty beer cans rolling on the pavement as they're blown out of recycling bins.

The trees say: "Look! Wind!"

My hair replies: "You're mistaken!"

A beer can in a recycling bin piles on: "*Quite* mistaken."

I make up a little story about why the trees are so out-of-synch with their surroundings: they uttered their lines too soon, before the wind walked onstage. Either that or the wind missed its cue. Nature is a staged spectacle, featuring actors not quite up to their parts.

But before I have a chance to fully explore the possibilities of that little story, another coalesces in my brain. Perhaps there are thin, translucent wires connecting all the tree branches to the arms of hidden puppeteers. *These puppeteers* are the reason why the branches (and only the branches) are moving.

The head puppeteer's name is Giuseppe. He runs a small corporation hired to perpetrate subtle hoaxes like this. One of my neighbors has hired them to fuck with me. Somehow, this corporation knows I walk each night around ten p.m. They waited for a completely windless night and set to work creating a pseudo-wind event.

Giuseppe is mute. So are all his employees. That's why they can pull off the ruse: they work in total silence.

I know there's no such person as Giuseppe. I mean, it's a rare name, in my part of the world. That said, there could be *someone* of that name in my neighborhood. It's not impossible. But what I'm saying is: I realize there's no such thing as a man named Giuseppe *who uses puppetry skills to make it seem like tree branches move in the absence of wind.* And yet, the world is more interesting when I pretend to believe my own little story about him. More interesting and, strangely, more satisfying. Some explanation is better than no explanation at all.

 A related truth: if one must interact with neighbors, it's best that those interactions be imaginary. For, now more than ever, flesh and blood interactions mean trouble. Not just trouble, disease!

Covid-19 might kill you, or it might maim your lungs, or it might hit you no worse than the common cold, or it might give you blood clots, or it might slow down your brain function, or it might result in chronic fatigue, or it might not cause you any symptoms at all. Everything's ambiguous until it's not, right?

As I round the corner from Tripoli Drive to Fort Niagara Avenue, I stumble over an uneven sidewalk. Tree roots have forced one slab of concrete to jut higher than the adjoining slab, and I trip over it.

This has happened to me about a dozen times in the fifteen years I've lived in the neighborhood. So far, I've been able to avoid a full-fledged, disastrous tumble. Tonight is no exception. I make a few tiptoe gallops to keep from falling. Then, a few sliding steps that slow things down. I feel myself whirling toward the ground, so I shift my weight to achieve balance. Then one more gallop on tiptoe. One more sliding step. Finally, I am upright and steady.

I suppose I should feel lucky I didn't crash onto the ground. Instead, I feel self-conscious. Embarrassed. Even though I don't see anyone, I suspect I'm being stared at. It's highly likely, when you think about it. Why *wouldn't* someone stare at me? My stumble was stare-worthy. When two people coexist on the same street, and one of them stumbles, the other will stare.

But is there anyone else nearby? Glancing about, I see no one.

I put little stock in this observation, though. Sight is the most deceptive of senses. Judging by sight, one would say the sun rotates around the Earth, rather than vice-versa. Judging by sight, one would say there's a face on the moon. Sometimes, you've got to ignore visual proof and rely on your intuitive sixth sense.

I may not *see* someone staring at me, but I physically *feel* a pair of eyes boring into me. And though I attribute this sensation to an "intuitive sixth sense", I should emphasize that there's nothing flighty or ethereal about it. It's a visceral experience. When I say The Eyes bore into me, I mean that they're sawing into me. I am a walking corpse and The Starer is performing a sort of autopsy with bonesaw eyes.

It's humiliating and frightening, to be stared at after stumbling. Even though I didn't fall onto the ground, I feel exposed. It would, perhaps, have been more dignified to allow myself to tumble to the ground. Of course, it would have hurt. I'd have abrasions on my hands and knees, perhaps even on my chin and cheekbones. But it seems to me that tiptoe gallops and sliding steps and whirling have a cartoonish quality to them. They made me look like a Warner Brothers villain, bumbling along in pursuit of a wabbit.

A burning sensation starts in my ears. Spreads to my neck and cheeks.

Yes, someone must be watching me. (Why would I start blushing, if I wasn't being watched? Such reactions don't spontaneously erupt, in the absence of stimuli.)

Perhaps The Starer is merely a neighbor looking out their window.

No, it can't be a neighbor looking out their window. The window would act as a buffer between their eyes and my flesh. It would soften the blow. Their eyes would feel like pinpricks, not bonesaws.

And the eyes feel like bonesaws. Yes, of that there is no doubt.

I take slow steps back to my house. I try to make it seem like I'm walking naturally. However, I'm taking things much slower than normal. Every step presents the risk of a cartoonish stumble. I vow to exhibit a gait free of cartoonish stumbles. I watch where I'm going.

The Starer does, too.

4

I keep hearing the windless wind noise, even after I go inside. Giuseppe and his cronies are nothing if not devoted. I suppose they plan to keep this up all night! I continue to feel vulnerable. Even inside my house, I'm fairly certain someone is staring at me.

If you feel tempted to question my sanity, don't. People know when they're being stared at. This is not a conjecture, but a fact. The next time you're stopped at a traffic light, stare at the driver next to you. If you stare long enough, they'll notice. Perform the experiment multiple times, and you'll find the results consistently replicated. To get away with staring, undetected, you have to keep things brief. One second. Two at most.

The person (or thing) who keeps staring at me must be a novice starer, because they far exceed the two-second limit. Well, either they're a novice, or they're fearless.

Yes, that's it. They're not a novice, not a mere starer. They're A Starer. They may, in fact, be a *virtuoso* in the art of staring. It's just that, in this case, they don't care if they're noticed. Perhaps they even *want* to be noticed. They want to pollute the darkness with their presence.

Or maybe I'm not the sole subject of their staring. Maybe I was initially, outside, but now they alternate between staring *at me* and staring *at all the clutter in this house*. Yes, it could be that the Staring Thing (or, if you prefer, The Thing That Stares) has never seen a messier house. It would like to do me harm but can't find a route to get to me, through all the clutter.

Too many *objects*. Piles of laundry. Stacks of unopened mail. Little plastic screws and metal coat hangers. Recycling I keep meaning to haul to the curb. Used books. Used bookmarks. Used bookbags. Cracked DVD cases. Wide-eyed ceramic owls. Holiday decorations. Gifts I never delivered to their intended recipient. Pictures of pets that have since crossed the rainbow bridge. A VHS copy of *Bridge Over the River Kwai.*

But how can The Staring Thing see all the clutter? The house is dark. I've not turned on the lights.

The Staring Thing isn't human. He can see in the dark.

A complication: all remains silent. I can't hear an intruder.

Maybe the intruder is mute, like Giuseppe and his underlings.

No, that's impossible. Giuseppe and his underlings aren't real. They're characters in one of my little stories. The Starer, on the other hand, is real.

Unless I invented The Starer and *forgot I invented him.* This is all just a little too much like Poe, isn't it? (By which I mean too much like "The Tell-Tale Heart".) It's the middle of the night. I'm old. I'm alone. I fear the presence of an unseen assailant. I'm just like the victim in the story.

In the story, when the old man begins to feel the presence of a Starer, he cries out "Who's there?!"

And now, here I am, crying out "Who's there?!"

No answer.

I keep my little tube of pepper spray with me. I hold it tight in my hands. I consider the idea of spraying the tube in random directions, on the off chance I might hit my target. But instead, I turn on the lights.

Nothing.

I turn on the television. I hate the television, but on nights like this the noise helps calm my nerves. Even the daily list of local catastrophes, read from a teleprompter by humanikins, is better than worrying about a Starer.

(A humanikin is a human being who has been possessed by the spirit of a manikin. Humanikins have taken over the media.)

I'm on the sofa, watching the eleven o'clock news. What could be more normal? I hear a weather report, prophesying an overnight low of twenty-nine degrees. "You might see some frost on your mums," a tall blond humanikin says to a rugged, broad-shouldered humanikin. The rugged, broad-shouldered humanikin chuckles. I have no idea why he's chuckling. The blonde didn't even make a joke. But he's chuckling.

Humanikins are always laughing at unfunny shit.

I want to stay awake. I keep my pepper spray at the ready. I put my feet up on the coffee table to get more comfortable. I watch commercials. I watch a national news item about Covid-19, dumbed down to a fourth grade level of understanding. The humanikins have sanded away all of the story's complexities. This angers me.

Anger at the news. Anger at the nation. Sweet, distracting anger.

Too sweet, actually. So sweet it softens into unfocused, vague, drowsy anger.

I need coffee.

Throughout this day, my brain has processed many words and phrases and feelings. Now, late at night, my brain fails. Discrete phrases and thoughts melt into each other. *I need anger. I feel coffee.*

And then, I'm hit by a wave of cognitive entropy. By which I mean, phrases drift apart from one another. Words and letters devolve even as I'm trying to reassemble them in my head.

I need anger becomes *Knee-anner.*

I feel coffee becomes *Fecal fee.*

And *then* (as if matters weren't bad enough), they devolve one more time. They can no longer even pretend to be words.

Knee-anner becomes *Nuh-ahn. Fecal fee* becomes *Feek-fuh.* The arc of consciousness is long but bends towards nonsense!

There's the nonsense of a brain on the cusp of sleep. Then there's the nonsense of the dreaming brain, the pulsing shadow shows. Earth flipping inside out. Air flipping inside out. Fire flipping inside out. Water staying just as it is. Dead tongues. Screaming skin. A slamming storm door.

I wake before sunrise, fearful of The Ghost of Nonsense Yet to Come. I fell asleep on the couch, with my feet up on the coffee table. That's probably why I woke up early. That position puts pressure on my back. I'm all fucked up with arthritis. Agitation plays a role, too. I fell asleep in a state of vigilance, therefore I awaken in a state of vigilance.

Or, at least, *drowsy* vigilance. A strange sort of vigilance that would rather go back to sleep. A strange sort of drowsiness that would rather spring into action. It takes a few moments for anyone to get their bearings, in such a state of mind.

Have I gotten my bearings? I can't say. All I know is that I'm looking around for The Thing That Stares.

It's gone. Yes, of that I'm certain. Gone, or at least, moved to another part of the house. I search all over. Under beds. In closets. Even under chairs and tables. (Who knows? The Thing That Stares might be an animal.)

Was it ever truly there, inside my home? Perhaps it was actually lurking *outside* the house the entire time. Yes, it could have been staring at me the entire time, through a window.

I open my front door to look for clues. Footprints in the frost, that sort of thing. This proves to be unnecessary. The clues find me! By this, I mean that my storm door is all fogged up. The Thing That Stares wrote a message in that fog, using its finger. The message reads:

HTAERB YM YB EM ON LLIW U

More nonsense! Perhaps a foreign language? A code? I have not yet had my coffee. I find my phone and take a photo of it, to document it, to prove it's real and not just one of my little stories. But the sun is hitting the storm door at an odd angle. Glare ruins the picture. So, I transcribe the message, instead.

After a few sips of coffee, I feel stupid. It's not a code! The Starer wrote the message from outside the storm door. I was looking at it from inside the house, hence reading it backwards. The message was meant to be read as:

U WILL NO (sic) ME BY MY BREATH

5

You might imagine I'm getting goosebumps. Maybe you think I'm dry heaving, or hyperventilating or whimpering. After all, that would be the *rational* response to an intrusion of The Irrational.

But my response to The Irrational is irrational. I feel a sense of relief, because the message scrawled in the fogged-up door proves The Starer exists. I might be in danger, but at least I'm not mad.

I make my coffee (instant, hazelnut). I sip my coffee. I run my fingers through my hair.

So, I will know The Starer by its breath?

A comical aside: does this mean it will have terrible breath? *Distinctly* terrible breath? Breath so idiosyncratically rank that it could be picked out of a lineup?

That's funny, I suppose. But only mildly funny. It's not up to my usual standards of hilarity. Therefore, it does nothing to calm my nerves. A mediocre joke is a deflating joke.

Maybe I'm being too harsh in my self-assessment. That's possible, I suppose, but irrelevant. Even if I am being too harsh in my self-assessment, the moment of mirth is gone. It's been replaced by a spirit of clinical detachment. A desire to face up to facts about my comedic skill (or lack thereof).

A shift. The investigation into my comedy chops gets over-shadowed by the need to collate and analyze all the known facts about The Starer.

Fact: I was observed by a Starer last night.

Fact: Using his finger this Starer scrawled a message on my fogged-up storm door. ("His" finger? Am I certain it's a man? Are there no other possibilities? The Starer could be a woman or nonbinary or even a ghost. The Ghost of Nonsense Yet to Come!)

Fact: I don't believe in ghosts.

Fact: The messenger wants to meet me. (Why else provide a clue about his—or rather, its—identity?) Yes, it wants to meet me. Or, at least, it wants me to recognize it at some future point when our paths cross.

And now my mood changes again! It starts with a physical sensation in my forehead. I get the sense that it's drooping down into my eyes, like a shar pei's forehead. At the same time, fatigue hits. I've pushed my brain too hard. It's not possible to sustain this analysis. Objectivity before breakfast is doomed to wilt.

And wilt it does.

My arms and lower back start to itch. I'm sweating. Dizzy illness rushes in to fill the void left by departed reason. My stomach plunges. I rush to the bathroom. Nervous diarrhea.

I'm on the toilet when Mother calls. I don't pick up, of course. I look at the vibrating rectangle and wish I could throw it in the toilet. Why not? Every word I speak into that machine is nothing more than verbal excrement. Not meaningful words, but rather the waste products of words. Perfunctory lies. ("Yes, of course, it's good to hear from you Mom.") Insincere valida-tions. ("I agree, that *wasn't* very neighborly of Mr. Cosgrove.")

My cell phone is a verbal port-a-potty but I carry it around in my front pocket all day and pretend it's not disgusting.

I'm still astride the toilet, wiping my ass, when I hear a bleeping-blooping sound. It's just my phone, informing me that Mom has left a message. This is a morning for messages! One, cryptic, scrawled in window fog. Another recorded with merciless digital clarity.

I would like to put off answering Mom's message, because I think I know the kind of statements that await me. Mom doesn't like leaving messages. You can hear the disdainful tone in her voice whenever she's forced to use voicemail.

Perhaps I'm wrong. Tone is, after all, in the eye of the beholder. Perhaps I'm reading something into these communications, hearing disdain where none exists. I suppose there's no way to know for certain (I mean, with *one hundred percent* certainty), that her tone is one of disdain. I should be wary of jumping to conclusions. That said, it doesn't take long to find corroborating evidence for my theory. For you see, it's not just the tone of Mom's speech that's disdainful. The *content* is, too. The guilt trips. The passive-aggression.

Take, for example, the message I hear coming out from my cell phone's speaker right now. "I'm sorry to bother you," Mom says. "I know you have a life of your own, in Indiana. But we're up to our necks in a terrible mess. It's all just a nice big mess. I thought you might want to know about it, even if you can't help."

Then, a click. (Her landline receiver plopping back onto its cradle.) No "good bye". No "I love you". Just a click.

I'm washing my hands, and wishing I could wash out my ears. You know, use disinfectant to sanitize them. Kill the drama germs. But she's my mother. I'm her daughter. Even though my umbilical cord rotted decades ago, in a bag full of medical waste, I remain connected to her. We share a history. We share a face. I look just like her. Well, I'm a foot taller than her. And, of course, I'm younger than her. She's gray-haired and wrinkled and crippled with arthritis. I'm still blond. My wrinkles are limited to laugh lines. My arthritis is more a nuisance than a disability. But it's pointless to focus on the differences. We share a face! Whenever I look at her, I'm looking at The Ghost of Me Yet to Come!

And now I can feel my pulse in my neck. And soon, my skin starts to burn. The physical manifestations of anxiety, mere thoughts transmuted into physical sensations. Words made flesh.

I'm inside the house. It's early morning. The sun has risen but it bears no heat. Nonetheless, my skin feels sunburnt! I'm flushed. Nervous. I don't want to call Mom back.

I call Mom back.

"I know you have a life of your own, in Indiana," Mom says. "But, oh, we're up to our necks in trouble."

This repetition isn't a sign of senility. Mom has always enjoyed repeating herself. I sometimes wonder if she scripts her calls out ahead of time. So often, she seems to be reading lines. So often, she seems to be performing the role of the woman scorned.

"Your sister has Covid. In the hospital. At least, that's what she claims. She's calling from the hospital. The caller ID says so. But maybe she's just calling from a *pay phone* in the hospital *lobby*, you know?"

Mom apparently hasn't gotten the news about the pay phone's demise.

"I mean, she just sounds like she has a bad cold, to me. Maybe she's saying she's in the hospital with Covid when in fact she's just too lazy to take care of your father."

Father is elderly. Father is a bed-bound invalid who does not remember who I am. Father requires constant care.

"I hate to ask you this, but can you help? Help your poor dear old mother? Help with your father, I mean. I don't need any help, but it's your father, you see, who needs it. Your father. How will I change his Depends if I don't have someone to help? I can't lift him by myself! Your sister used to help, but she says she's sick."

The government has discouraged interstate travel. Driving cross-country entails risk, even in the best of times. I don't relish the idea of driving seven hundred miles, over the Appalachians, to visit a home boiling over with empty ugliness. Redneck dysfunction on par with *The Jerry Springer Show*. Tragic madness on par with a Russian novel.

But do I want to stay at home, stalked by The Starer?

I mumble certain meaningless phrases into my phone. Verbal farting. Verbal feces. Buying time, trying to figure out the right answer. I know she must be desperate, if she's asking me. And even if she's asking disdainfully, she *is* asking.

I want to say something meaningful to her, but I don't think she can handle anything meaningful. So I spout platitudes. "I love you. I want to help. Such a difficult time for everyone. The world has gone crazy. I just don't know."

But then there's a shift. The burning sensation becomes a scalding sensation. Right there, in my living room, I see heat waves. Or maybe heat has nothing to do with it. Whatever the case, the air's wrinkling, twisting, wrapping itself around my neck like a noose. I can no longer speak into the phone. I can only whimper and wince. I can no longer hold on to the phone. The world starts to tilt. Everything gets foggy. My eyes start steaming up like a bathroom mirror. A weakness seizes my knees. I'm still talking to her, but my speech has devolved into glossolalia.

Or am I just speaking backwards?

6

When I come to, I'm driving.

No, that's not the right way of putting it. "Driving" implies that I have some control over the vehicle. I don't. I'm drifting in and out of lanes. Horns blast against my ears like flak against a warplane.

A strange vocalization escapes my mouth: a kind of gurgling, inhuman wail. I flail my hands around the steering wheel, hoping to steady the car. It works. No accident! You would think the other drivers would be grateful for my efforts! But no. As they race past me, more horn blasts (this time accompanied by middle fingers). A filthy, gaunt old man crossing the bridge on a moped has the gall to turn his head, stare at me, and scowl.

So, I try to suddenly transform myself into the archetype of a responsible driver. I get my bearings. There's a gray sky above me, gray steel beside me, and brown water below. In the background, the humble, gray skyline of Louisville. Only a dozen modest skyscrapers. The biggest of them looks like a great gray dick (a long shaft crowned by a rounded tip).

Such observations can only lead to one conclusion: I'm crossing the Ohio River on the Kennedy Bridge. Yes, I'm on the Kennedy Bridge, technically still in Indiana. But now... *now*...a sign says I'm no longer in Indiana. I have crossed over into Kentucky. "Lincoln's Birthplace", the sign declares. Did you know that Abraham Lincoln *spent his boyhood and adolescence* in Indiana, but was an *infant and toddler* in Kentucky? Therefore, in a way, it's almost like I'm traveling back through time.

Such a weird thought! I don't want to be weird. My brain's just wired this way. At least I'm not speaking in glossolalia anymore. Nonetheless I'm jumping to conclusions. I'm drawing a comparison between traveling across a state border and traveling through time. I'm making weird associations, but at least I *know* I'm making weird associations. Just as I was able to straighten the trajectory of the car, I'll be able to rein in the wildness of my thoughts.

No, I won't.

I won't, because glass is breaking. Not *shattering*, mind you, but cracking; making a spider web pattern on my windshield.

And I won't, because some small bird is croaking and wheezing and spitting up blood on my windshield.

And I won't because this bird wasn't simply mangled by the collision. It was deformed beforehand. It has too many eyes. Maybe ten?

Quite possibly ten, and they're all staring at me from odd places on the bird's body, places where there shouldn't be eyes. On the bird's chest. On its wings. They're all staring. Accusing. Many of them are bleeding. A few seem to be crying. I feel like each and every one of them possesses a soul, and they all blame me for their death.

And I want to speak to the eyes. Explain to them that, at the time of the collision, I was no longer weaving in and out of lanes. I had regained control. The collision is their fault, not mine. I'm on the verge of actually opening my mouth and talking to those eyes…

But then I realize I'm mistaken. Birds don't have ten eyes. And while birds might bleed from their eyes, I'm pretty sure they don't cry when they're upset. The eyes aren't eyes at all. They're just odd patterns in its plumage.

And another correction: it isn't dead. It's struggling. It's struggling and, I swear to…Something…it manages to recover and fly away. (I say "Something" because I don't believe in God.)

Things calm down after that. They would almost have to. Intense strangeness can't go on forever. The Earth gets bored of it after a while. Yes, every time the Earth gets tired of playing make-believe, normality returns.

I'm tired of playing make-believe. This must be make-believe. The bird that hit my windshield wasn't a bird but a large moth. It didn't have a dozen eyes, it just had an odd pattern in its wings. I'm not going back in time. I didn't suddenly come to behind the wheel, I just dissociated for a while. It happens to everyone. There is no such thing as a Starer. There was no message in my fogged-up window. It had started to de-fog and condense into water. The message was just little trickles of water that coalesced into something that *seemed like* words.

Mircea Eliade's *Myth and Reality* is to blame. Granted, Eliade is no true believer. He's merely documenting beliefs across cultures. And yet, the book has stirred up something Jungian in my heart. I don't like it.

Unfamiliar papers catch my attention. They're on top of the dashboard. I grab them, give them a glance. Hotel reservations. Beckley, West Virginia. A place called The Zodiac. A ridiculous name, in the Appalachians!

I've stopped in Beckley plenty of times while traveling east. I'm too old to drive the ten hours straight through to Maryland. I've never stayed at a place called The Zodiac. I've never even *heard of* it.

A GPS app speaks up. The bland white female voice reminds me of the humanikin news anchor. "For the next two hundred and forty-five miles, stay on I-64 East."

I shouldn't comply, but I do.

7

Kentucky is called The Bluegrass State. Everyone learns in kindergarten (or preschool, or even *before* preschool) that grass is green. But Kentucky is called The Bluegrass State. This moniker hints at a broader truth: Kentucky is a state where Things Are Not as They Should Be.

This, of course, is just a little story I tell myself to pass the time. It's been a while since I've told myself a little story. It's a relief to know I can still do it. I haven't confided this in you before, but I had been afraid The Starer had somehow robbed me of my storytelling ability. This would have been a huge loss.

I tend to do better, mentally, when I'm making up little stories. When I'm making up little stories, I know that I am the creator and the story is my creation. There's a pecking order, right? And I'm at the top of it. I've never been at the top of any hierarchy before. It feels good and safe to be in charge of *something*.

Another advantage: when I make up little stories I'm able to simultaneously confront and evade the truth. For example, my little story about bluegrass helps to express my concern that something Unreal is going on, while at the same time keeping that belief at a distance.

I don't see a lot of grass (of any color) on I-64. I see tractor trailers, commuters, and out-of-state cars towing kayaks. There's traffic, but it isn't traffic. What I mean is, the locals will complain about morning traffic, but it's nothing compared to the traffic on the East Coast. I know that when I get to the Baltimore-D.C. corridor, I'll be in Hell.

But there's a long, long way to go.

Cars pass me on both sides. *Whoosh-whoosh!* The speed limit is fifty-five and I'm going sixty-two. I always go seven miles over the speed limit because seven is a lucky number. Everyone else goes twenty or thirty miles over the speed limit. They're in a hurry. I should be in a hurry, but I'm not. In fact, part of me would very much like to get lost.

A memory: when I was nine years old I used to fantasize about being lost in the woods. I grew up close to lots of wooded areas. I grew up in Maryland, yes, but it was an Indiana-esque part of Maryland. A small town. Property adjoining a farm. Forests everywhere.

Every Friday night, Dad would drive us to a nearby town for dinner at McDonald's. Every Friday night, I would look out the car window and stare into the woods. I would pick a spot at random and imagine walking into there with the goal of getting lost. In these daydreams, I was alone. Lost and alone and at peace.

In about a third of these daydreams, my family created a search party to find me. In the aftermath, they showered me with positive attention. I knew I was loved. In the rest of the daydreams, I simply wandered around the woods. I made a life for myself out there. Or I died out there. In either case, it was peaceful.

Jerry Springer isn't peaceful. Russian novels aren't peaceful.

Yes, even now, it would be very helpful to get lost. If I were lost, I could call Mom and tell her I couldn't make it to Maryland. This failure wouldn't be my fault. Something had gone wrong. Somewhere along the way, I had taken the wrong road. Ended up in some backwater.

How far could I push this excuse? Would she actually believe I was so utterly lost that I couldn't possibly find my way to Maryland? No. Even at her advanced age, she would know better. But I could delay my arrival. Yes, certainly, she would believe I was delayed. And that delay might give me time to better prepare myself.

And, of course, I could always exercise the nuclear option. I could fake having Covid.

Could I fake having Covid? Am I really capable of doing that? Would I be able to live with myself in the aftermath, knowing Dad was stuck in a pair of poop-filled Depends because I was too anxious to help him?

No, I couldn't. So, I obey the GPS voice and continue driving on I-64 East.

The sun rises in the east. Therefore, when one travels east one travels back to one's beginnings. My nation began on the East Coast. My life began on the East Coast. That sense I felt on the Kennedy Bridge, the sense of traveling back in time, reasserts itself. Now, it's even stronger than before.

Maybe that sense is bullshit. Yes, I'm being overly dramatic when I say I'm traveling back through time. I'm simply traveling back to the place of my origins. To the place of my nation's origins. That's not the same thing as time travel. At least, I don't think it's the same thing.

I'm seized by a sudden desire to find out what Mircea Eliade thinks about all this. My copy of *Myth and Reality* sits on the passenger seat. I don't remember bringing it, but there it is.

And so now I'm pulling over at a rest stop so I can search the index.

It's far too early in the journey for a rest stop, but I must have answers and I don't want to attempt reading and driving. If only I'd discovered *Myth and Reality* as an audiobook, I could finish it during the drive. It would take longer to find the answer to my question. There'd be no index to search. However, I wouldn't have to stop.

Probably, back in the day, there was a book-on-tape version. You know, a version recorded onto old school audio cassettes.

I'd bet you anything Charlton Heston did the narration. Of course, my car doesn't have a cassette player, so none of these musings amount to a hill of beans.

Anyway, I'm looking for a parking space at the rest stop now. It's the one right after the Shelbyville exit, the cleanest rest stop I've ever visited. The parking lot's only one-third full, but I don't pull into the first available space. I have standards.

What I mean is, I need for there to be at least two empty spaces between me and the closest car. I don't know why I have that requirement, I just do. So I wait until I discover a spot that meets my criteria.

There's one, over to my right.

Some rednecks park their pickup right next to it.

Now (because of my criteria) I have to look for another spot. I coast around the lot some more. I find another space that fits my criteria. A minivan swoops in and takes it. A large Middle Eastern family disembarks. The little boy is hopping around doing the pee pee dance. I harbor no ill will to these folks for taking the spot I had in mind. Potty emergencies take precedence over OCD.

In the distance, about thirty feet away, I see what might be another dream spot. I'm in such a hurry, my tires squeal as I take off for it.

"Hey!" the little boy's father yells. "Hey! Slow down."

I hit the brake. This just makes my tires squeal again. I look in my side view mirror. The father's shaking his fist at me.

I didn't mean to make my tires squeal. I'm embarrassed. I feel even worse when I notice that I've startled the little boy. He's bawling now. His mother is trying to comfort him. A damp circle is spreading from his groin to the hem of his shorts. Urine drips onto the sidewalk. The mother glares in my direction. I hate to be the cause of so much frustration. I can't look anymore.

I coast toward the parking spot that I thought might meet my criteria. I go no more than three miles per hour as I do so.

The spot still meets my criteria! I pull in and notice I'm sweating. My shirt clings to my chest. Even though it's November, I turn on the A.C. That helps calm me down. At around the same time, a whimsical new distraction comes along: an old lady in huge sunglasses. She's walking a skinny, wrinkled poodle on a leash.

Both are decrepit. Neither seems to let it bother them. I observe them carefully, noting the arthritic shuffle each makes along the sidewalk. It's fun to watch them. Decrepit moxie is quite entertaining. I decide that when I am an old lady, I will get a poodle and a pair of huge sunglasses. I am an almost-old lady now. Middle-aged. Before you know it, I'll be eligible to own a poodle and a pair of huge sunglasses.

People use the rest stop to take human toddlers and geriatric poodles to the bathroom.

I suspect I'm the only person pulling into this rest stop to consult a book. Books are far less powerful than they used to be. No one even needs to consult a road atlas these days. But here I am, skimming *Myth and Reality* by Mircea Eliade.

I want to look up "origins" in the index, but I open it up to the table of contents, instead. There, I'm reminded that the second chapter (which I've already read) is titled "Magic and Prestige of 'Origins'". I've underlined many passages. *Too many* passages. People underline those passages in books that strike them as uniquely powerful; the passages that stand out from the rest. But if I underline most of the passages in a chapter, then I'm saying most of the chapter is uniquely powerful. And that can't be the case. When everything's special, nothing's special.

I skim through the underlined passages until I find something that seems Truly Special, a passage on page thirty-three: "When a child is born among the Osages, 'a man who had talked with the gods' is summoned. When he reaches the new mother's house he recites the history of the creation of the Universe and the terrestrial animals to the newborn infant. Not until this has been done is the baby given the breast."

Alas, no one related the story of the Big Bang to me. No one read from Darwin's *On the Origin of Species*. I was allowed to latch onto Mom's breast without understanding the larger context of my existence. Maybe that's why I've felt so confused all these years.

So, to go back to my original query: What would Mircea Eliade think about this trip back East, this return to my origins? Would he say that it constitutes a kind of time travel?

No. He'd say it was superficial. Well maybe he wouldn't be *that* harsh, but he'd point out that it lacks a sense of mythic grandeur. My birthplace in Maryland is *a* point of origin, but not *The* Point of Origin.

If we believe in The Big Bang, then we conclude that *The* Point of Origin was literally that: a single *point* of infinite density. But if that's the case, how can one possibly go back to *The* Point of Origin? Not literally. I would have to involve ritu—

"Sammy! Sammy!"

I hear muffled shrieking from the other side of the windshield.

It's the old lady with the poodle. The dog is having seizures on the sidewalk. This frightens me. To be brutally honest, it irritates me, too. The old lady obviously didn't read my script. She and her poodle were supposed to be adorably feisty distractions, nothing more.

First the little boy, and now the dog. Why is life interrupting my introspection and speculation? I hate being hurled away from Mircea Eliade, and the macrocosm, and The Point of Origin and mythic grandeur. I hate being forced to use more of my already-strained supply of empathy.

I should take some sort of heroic action. Or, at the very least, comfort the old woman. That would be the humane thing to do. Right now, she's crashed in utter despair. Another dog walker, some suburban corporate douchebag type on vacation, seems to notice the old lady's upset. He doesn't do anything, though. He's hurrying his dog off in the opposite direction.

I probably should hurry off, but I don't. I'm looking at the old lady. You might even say I'm *staring* at her. Why am I staring at her? I don't know. I just feel compelled to stare at her.

I'm pretty sure she knows I'm staring at her. I get the sense she'd like for me to stop staring. She gazes back at me, and I feel like I've been caught.

(Well, I *have* been caught. Caught *staring*. That's indisputable.)

But that's not what I'm talking about. The old lady's eyes are staring back at mine, and her face is contorted into a frightened grimace. It's like she caught me committing some crime far worse than mere staring.

Now she's hyperventilating. The poodle just keeps on having seizures. I'm not looking forward to arriving in Maryland. I really don't want to change my father's Depends. But my anxiety is even worse here at the rest stop. I can't deal with it.

Soon, something like shit leaks out of the animal's butthole, and it stops twitching. It has made the transition from pet to corpse. The old lady is wailing. Her sunglasses have fallen off her face.

I pull out of there. My wheels squeal yet again. This time I don't care. The whole thing's just too much for me. As I veer back onto I-64, I nearly collide with a tractor trailer. The driver looks like he wants to kill me. An irrational thought arises: he's judging me. He knows I failed to comfort the old lady.

8

I want to forget about the dead poodle, so I turn on an audiobook. Not *Myth and Reality*, unfortunately. Rather, it's H.P. Lovecraft's "The Rats in the Walls" performed as a radio play, with the lead role voiced by a manic redneck. It was recorded at some convention in Paducah. It's about an hour long.

I'm not sure why I like that audiobook so much. Certainly, it seems like a poor selection for this particular road trip. "The Rats in the Walls" is a story of hereditary madness, and I'm dreading a return to my mad family. In the end, as the narrator shrieks "The rats! The raaaaaaaattttss!", I begin to fear that a subterranean chamber might lurk beneath my parents' tiny house. An image flashes in my head: my father as a "fungous, flabby beast". He is a subhuman thing, being driven onward by a cloaked shepherd. It's not a long, lingering vision. It's a little vision. You see, just as I sometimes tell myself little stories, I sometimes experience little visions. I don't believe my little visions are psychic visions. I just treat them as daydreams.

Still, I'm disturbed. Why would my brain go there? Why would it cast my father in such a humiliating role? Yes, of course, he's a babbling, bed-bound stroke victim who needs to have his adult diapers changed three times a day. But that doesn't mean he should be seen as less-than-human.

I want to think of him as human. In fact, I'd like to think of him as a particularly honest and kind and hardworking human. But in order to *think* that, I'd have to first *feel* it. And, anymore, I struggle to feel anything about him. The stroke happened five years ago. At first, I grieved the loss of his mind, his jokes, his warmth. I grieved that he no longer remembered me. But, for better or worse, grief (like empathy) is a finite resource. Feelings, in general, are finite resources.

Actually, that's not true. Well, what I mean is, it's *half*-true. It's an okay metaphor, but not *the perfect* metaphor. It's more accurate to say that feelings are mortal. They're not merely "used up" (like coal mines). They die.

Some feelings become ghosts after they die. I felt grief for my Dad when he failed to recover from his stroke. Then, at some point, my grief died from exhaustion. And then my grief became a ghost. This is why I can be so cold toward him. I no longer have feelings about him, I only have *the ghosts* of feelings.

I'm passing through an area called "Midway" now. (If I'm not mistaken, the name comes from the town's position halfway in between the Kentucky capital, Frankfort, and the city of Lexington.) There are horse farms out this way. The traffic thins out. I pass meadows where the grass seems blue.

It's a trick of light, I suppose. The sky seems deep blue; so blue the sun can't conquer it. In fact, if anything, the *sky* contaminates the *sun*. (By "contaminates", I mean that it seeps into it, takes it over.) Thus, the sunlight is blue light. And, when the blue light falls onto the green grass, you get bluegrass.

I pass buildings along the way. Clusters of buildings, really. Developments. Outlet centers. McMansions. Churches. They look like new construction. There's something clean, fresh, and sturdy about them. They're not at any immediate risk of falling apart. And yet, I can tell they've been constructed with cheap materials. Picket fences made of cheap white plastic (tinted blue by the light). Cheap red plastic signage (tinted blue). Cheap blue plastic awnings (made a deeper shade of blue by the tinting). These objects are not at any *immediate* risk of falling apart. But I feel, intuitively, that they'll begin to fall apart in three years.

Then again, the world might not survive for three more years.

Dad might not survive three more years.

The image of him, half-paralyzed, being poked and prodded onward by the cloaked shepherd, pops into my head once again. Not for the first time, I am repulsed by my own imagination.

I would like to listen to something relaxing, but there's no music or audiobook or podcast out there that can relax me. Every mile carries me closer to a duty I'd rather shrug off. I wish I could buy into Ayn Rand's stuff. Then I, like her Atlas, could shrug. But I suppose I'm too human for that. No, not too human. Too cowardly.

So I resist my urge to shrug. Instead, I wail. Well, not exactly 'wail'. I scream! "AGHHHA-FAHHHHH-AHHHHhhhhh!"

There's no penalty for screaming inside your own moving vehicle. What I mean is, there are social penalties levied against public screaming: the embarrassment, pity, or condemnation of bystanders. Hell, if you scream long enough and loud enough in a public place you might even end up in jail.

But reality is altered inside your own vehicle. At least, it's altered if you're *alone* in your own vehicle. Then you can scream all you want, without fear of repercussions. The worst that can happen is that you'll fuck up your throat for a while.

During a long, solo road trip the inside of a vehicle feels like an autonomous island. No, that description doesn't go far enough. Under such circumstances, the inside of the vehicle is like its *own little world*.

I tell little stories and have little visions inside my own little world.

My consciousness isn't an ordinary consciousness. You may have already gathered that. I'm not crazy, though. I'm just a mutant.

Of course, I don't mean that literally. I'm not a mutant, I'm just agitated. Quite agitated. Some of you may be thinking to yourself: "Of course, she's agitated. The entire world is agitated these days. No one alive has ever seen such a pandemic." But the plague has nothing to do with any of this. Don't get me wrong: I know it's real. It's just that the real is of precious little concern to me right now. Here, in my own little world, the unreal reigns.

For example, I'm now driving out of a gas station parking lot. My tank is full, and I seem to have acquired three bottles of Starbucks mocha latte. Once again, I've spaced out. I don't remember taking this exit.

There's a circus peanut in my mouth. You know what I'm talking about, right? One of those oblong orangish/pinkish candies. Little more than a thick glob of sugar and preservatives. I like them when they're stale. The one I'm chewing is stale. I don't remember buying it. I just know I'm chewing it. I'm not sure if I should swallow it. Something seems…off. I consider spitting it out. Instead, I hold it in my mouth. I don't swallow or spit.

Swallow or spit? That sounds crude. I didn't mean it to be crude. However, my subconscious may have meant it to be crude. What would Freud say about it? He'd say I had a hankering to suck cock. (In fact, I'm horrified by the very idea.)

He'd say the circus peanut is a phallic symbol. To him, every oblong object was a phallic symbol. Already, in his time, there were too many objects and not enough meaning to go around.

Instead of purging objects in deep evening dark, he thought up a different trick: by linking a meaningless object to a meaningful one, he made the world seem less junk-strewn.

Yes, Mr. Freud would say a "circus peanut" isn't meaningless, because it's actually a sublimation of the phrase "circus penis". He'd say my choice of roadside snacks means I want to suck clown dick or sideshow dick or the dick of some trapeze artist.

Disgusting! Ridiculous! *Quite* ridiculous! The only thing more ridiculous than that assertion is...

9

...driving through West Virginia. The governor is running for re-election. Campaign billboards every ten miles. He's a bulbous cartoon of a man wrapped in an ill-fitting suit. He looks like he slept in that suit. (Or at least *tried* to get some sleep in that suit. He has dark, insomniac circles under his eyes.) Something's wrong with the knot in his necktie, too.

After repeated exposures to his image, it dawns on me that he looks like an out-of-shape toad. Yes, an albino, brain damaged, out-of-shape toad made to wear an ill-fitting suit. A *mutant* toad, truth be told, with tiny, weary eyes. No wonder his necktie is all wrong. Nobody with webbed feet can tie a knot!

West Virginia is a state that allows toads to run for office.

On many of the billboards, he's pictured alongside the president of the United States. (Another bulbous cartoon of a man, wrapped in a slightly better-fitting suit.) He, too, looks like an out-of-shape toad with tiny eyes. An orange toad, slightly less brain damaged than the governor. The president is the alpha toad. If observed in a vacuum, he might not even seem like a toad. It's only when he's presented side-by-side with the anthropomorphic toad-governor of West Virginia that you make the connection.

"VOTE TOAD!" the campaign billboards say. "ALPHA TOAD SEZ OUR WEST VIRGINNY TOAD IS TOAD-ALLY AWESOME!" The signs don't really say that, but they might as well. I tell myself a little story. If I had magic glasses, I could put them on and see the signs as they really are, with the toad references intact. Like Roddy Piper in *They Live*.

Despite all this toad nonsense, West Virginia isn't an *entirely* ridiculous state. What I mean is, ridiculousness doesn't rule alone. There are other forces at work here, too.

For example: the mountains grant the state a dash of grandeur. They're more than hills. They really are mountains. Not big mountains. Nothing like what you find out West. But they're mountains. Thus, they possess a sort of grandeur. (Or at least a *hint* of grandeur.)

Ridiculous grandeur.

And that's not all. One must also take into account a *third* force: emptiness. And I'm not just talking about superficial emptiness (geographic isolation, low population, etc.). I'm talking about an emptiness of the soul, too. Looking out my windshield, the world seems only half-alive.

Thus, an unholy trinity:

Grandly ridiculous emptiness.

Emptily grand ridiculousness.

Ridiculously empty grandeur.

The Bluegrass State was unreal, yes. Unreal and plastic and cheap. But at least it was clean. The buildings weren't sturdy. I mean, *truly* sturdy. But they *seemed* sturdy, from a distance. They at least had the courtesy to *try* to appear sturdy. I found that courtesy comforting.

But West Virginia, well…how can I put it? It's a wounded state. Yes, that explains a lot: it's only *half*-alive because it's wounded. It's held together by train track stitches and rusty scabs.

No. I'm mistaken. This is an unfair assessment. John Denver described this same landscape as "almost Heaven", and (presumably) Heaven isn't held together by stitches and scabs. My judgment is off, because I've been driving too long. (It's already late afternoon!) Fatigue has tainted my impressions.

Yes, I'm tired and—even worse—arthritis chews on my joints. My back wants to break. My knuckles seem on the verge of shattering. The road doesn't cut me any slack. I veer a little too far to the right. Rumble strips growl.

My throat needs moisture. My eyes need moisture. Shadows bruise green mountains. Dark sunlight stains the valleys orange. Bridges span muddy rivers. Abandoned, half-completed road work forces traffic into a single, crumbling lane. It's a slow, bumpy ride. I hear the clinking and clinking and clinking of glass. I ignore it until I can't ignore it. Looking down, I spot three *empty* bottles of Starbucks mocha latte.

I don't remember drinking them, but surely I must have drank them. I mean, it's not like I would have simply poured them out. But if that's the case, why am I still drowsy? The answer pops into my head: it's possible to be both caffeinated and drowsy.

And now, I'm out of the construction area.

The road opens up. Traffic accelerates. The road reassumes its visual rhythm: blurry asphalt and blurry asphalt and smokestacks. Smokestacks and smokestacks and tractor trailers. Tractor trailers and tractor trailers and billboards. Many advertise the anthropomorphic toad. Others advertise porn shops to the truckers. Some show me the wounds of Christ and warn that HELL IS REAL.

The Interstate feels congested. Even though I can only see

three other vehicles, we're all knotted up together. Claustrophobia and claustrophobia and factories.

There's a crustiness, a raggedness, about it all. Have you ever seen a Van Gogh painting up close? I have once, at the Cincinnati Art Museum. It's violent, isn't it? I mean, the way Van Gogh slapped rough, semi-angular globs of color onto the canvas. I think the West Virginia landscape had rough semi-angular globs of color slapped onto it, as well. Maybe that's why the mountains seem bruised.

There's only one difference between the two, but it's a *key* difference: the West Virginia landscape wasn't painted by Van Gogh, with brushes. It was *finger-painted* in an art therapy class by a demon who had suffered a severe stroke. There's a nursing home in Hell, you see. They give the patients arts and crafts to complete as busywork. That's how all the world's ugliness comes into existence: brain-damaged demons doing busywork.

At least, that's the little story forming in my head. I don't like the odor that has begun to waft up from my armpits, so I need a distraction. The tractor trailers are trying to smother me, so I need a distraction. Little stories distract me.

You may think it's a *silly* little story. After all, Dante didn't include a nursing home in his *Inferno*. But think about it: what's to stop demons from growing old and decrepit? If Hell is a physical reality (as some believe), then its demons must be physical entities who fart, fuck, and age.

Let's suppose there once was a demon who'd had a stroke. And let's say the orderlies shouted at him: "Paint with your fingers, you decrepit loser!" And let's say that, in a fit of sarcastic rage (or perhaps a fit of post-stroke stupidity), he took the command literally, bit off his own finger, and used the stump for a brush!

And let's say that the demon's blood stank worse than a sewer. And let's say his blood was thick and half-clotted even as it seeped from the wound. The perfect paint! And let's say the canvas he'd been given was the tanned skin of a dead poodle named Sammy. And let's say the demon had, at one point, been a legitimately great painter, but the stroke had impaired him to the point that he could only produce a demented *parody* of beauty.

And let's say that Satan (the oldest demon, occupying a large suite in the Infernal Nursing Home) had picked the lock to this painter-demon's door as he was wandering about. And let's say he noticed this "decrepit loser's" finger painting, and said "I like the look of that. Bruised mountains! Sun stains! Crustiness and emptiness! Raggedness and congestion! Let's redecorate, so to speak, some out-of-the-way corner of God's creation so it looks like *that*. You know, someplace so remote He won't even notice."

And that's how West Virginia came to be.

"Yes," you're saying, "what a fanciful little story!" But if you've ever driven through certain stretches of I-64, you know it explains a lot. Even the air in West Virginia feels spiky and cluttered, you see. The hills and gorges hunger for souls. The roads always twist away from themselves. The people twist away from themselves, too.

Please don't take any of this the wrong way. I don't mean to malign West Virginia. Its bruises and stains appeal to my perverse aesthetic sense. Nor am I maligning stroke victims. Quite the opposite! I believe the demonic stroke victim who painted West Virginia to be *superior* to Van Gogh. After all, the demon's creation eventually took on three dimensions.

10

But these are cerebral concerns, right? Not just cerebral, but aesthetic. And, if I learned nothing else from my blue collar background, it's that aesthetics are dispensable. Best to focus on a mundane, but more consequential issue: my left front tire is going bad.

This raises questions.

Was it going bad when I left my house? Well, if you'll recall, I don't *remember* leaving the house.

Was it going bad when I had that stale circus peanut in my mouth? No, it wasn't. Of that I can be sure. At least, I *think* I can be sure.

Anyway, I hear a scraping noise—the sound of my chassis dragging against the road. My tire's *that* fucked up. It no longer elevates the chassis above the asphalt. Only, I don't know that my chassis is scraping against the road. Not at first. At first, I think I've hit a dog. Mind you, I never saw a dog on the Interstate. Not a single floppy ear. Not a fraction of a tail. But still, the fear curls up inside my brain: *I've hit a dog. It somehow got stuck in my chassis. I'm dragging it over the asphalt.*

Sammy the Poodle was tragic enough. I have no wish to look upon more canine suffering! The scraping's getting worse. Pictures of a skinned snout and lacerated doggo guts gallop through my head. By providing these grotesque images, my brain is trying to prepare me for the worst.

But, of course, the worst didn't materialize. I didn't hit a dog.

No, strike that. I erred in saying "the worst didn't materialize", because from a self-centered point of view a flat tire on a road trip is worse than hitting a dog. Yes, it would have been terrible to be involved in vehicular dogicide, but once the corpse was dislodged from my chassis I could have driven off. A flat tire, on the other hand, is a more complicated issue. At least, *for me* it's a more complicated issue. A dead dog could be extricated from a chassis in a matter of seconds with a reasonably strong stick. A flat tire requires more time, energy, and expense.

I pull onto one of the Huntington exits. Coast into an abandoned strip mall. Butcher paper covers the windows of a failed bar and grill called Crawdaddy's Place. It looks like the kind of establishment the local cops would have been happy to see fail. There's a black, three-foot-long stain on the crumbling brick facade. Mold? Oil? Soot? All three? I wish I had an answer, but I don't. In the lower right hand quadrant of the stain, someone has spray painted a golden pentagram. Appalachian kids trying to be edgy, I'd bet.

There's a portable air compressor in the back seat. I plug it into the cigarette lighter, hook the nozzle up to the valve stem, and watch the tire inflate. All the while, I'm brandishing my little phallic tube of pepper spray. I keep one eye on the tire and another on Crawdaddy's Place. For all I know, some lecherous vagrant has taken up residence nearby.

Inflating a flat tire with an air compressor isn't all that difficult. A kid could do it. Nonetheless, I feel a surge of confidence and relief. The tire seems to be holding air.

It strikes me, just now, as I think about things, that it's pretty damned gauche of the universe to curse me with one dying tire. It's like only having one foot pedicured, or only wearing one shoe. It's asymmetrical, and therefore in bad taste. Perhaps I'm being ridiculous, hoping to find good taste in the parking lot of an abandoned restaurant in Huntington, West Virginia. Maybe the state's Ridiculousness is contagious, and I'm beginning to show symptoms!

More Ridiculousness: if the right front tire was failing, along with the left front tire, then I'd at least be able to appreciate the symmetry. Symmetry can be aesthetically pleasing, and that would provide a silver lining to my distress. Hell, even an asymmetrical state of affairs can be aesthetically pleasing, if it's the right sort of asymmetry. Consider, for example, how I might feel if my left front tire was going bad at the same time my rear right tire was going bad. The pairing of opposites can be beautiful.

Yes, more Ridiculousness, and more aesthetics! I was born into the working class, and I've never quite managed to escape it. That said, I'm not very good at being working class. My mind keeps wanting to drift back to aesthetics, which have little value in a working-class life. Even worse, I make unironic use of words like "gauche"!

So now I will focus on practical matters. If my father were not a bed-bound, infantile stroke victim, he'd want me to focus on practical matters. By focusing on practical matters, I will honor his spirit. For, you see, he was a very practical man.

I didn't mean to refer to him in the past tense. I suppose, in his stroke-victim sort of way, he *remains* practical. In fact, being a stroke victim is probably the most pragmatic state of mind one can achieve. Your day is consumed with concrete obstacles, like swallowing food without choking, or walking the tightrope between constipation and diarrhea. You never use the word gauche, nor does anyone ever use it to describe your actions. (No one will ever call a stroke victim gauche for shitting his pants, because it's not his fault.) Most important of all: you never have to entertain aesthetic considerations.

So, I will endeavor to (metaphorically speaking) channel the spirit of my working-class stroke victim father, and refocus all my energy on the ongoing, practical challenge presented by the tire. Yes, ongoing. Because, unfortunately, the tire isn't truly holding air.

Well, what I mean is, it holds air *for a little while*. For twenty
minutes of Interstate travel. Blurry asphalt and blurry asphalt
and toad-men and smokestacks and smokestacks and tractor
trailers and blurry asphalt and HELL IS REAL.

Then I hear that scraping sound again. Fortunately, a sign
tells me a gas station will soon be in reach. This will afford me
a safe place to reinflate the tire. I'll go inside, take a piss, buy a
can of Fix-a-Flat, and the tire will hold air.

Unfortunately, the sign lies. I mean, it lies by omission. It
neglects to mention that the gas station is an *erstwhile* gas station. Derelict. Empty. Locked up. Available for lease.

Therefore, for the second time today, I find myself in the
parking lot of an abandoned business. This one was called
Pop's Market. The gas pumps have been removed from the
parking lot. The windows have been battered by high tides of
dust. A newspaper vending machine stands guard by the door.
Through cracked glass, I see a headline: VICE PRESIDENT
TO VISIT CHARLESTON. I see a picture: a bulbous, be-
spectacled man with a crooked mouth (a mouth twisting away
from itself). Melting icebergs of white hair linger on the sides
of his head. The average person, however, would describe him
as "bald".

I haven't seen a picture of Dick Cheney in over a decade. Today, I see him as I've never seen him before. I realize he's part
toad. For some reason, this realization is frightening. Dread
oozes down my soul.

I need to take a piss. This is undeniable. More urgently,
however, I need to leave this place. My soul can't endure so
much dread.

I won't be able to buy a can of Fix-a-Flat, but I still have that
portable air compressor. I can use that to reinflate my tire and
hope it lasts long enough to get to another gas station, one that

isn't closed, right?

Well, yes and no.

I must have mishandled it outside of Crawdaddy's Place. Maybe I shoved it into the cigarette lighter too roughly. In any case, I seem to have damaged the wire, because now it has a short. Therefore, it doesn't work.

Well, to clarify: it works, and it doesn't work. What I mean is, it only works if I bend the wire at just the right angle, with just the right amount of force.

Fortunately, I can find that magic angle pretty easily.

Unfortunately, I find it too easily. What I mean is, I blow the fuse in the cigarette lighter. I asked too much of it and it gave up.

On the facade of Pop's Market I see a black smudge about six feet long. Could be oil or mold or soot. In the upper left quadrant of the stain, someone has spray painted two golden pentagrams. Appalachian kids trying to be edgy, I hope.

11

I should call someone. I should call Mom, to let her know I'm having car trouble. But what good would that do? I would probably interrupt her while she was changing Dad's diaper. And then I'd worry her.

"Don't get raped," she'd tell me. "You should have flown out to visit, instead of driving all that way. If you would have flown out, you wouldn't have to worry about getting raped."

I'm not attractive. At least, not in any conventional way. But I know I could still get raped. I have no co-pilot on this road trip. Not even God. I'm a woman traveling alone through West Virginia. I feel vulnerable, but I keep pepper spray at the ready.

Yet, how much faith should I put in the bottle of pepper

spray? I would feel more confident if I'd actually had a chance to practice using it. As it is, I don't know if the pepper spray actually works.

I live in southern Indiana. The Midwest is teeming with gun ranges, where people can practice firing lethal weapons. Those of us packing non-lethal force have no similar place to aim at targets. While it's true that our weapon is dispersed as a spray, rather than a projectile, that shouldn't make a difference. We deserve our own equivalent to shooting ranges. We deserve our own subculture, too.

I start to make up a new little story. This one is about all the redneck gun shows getting replaced by redneck pepper spray shows. I imagine dudes going overboard by purchasing pepper spray howitzers. I imagine dudes toting huge canisters of pepper spray—I mean, the size of fire extinguishers—to Second Amendment protests. But that's just my brain entertaining itself with absurdity. And, if I've learned nothing else from my blue collar background, it's that a sense of the absurd is best kept to oneself.

Indeed, I probably shouldn't indulge in absurd musings. I probably should use my iPhone to search for the nearest auto repair shop. I probably should focus on the solid world of rubber and road.

I should. I know. I should!

But I can't.

I can't because I'm an absurd person. You no doubt have already concluded that I have an absurd soul, but did you know my *body's* absurd, too? I imagine my soul is a gray ghost inside my chest. I imagine there's a membrane separating it from the material plane. I imagine my soul's absurdity swelled so much the membrane ruptured. I imagine the absurdity then leaked out of my soul and into my body.

This is a little story I tell myself to explain why I'm a female scarecrow, too tall and too thin. It also explains why I'm too nearsighted, too neglectful of my hairstyle and nails, and too sloppily attired. For that matter, it might just explain why my glasses are always too smudged, and why they're always sliding off my nose.

What sort of impression would I make if I were to show up at some random West Virginia repair shop? They'd probably think I was a junkie. I'm not a junkie. I've never done hard drugs and I haven't even drank or smoked weed in months. Nonetheless, people think I'm a junkie. Why else would I look the way I do?

The repair shop would think I was a junkie.

And they'd know I was a woman.

And they'd see my out-of-state tags.

And let's assume the best-case scenario: they *didn't* rape me. They'd still find a way to take advantage of me. They'd charge way too much to patch my tire. Or, they'd pretend the tire couldn't be patched. They'd say I needed a new one.

For that matter, what if the *tow truck driver* tries to rape me? Or murder me? Or both? Yes, I have my little phallic bottle of pepper spray on hand. But, because there are no pepper spray ranges where I can practice, I have no idea if it would work.

This is all too much to consider.

I've long been an anxious person. My father was an anxious person, too. Perhaps that's why he had a stroke. I hope I don't end up having a stroke. But if you worry too much about having a stroke, you can worry yourself *into having a stroke*!

I must not allow myself to fall victim to a stroke. So, I try to calm down. I force myself to think happy thoughts. I imagine arriving at The Zodiac sometime after ten p.m. I imagine a hot shower and fast food.

I imagine tomorrow will be better. I imagine pulling out of Beckley and looking at West Virginia with transformed eyes. It won't look like a fingerpainting by a senile demon. It will be John Denver's "almost Heaven". In fact, I'll regret leaving West Virginia to cross into Plain Old Ordinary Virginia. I'll regret leaving Plain Old Ordinary Virginia to cross into my native Maryland.

I imagine arriving in my tiny little hometown, which is no longer my hometown, not really. My home's in Indiana. But the tiny little town is my erstwhile home. It's my family's home. And that's why I'm traveling all this way, to help my family.

I try to imagine my father as something other than a geriatric infant who spends his days babbling, gibbering, shitting and choking. I try to imagine him as being capable of intelligent thought. *Dad is an intelligent life form.*

No, that's a lie. Or at least an *exaggeration.* I tell myself Dad is an intelligent life form because I want to avoid the painful truth.

I know that sounds cruel. I should be able to at least *fake* respect for my father.

But before you judge me, please bear in mind that I really can't do much of anything, right now. I'm too exhausted. I know I should do…something. But I'm tired of doing things. I don't want to die, but I don't want to do things. I'd like to stay numb for a while. Frozen. Still.

For a moment, I contemplate what it would be like to just give up on driving home. Give up driving *to my parents' house,* I mean. I could just turn around and go back to my house.

Or…

…I could also give up on driving back *to my house.* I could just stay here, in this parking lot. Instead of fearing vagrants, I could *become a vagrant.* It's an idea I've often kicked around.

I've never had the guts to try it, though. It takes guts to do such a thing, you know. You're abandoning all convention, and with it all comfort. You're risking jail. You're risking rape.

I know, I know—I have a preoccupation with rape. That's because I've been raped.

An intrusive memory: The dark filthy shape looms over me.

I shove the image out of my head. It slinks off to a dark corner, pretending to leave. It will be back.

It happened over twenty years ago, this dark filthy shape incident. I don't want it to happen again, so I keep my guard up. Don't feel bad for me. It's happened to more people than you think. Besides, it actually feels good to have my guard up. I know that sounds weird, but it's true. When I have my guard up, I feel like I'm in control.

I'm not in control. People who are in control take action when they get a flat tire on a road trip. They don't sit in an abandoned gas station.

You want to know just how out of control I am? I'm shaking. I'm shaking and I'm seeing shit. Bipedal shadows leaping around me, dancing around me, like cultists around a sacrifice. Actually "bipedal shadows" doesn't quite do them justice. Sometimes I think I can see part of their flesh. It's like they're half-flesh and half-shadow and the two halves are always changing places. For example, I'll see a taut, well-muscled leg for a moment, but as it leaps through the air the leg gets lost in a fog of shadows. And then I'll notice the thick neck of another dancer, but it's only there for a moment before disappearing.

I'm shaking and I'm whimpering and I need to pee and I'm freezing. The sun has gone down. I can't say how long ago it went down. I wasn't paying attention. It was eighty degrees this morning, back home in Indiana. And now, here in West Virginia, it's well…I don't know the exact temperature. But it's cold. Cold enough to see my breath.

Cold enough to see the other breath. The one coming from the back seat. The one I feel against my neck.

A glance in the rear view mirror: nothing.

But I see a second puff. A little cloud. And I hear something like the start of a cough.

I wail. I run, leaving behind my canvas bag (the closest thing I have to a purse), leaving behind my phone, leaving behind this whole pointless errand to visit a father who isn't really there.

Wind shoves the cold in my face. There's something wrong with this gust. It has a texture. All gusts of cold hard wind are supposed to feel the same. This one, however, feels crusty. This isn't to say that the wind is carrying something crusty *along with it,* and that this crusty something hit my face. No, the wind, *itself,* has a flaky, granular quality to it. It feels... diseased. It's not an intact, healthy wind, but rather the scab of wind. Yes, the wind feels like a gaseous scab. I try to run from it but it's coming from all directions.

This is wrong. There's no such thing as a gaseous scab. Winds can't blow at you from all directions at once. My sensations and perceptions don't make sense. But they persist. They *don't care* that they don't make sense.

And as my legs stride and my arms pump, something inside my chest twists. And all the things in my stomach twist. My heart is gnarled, no less than my arthritic joints. My intestines feel three times their normal weight. Something wet and humid and foul leaks out of my butthole. I piss myself, too.

I'm drowning in air. I'm gasping and running. I'm tripping over...a curb?

I make a few tiptoe gallops to keep from falling. Then, a few sliding steps that slow things down. I feel myself whirling toward the ground, so I shift my weight to achieve balance. Then one more gallop on tiptoe. One more sliding step.

It doesn't work.

I'm falling. I try to land so I don't hurt myself, but I don't land. I plunge down a pit of scabby blackness.

Plunging.

Howling.

Cursing.

Plunging.

Cursing.

Crashing. Crashing. Not so much *landing* as *crunching*.

A tornado of broken bones whirls inside me. Raw whines. Sobbing. "Oh, fucks!" SHRIEKS! The sharp edges of certain fragments lacerate my guts. I am a dead dog. The dead dog is me. Time stops…

12

…and starts again. I'm on my back (or what's left of my back). So much throbbing and stinging and chaos. The ruthless burn of piss-stench. Turd-stench gagging me. Soaked, soiled underwear. Am I crying? I feel like I might be crying.

No, I'm not crying. I'm bleeding. Or maybe I *am* crying and the tears are mixed with blood. My eyes feel weird, too tight for their sockets. It's like they've swollen. Is that possible? It doesn't matter if it's possible—it's happened. Yes, my eyes do feel as though they've expanded beyond their former boundaries. Maybe they're bulging out from their sockets, like the eyes of a hungry cartoon character gawking at a steak.

But I'm not a cartoon character. So, why has this happened?

I should get up and run back to normality. Only, I can't. I'm paralyzed.

I mean. I'm not *exactly* paralyzed. I can feel pain. So it's not like my body is numb all over.

But I am paralyzed, in the sense that I can't move my extremities. All I can do is look up at the starry night, which looks like Van Gogh's "Starry Night". You might think this is a beautiful sight. Think again. Sure, *on a canvas*, Van Gogh's stars look pretty. But in *real life* they're grotesque, swollen beyond all natural possibilities. They're rough, angular, yellow blobs. They're cancerous stars, metastatically consuming the world.

Are my eyes as swollen as these stars? Might the swelling of the stars be an illusion? Am I only seeing swollen stars because my eyes are swollen? I didn't notice any stars at all, before my tumble. You'll recall that when I fell, I plunged into blackness. No starlight illuminated the scene. Now, the sky is infected with swollen stars. They rain down angular blobs of light. I feel like I'm a character in a movie. My scene has been altered in post-production to make day seem like night. This night is unreal.

But I'm not a character in a movie.

At least, I'm not in a *live action* movie. If I am a character in a movie, the evidence (e.g., bulging eyes) would suggest I'm a cartoon character in a cartoon movie. After all, cartoon characters have been known to see a circle of stars parade around their head, like a living halo, after suffering a knock on the noggin. Perhaps I am a character in a cartoon created by Van Gogh. Not a children's cartoon, but a mad cartoon in which stars are portals to unpleasant places.

No, upon further review, I'm not a character in a Van Gogh *cartoon*.

Van Gogh's worlds are constructed from thick, paste-like paint applied with thick brushes or knives. His paint is like embalming fluid. He takes a living, breathing night and makes a taxidermy of it. This method makes animation impossible. Maybe I'm made of thick paste-like paint. At the very least, the shit in my pants feels like thick paste-like paint.

That might explain why I can't move. Maybe I'm a figure in a Van Gogh painting. Perhaps if you stare long enough at Van Gogh's "Starry Night", you'll notice me sprawled on the ground. That might explain why my world seems embalmed right now. Inert.

For a moment, this seems like a real possibility. The only problem is that my shit doesn't smell like paint. It smells like shit. Further proof I'm not a figure in a painting: flies begin to swarm around my pants. I'm no painting. I'm not art. I'm biological. I'm an animal.

Now, I hear sounds: shoes tramping their way through tall grass. A cough.

A figure, a shadow, leans over me. I see a flash of teeth, followed by a cloud of breath. "I'm cold," he announces. The voice is nasally, high-pitched and hoarse.

A few moments pass. More puffs of cloudy breath. "I mean, that's my surname. Cold. You look frightened. I suppose that can't be helped, but it's a waste of energy. There's no reason to be frightened. I'm no killer. I'm a searcher. Do you know what a searcher is?"

I want to debate him. He can't fool me. He's no 'searcher'. He's a *Starer*, ergo a *creeper*. I want to say all these things, but can't get my tongue to work.

Then the following statement inserts itself into my consciousness: *Let your brain be your tongue. Answer me by way of telepathy.*

I want this all to end. Even though I crashed onto the ground, I feel like I'm still falling.

Then another statement inserts itself into my consciousness.

You don't need for things to end. You need a new beginning.

Sounds like the sort of message I'd find crammed inside a stale fortune cookie. I hope this so-called Mr. Cold actually *is* communicating with me via telepathy. I'd hate to think that *my own thoughts* were so trite!

You need proof of what I can do. This isn't a problem. I want to help you. If you let down your guard, I can fix all of this.

I'm not about to let down my guard.

Mr. Cold isn't leaning over me anymore. He's sighing (vocally, not telepathically). Sighing and puffing out air. He's walking off; I'm left to look up at the apocalyptic sky, monstrous with metastasis. And I'm left to contemplate the foul ammonia scent in the front of my pants, and the foul smell of mashed-up turds around my anus. And I'm listening to the buzz of flies, and I'm feeling one land on my nose. And I know they like the way I smell. And I'm thinking about my father. I'm aware of how he, too, will draw flies if his diaper is left unchanged.

And I'm thinking of how I had a birthday recently, and how I called my mother, and how she coached Dad on what to say to me, because he had no way of creating the words on his own.

"Tell her that you love her," Mother said.

"I love her," Father said.

"No," Mother coached. "Say: 'I love you.'"

"I love you. I love you. I love you," Father said.

These were the so-called conversations I had with my so-called father. I suppose I should be grateful he's not dead. I can still hear his voice. But that's the thing. It's not even his voice anymore. The stroke changed it. Made it more nasal.

More nasal and high-pitched and hoarse. Like Mr. Cold's. In fact, *quite a lot* like Mr. Cold's. The difference is that Cold's voice carries genuine emotion. He isn't my mother's ventriloquist dummy.

I hear shoes wading through the high grass again; starting close by but then fading. Other sounds follow. Footsteps on asphalt. Car doors opening. Car doors slamming shut. Jangling keys. Then more footsteps. Grunts. Finally, shoes wading through the high grass again, approaching me.

I see a puff of breath overtop me. This time, it strikes me as being more of a fog, a mist, than a puff of air. Mr. Cold's mist catches the swollen starlight, reflects that light or refracts it or whatever. I suck at science. The gist of what I want to say is that, for a moment, I can see a tiny rainbow in the midst of his mist.

(Technically, I suppose, a *moon*bow.)

A thought gets inserted into my head: *When you ran off, you left your keys behind. Which means you also left behind your self-defense spray. How odd that, when you wanted to keep your guard up, you accidentally let your guard down.*

After a pause, Mr. Cold inserts another thought. *Anyway, please accept this gift as proof of my good intentions.*

Keys jangle. Then they stop jangling. Then I feel cold steel and plastic in my right hand. He's returned my keys to me. And not just my keys, but a tiny phallic tube as well.

Do you require any further proof that I'm harmless? Searchers do no harm. If I had wanted to harm you, I wouldn't have given you back your toxin.

An odd way to put it, but I understand what he's trying to say. He has a point. I don't make a conscious decision to let my guard down, but I let my guard down. Which is to say, I relax.

Good. Now I will raise you back up into the world.

And what happens next is freaky. Yes, of course, this entire episode is freaky. I am living in a deformed reality. Perhaps I have always lived in a deformed reality, but now my reality is becoming deformed to the second power. My reality is deformity squared.

I say this because Mr. Cold ascends toward those hideous Van Gogh stars, and takes me with him.

I'm not taking you to the stars. Not yet, at least.

My keys are in my right hand. He grabs onto my left. Pulls me up onto my feet. We're floating upward, out of this pit. Floating slowly, with an almost-mechanical steadiness. Floating like we're passengers in an elevator.

Multiple, conflicting emotions collide in my heart. Relief. (I'm able to move again. I'm no longer paralyzed, or half-paralyzed, or whatever.) Disgust. (Mr. Cold's hand feels like frozen beef. I mean, it's literally covered in a thin layer of frost.) Terror (my hand starts to slip away from the frost). More relief (he wraps both his arms around my waist, ensuring my safety). Despair (I now feel like I'm bathing in ice cubes).

We're going back to the gas station. Way back, *to the gas station. Which is to say, we'll be traveling back in time, to 2007, when the American Vice President visited Charleston and this refueling station was still operational.*

13

I'm back in my car. I'm wearing clean underwear and jeans. A shadowy figure in a ball cap and overalls is shoving a clipboard through my open driver's side window. "Ma'am? You need a pen? Ma'am?" His breath makes puffy clouds in the darkness.

On the clipboard, a credit card receipt. Forty-seven dollars. Seventeen dollars to fill up my gas tank. Thirty to patch my tire.

The moment I sign, there's a gust of wind. The receipt flaps against the clipboard, then rips loose. "Awww, shit. You need another copy of that, Ma'am?"

I shake my head.

"Okay, then. Safe travels."

I nod.

"Give your dad a call. This was a good year for him. You can hear him the way he used to be."

My hand starts to shake. I want to scream. I want to thank him. I want to scream. I *start* to scream. I'm not screaming any particular word. I'm just screaming. I'm not logical. The world isn't logical. The word "logical" is derived from the Greek word "logos" (roughly translated as "word"). I'm not logical, therefore I indulge in wordless wailing, a sort of animalistic ululation that dissolves into a whimper.

"What you upset about? All I said was it weren't so bad at all. This tire's a Goodyear. You can heal them with a patch, you see."

That's not what he said. What kind of mechanic talks about "healing" a tire with a patch? And why would the brand matter? Surely, *all* tires can be patched. There's nothing special about Goodyears!

Mr. Cold has performed magick. *He's* the mechanic. *He's* informing me that (since we're now back in 2007) I can speak to my father as he existed before the stroke. In other words, he's telling me I can talk *to my father*. My *true* father, not the ventriloquist's dummy.

I didn't own a cell phone in 2007. I am a late adapter to all technology. But in this alternate version of 2007 provided to me by Mr. Cold, I do have a cell phone. A first generation iPhone, to be precise. And, since my parents have always had the same landline number, all I have to do is dial.

And, of course, I don't mean "dial", literally. Because iPhones don't have the old rotary dialers on them, the ones I used in my childhood, that whirred when you physically moved the dial in its predestined, clockwise arc. No, this "dial" is a series of buttons. And they're not even "buttons". Because cell phones no longer have literal plastic "buttons" on them.

I miss dials and buttons. I miss the way the numbers printed onto the buttons would fade away, over time. (Presumably because some oil in your skin ate away at them.)

The buttons I'm pushing right now are graphic images that appear after I click on the phone icon and disappear as soon as I'm done. Ephemeral, cartoon buttons fitting for an age of ephemeral, cartoon communication. I press those impermanent buttons so I can talk to my impermanent father.

The electronics purr at me. I wait for Mom to pick up. If I recall correctly, Mom was the one who always picked up the phone. Dad never picked up.

But surely that can't be the case. No, I was mistaken. Before his stroke, Dad answered the phone. I had just forgotten this fact, because I have a hard time imagining him involved in any meaningful conversation these days. "Hah-low???" he'd say. Yes, I recall now. He answered the phone with a question. (His *answer* was a *question*. Ha!)

So I brace myself to hear that "Hah-low???", and I start to think about what I'll say to him. I'll tell him I love him, and he'll tell me he loves me. Yes, that will be enough. I want to hear a genuine, spontaneous expression of love from him. Not a ventriloquist dummy's love, but a father's love.

Unfortunately, Mom picks up instead. She doesn't answer it with a "Hah-low???". At least, not exactly. She answers it with a "Hel-LOW!!!!" Note the multiple, superfluous exclamation points, indicative of exasperation. Any time she ever picked up the phone she was exasperated. And tonight there's a raspy trace of a growl in her voice, too. She might even be answering through clenched teeth.

"Hi Mom."

"What do you want?"

"I just called to say hello."

"Called to say hello?! It's three o'clock in the morning!"

In the background, I hear Dad's voice. "What's wrong, hon?"

"It's your daughter. She's drunk."

"I'm not drunk!"

"Only drunks call their parents at three in the morning. What's the matter?"

"What's the matter?" Dad repeats, in the background.

"Here, Steve. You take the phone. She never did listen to me. Ask your daughter what's wrong with her. What sort of daughter prank calls her parents at three a.m.?"

"I'm not prank calling…"

How do I make her understand? I think I have a solution. "I'm just calling from another time zone. I'm…traveling."

Mom, in the background. "It would be awfully nice if *we* could travel every once in a while. But after we helped you pay for that bankruptcy lawyer, we're a little short of funds. She's kicking up her heels again. Probably charging this trip on a credit card. Ask your daughter what's wrong with her. Ask her what she wants. What she *really* wants."

Dad complies, as he has always complied.

Even before his stroke, he was her ventriloquist's dummy. He's always been her ventriloquist dummy. ("What do you really want, Nancy? What do you really want?")

And then, I run afoul of a pothole. Yes, a pothole on the Interstate. And my car (which is, as you may recall, my *world* during this road trip) shakes. And the steering wheel vibrates in my hands. And blue sparks appear in my peripheral vision and red sparks appear right in front of me. The pothole isn't a pothole. Or, at least, the pothole isn't *just* a pothole. It's a sign. It means the time travel spell is ending. No one *tells* me this is the meaning. Mr. Cold isn't inserting the thought into my mind. (At least, I don't *think* he's inserting it into my mind.) Somehow, I'm simply *aware* of it, intuitively. The present will soon re-assert itself.

There's a distortion in Dad's voice. It's shaking. Just as my car shakes, his voice shakes. And it changes as it shakes. Grows more nasal and high-pitched and hoarse. It's like the stroke is happening all over again. The spell is coming to an end.

I would like to think everything is returning to normal.

I mean, strangeness can't go on forever, right? Strangeness— I'm talking about *pervasive* strangeness, the sort of strangeness that makes the whole world seem blotchy and angular—eventually exhausts itself. The Earth grows weary and can no longer sustain it. Humans have a momentary brush with the paranormal, and then things revert to the simply normal.

Only, so far, things haven't returned to normal.

I'm driving headlong into a savage wind. It whistles and groans. My car crosses into the other lane. I didn't want it to go into the other lane. I don't have control over this car (this world). The wind is a cat. My car is a mouse. I'm being batted from one gaseous paw to another.

No, the wind isn't gaseous. It's palpable. I see now that the wind is paint, applied by a mad, swatting brush. Applied in angular blotches. My car is the canvas. There is no escape. I am at one with The Strange.

14

"You have arrived at your destination: Zodiac Hotel and Conference Center."

The parking lot is full of Objects. Cars, cigarette butts, abandoned soda bottles, shrubs, street lamps, construction equipment. Lots and lots of construction equipment. Mud-splattered construction equipment.

No. Not exactly. It's not *construction* equipment, but rather electric company trucks. Or maybe tree-cutting trucks. Trucks equipped with mechanisms to elevate workers up in the air so they can fix power lines. I assume severe thunderstorms have plagued the area recently. That's the only reason I can imagine for so many electric company trucks (or tree-cutting trucks) to be assembled at a hotel. I mean, these professions don't host conventions, do they?

I make up a little story: these trucks belong to Giuseppe the Puppeteer. He and his employees used them to attach strings to the highest tree limbs.

The hotel is a single tower, rising only four or five stories. On one of the floors, about halfway up, nearly every room is lit up. All the other floors are dark, but flood lights illuminate the crowning spire. To enter, I have to first walk up three dozen steep granite steps. Have you ever heard of such a thing? It's like I'm walking up to an art museum or courthouse, not a roadside hotel.

I've been through too much already. Too much driving and sweating and falling and screaming. And now, I'm being forced to march up three dozen steps? Perhaps I'll leave a Yelp review. One star. Two words: "Terrible entrance."

The clock behind the front desk tells me it's four o'clock. A bedraggled clerk is seated directly beneath the clock. There's a scruffy beard lurking beneath his blue surgical face mask. There are dark circles beneath his brown eyes. A year ago, he would have been a very strange sight. A year ago, the only place I would have seen a hotel clerk wearing a blue surgical face mask would have been in one of my stranger dreams. Now, such sights are commonplace.

A strange, dreamy epiphany: *I'm wearing a face mask, too!* I don't remember putting on a face mask, but I feel its straps cutting into my ears. I must have been wearing it for quite some time. Was I wearing it when I talked to Mom in 2007? Did it make my voice sound muffled and groggy? Is that why she thought I was drunk?

"It's f-four a.m.," the clerk stammers (as if I couldn't tell time on my own). "I w-wasn't certain you w-would make it. Even after your dad said you were coming, I had my doubts. But you m-made it, eh?"

He's mistaken. My dad lacks the cognitive and motor skills required to make a phone call. Moreover, there's no way Dad could have known I'd planned to stay at this particular hotel, in this particular town.

But if Dad didn't call him, who did? Maybe I did. Sometimes my voice gets mistaken for a man's voice. It's possible that I called to say I was en route, but subsequently *forgot* that I'd called to say I was en route. Perhaps I tried to explain that I was traveling to visit my dad, and the clerk thought *I was my dad.*

Or maybe Mr. Cold called (ha ha! "cold called") and impersonated my father. His voice sounds similar to Dad's, after all. But then again, there's no way the night clerk would *know* it sounds similar.

I don't want to live in a world where Mr. Cold can call a hotel and impersonate my father. This is not to say that I want to commit suicide. In the past I've wanted to kill myself, but not now. I just want to leave. Somehow, it seems like I would be better off if I had pulled onto the shoulder of I-64 when my tire went flat and waved down a cop for help. But how could I have been sure that was safe? How could I have been sure the cop wouldn't rape me?

The only thing I like about this hotel lobby is that it's well-lit. Well, that's not the *only* thing. I also find it refreshing to hear a human voice. Not the voice of a humanikin news anchor. Not a ventriloquist dummy's voice. Not a telepathic "voice". No—a mundane, run-of-the-mill voice.

Pardon me while I second guess myself. Mundane? Really? Is that an accurate adjective?

No. The clerk has an *almost*-mundane voice, but it isn't *purely* mundane. A mundane voice wouldn't be so shaky. He's a nervous man. Yes, an extraordinarily nervous man! Maybe he's nervous because my eyeballs are swollen. Yes, I would be nervous, too, if I were working third shift at a hotel and ran into a swollen-eyed traveler. It would lead me to think I was hallucinating.

But my oddity doesn't explain away his oddity. He's not just nervous. He exudes an aura of sharp blotchiness. The dark circles under his eyes look as though they might have been slapped onto his face by a knife or thick brush.

I think he's a little dangerous. Or, at least, he's *acquainted* with danger. I'm probably making too much of a small matter. In all likelihood, he's just high on opiates.

He seems to be in his late thirties. Old enough to have fallen from grace. Young enough to get up and make another go at things. How do I know this? As I've already informed you, I like to make up little stories. What I haven't yet told you is that I have a particular talent for making up little stories about the people I meet in hotels.

Take this nervous night clerk. I make up a little story that he suffers from multiple sexual compulsions. Once, he was an idealistic public defender. After a year, he found himself transformed into a less-than-idealistic public defender. After another year, he found himself going through the motions. It was at this point that he started cruising for sex in public parks.

Being neither attractive nor unattractive, he found himself quite popular. If he had been either attractive or unattractive, then his face would have been memorable. And people who cruise for sex in public parks don't want to remember the faces involved. They want a blank slate upon which they can project their fantasies.

I mean, I don't know this for a fact. I could be totally off the mark. This is just a little story I'm making up.

Anyway, as I was saying, he had the sort of average looks coveted in the cruising world. His dance card was always full. One day, he went to the park very early in the morning and stayed far too long. He missed a client's bail hearing.

As a result of that, his client (a wife beater) remained in jail. While the defendant in question was quite the tough guy when torturing petite women, he was utterly aghast at the prospect of another day behind bars. (This fear was well-founded. A disgusting trauma had been visited on him at four a.m., the first night he was locked up.)

So, after his bail was set exceedingly high, he hanged himself with his own underwear. At first the man behind the hotel counter, the erstwhile public defender, faced no consequences. He told a story about illness and promised to have his physician write him a note. When pressed on this, he managed to produce a reasonable forgery by cutting and pasting letterhead.

If anything, the man behind the hotel counter (the erstwhile public defender) felt emboldened by this whole series of events. His client had been a horrible person. No one would miss him. Therefore, his dereliction of duty had actually yielded a benefit to society!

Yes, he gave himself many pats on the back. He began to think of himself as a Spiritual Rebel. To have sex in the woods was to return to Eden. Or at least, to Nature. (Which, if you think about it, is even better than Eden. You can't have Eden without God, Judgment, and a Fall from Grace. Nature, on the other hand, implies freedom, amoral ecstasy, and the ascent to a higher state of consciousness.) No longer was he living as a servant of the law. He was a servant to nothing but Nature, which was to say that he was a servant only to himself. That is, to those appetites infused in him by Nature.

But you can only miss court so many times.

So he found himself fired. And he bounced from job to job, park to park. Until one day he was arrested for indecent exposure. He'd been drunk that day. Blackout drunk. When he came to, he was told he'd been masturbating in front of an old bird-watching couple. Or at least, trying to masturbate. The vodka had made him limp.

The police report indicates he had tried to convince the older couple to cavort with him in a threesome. He couldn't remember enough details to counter the allegation. The erstwhile public defender had no viable defense. He made up a story that it was consensual. No one believed him. His jail sentence was suspended, but he's in year two of a five-year probation.

He doesn't want to be working third shift behind the front desk of a hotel in Beckley, West Virginia. He wants to be a lawyer again, back in Morgantown. He'll never be a lawyer again. Nor will he ever return to Morgantown.

That's the little story I make up about this fragile man who looks lost in the maze of his own hurt. It only takes about thirty seconds to tell the whole tale. I have to sign a form to check in. The form requires me to write down the odd alphanumeric jumble which adorns my license plate, as well as the name of the state that issued it. Of course, I know where I come from. But I never remember the odd alphanumeric jumble. So, I walk outside to take a glance at it. This takes thirty seconds. I tell myself the night clerk's tale while completing the chore.

I don't like to talk about this, but sometimes I think I might be psychic. Earlier, I may have told you that I don't believe I have psychic visions; that I just have daydreams. I was lying.

Sometimes, rarely, I do believe I'm psychic. Not that I've ever thought of putting out a shingle for a fortune telling business. I don't think a real psychic should take money. Nor should they pursue fame. They should quietly use their gift to do good. Or, at least, to avoid harm.

One caveat. Just to be clear, I'm not absolutely *convinced* that I'm a "*real* psychic". Sometimes I believe it, but that belief is always shaky. I remain skeptical about the whole thing. I believe we live and we die and we rot. There's no room for a magician in that circus!

Nonetheless, I have these nagging, brief, intermittent episodes of belief. I think I can sum up a person's life simply by looking at them. I can almost hear the jeers now: "You're no psychic, you're just stereotyping." But that's not really the case. I don't just look at the obvious external clues (manner of speech, manner of dress, gestures, etc.) to come to a decision. I look in their eyes. I see their smile. I compare their eyes to their smile. Do they seem to naturally, in some relaxed way, work together like intermeshing gears? Or, are they at odds. Does the smile say "I'm happy", while the eyes say "I'm acting!"

Of course, the clerk has no visible smile. He's wearing a mask. But his is a unique case, in which the eyes are so visibly tormented that they suffice to tell the tale all on their own.

That's how I came up with the hotel clerk's tale. That, and a subjective sense that he was well-educated and out of his element. He reminds me that check-out is at eleven a.m. "Try to get whatever sleep you can," he says.

15

The next thing I know, I'm floating. What I mean is, I'm in the elevator. I hold car keys in one hand and room keys in the other. Not room *keys*, exactly. Just *plastic cards* that serve the same function as keys. I've been given a small envelope containing two of them. I mean, I haven't yet looked inside the envelope to confirm there are two of them. I take that on faith. Hotels always give you two, right?

The elevator makes a soft, antiseptic chiming sound when its doors open. As I walk out into the hallway, I realize several rooms are hosting loud, crass parties. All the doors are closed, so the noise is muffled. Alas, that doesn't help much. Yes, it's like a Chuck E. Cheese party is being held in each room; a Chuck E. Cheese party *for sketchy adults* instead of children.

In one room, an Appalachian woman lets out a drunken belly laugh. In another, a woman with a Chicago accent is getting thoroughly plowed. In a third, a man of indeterminate origin belches proudly, while some dude from the Bronx wails "Calluses suck!"

The Appalachian woman laughs again. Then, a ferocious thump. Someone (or some*thing*) has been rammed up against a door. Then a moment of celestial quiet, interrupted by noise from a *fourth* room: a Don Knotts rant. It goes on and on, becoming increasingly manic. Quite the monologue! I'm trying to discern if it's from *Three's Company* or *The Andy Griffith Show*. Probably the latter. On *Three's Company* he didn't have as much screen time.

In any event, canned laughter ensues. Then, the dude from the Bronx again. "Lick it!" he shouts. Then he giggles. His giggles merge with the sitcom's laugh track. Don Knotts has wrapped up his monologue, and the audience loves it. At least, that's what we're made to believe. There was no live studio audience for *The Andy Griffith* show. The laughs were pre-recorded. You could even say *disembodied*.

I'm worried I won't be able to sleep through the cacophony. First things first, though. I can't even find my room.

According to the little envelope holding the key cards, I'm staying in Room 313. However, I can't find Room 313. I see 311, 312, 314 and 315, but no 313. I look across the hallway. I look down the hallway. No dice. Has the night clerk played a practical joke on me?

Perhaps he really didn't save a room for me. Maybe there is no Room 313. Maybe he was just too embarrassed to admit he gave away my room, so he made up the name of a phantom room. Maybe he's hoping I'll wander around for a little bit, shrug my shoulders, give up, and drive away. Or maybe he's hoping I'll slink off to an obscure nook of the stairwell, curl up into a ball, and cry myself to sleep.

In the midst of this cacophony, I hear someone fidgeting with a lock. The door to Room 312 opens. A deep, hoarse voice speaks. "Hey, man. They gave you 313?"

Something's wrong with this guy. He's unsteady on his feet, wobbling in place. He's wearing black sunglasses indoors, at night. There's something wrong with his stomach. It's not so much that *he's fat* as that *his belly is distended*. His legs are thin, but his belly is swollen.

 This is all the more apparent because he's shirtless. He's only wearing long black shorts and black flip-flops. His skin bears an unhealthy yellow tint. Much to his credit, he's wearing a black surgical mask. He doesn't look like the kind of man who would wear a mask in a hotel hallway. He looks like a redneck anti-masker, but he's obviously not.

However, just because he's *not* an *anti-masker*, I can't assume he *is* a *pro-masker*. I have a gut feeling that he's too complicated to be pigeonholed. This frightens me.

All this time, as these thoughts slosh through my brain, the hotel cacophony continues. The Chicago woman (who has just gotten fucked) is sobbing and wailing. "You aren't the man I thought you were!" she screams. The Bronx guy shrieks: "Forklift drivers REPRESENT!" A slap, probably a high-five, follows. The Appalachian woman is still giggling. "I swear by Judas's neck, it's true!" she says in between giggles. "By Judas's neck!"

And the Swollen Man, he's talking too. Even worse, he seems to expect an answer! "Hey, man… Hey, man! I asked you a question. Did they give you 313?"

What's with this "Hey, man"? Is he using "man" generically? Or, does he think I'm a dude? Sometimes, I get mistaken for a dude. It's bound to happen to a tall, unattractive, poorly groomed woman like myself. But he's probably just using it generically. Yes, that's it. So I stop worrying about being misperceived and answer his question with a nod.

"Well," he says, "to get to 313 you have to go through 312."

I don't believe him. He wants to lure me into his room. To rape me? That's entirely in the realm of possibility. To murder me? A longshot, but possible. To kidnap me and hold me for ransom? That requires multiple steps. I don't think he's up to it. Whatever his precise motive might be, I'm sure it's sinister. So, I mutter an excuse. A fib. "I need to go down to my car to get my bags."

I don't even know if I packed any bags.

"Hey, man. Your bags are already inside. Your dad brought them up a couple of minutes ago."

My bowels clench. My throat tightens. My brain spins around in my skull. I brace myself against the wall. I pretend I didn't hear him. I pretend my sister doesn't have Covid. I pretend my father never had a stroke. I pretend I'm dreaming all this nonsense. I'm not in West Virginia, because I never needed to travel east. I'm not in a hotel, I'm safe at home. There was never a Starer. The Starer was a little story I made up to entertain myself. Covid was a little story I made up to entertain myself. President Trump was a little story I made up to entertain myself. None of it's real.

I pinch myself. I click my heels three times and think to myself: *There's no place like home.* I expect to find myself back in Indiana, back in bed, staring at my ceiling fan.

Alas, I'm still in The Zodiac, having an unpleasant conversation with a Swollen Man. I grab a tight hold onto my pepper spray. Stagger away, toward the elevator.

I will leave the hotel. And then, I'll…

I don't know what I'll do after leaving. Perhaps I'll find some nearby patch of forest and get lost. Maybe I'll take this opportunity to become a hobo. A *female* hobo. A hoba? Images flash through my brain. I'm tying a bundle to a long branch. I'm stowing away on freight cars, stealing discarded food from trash cans to get by. Sleeping under the…

A new eruption of Ridiculousness interrupts my Hobo Daydream. The hallway's shaking.

Is it an earthquake? No, earthquakes are few and far between in West Virginia. It's the Swollen Man. As he runs down the hallway, the floor shakes. He's not alone. What I mean is, he's apparently not the only Swollen Man! There are three others.

They all have distended bellies. They're all jaundiced. They're all wearing black shorts, flip-flops, sunglasses and face masks. They're all panting and bounding down the hall. They all have their arms stretched out to grab me.

I flip open my pepper spray. Push down on the nozzle. Aim at the eyes of the first Swollen Man to approach me. I expect him to howl in pain, possibly shriek, and then collapse onto the floor. Instead, something Ridiculous occurs.

The air smells like rotten eggs. The Swollen Man's eyes widen. I keep waiting for him to scream, but he looks closer to laughing. He rips the pepper spray out of my hand, takes a closer look at it, and giggles.

"Hey man, I've been in a lot of rumbles, but this is the first time I've been attacked with fart spray!" He grabs me by the hair and shows me the little pink phallic tube. A tiny label reveals that it isn't pepper spray at all, but rather "Dr. Colon's Fart Attack Spray!"

Mr. Cold didn't give me back my pepper spray at the gas station. He tricked me with the old switcheroo!

THUD!

The Swollen Man tosses me to the floor. I tumble down chin-first. I'm freaked out and rug burnt. I'm screaming. And then a thought is inserted in my head. A thought, inserted by telepathy: *Necessity is the mother of deception. It would be a grave mistake for you to continue your journey east. Steven Coughlin is not your father. My name is Indrid Cold, and your true name is Nid Cold. You are my long-lost daughter. I've come to take you away from this dimension. I've come to take you back to our Homerealm.*

A freezing wind blows over me, freezing flesh envelopes me. Numbness wins a victory over pain. I'm in the arms of Indrid Cold. He's lifting me off the floor.

The lowlife Chuck E. Cheese party begins anew. The Chicago woman is hoarse and screaming accusations. "You took my pills!" The Bronx Guy is bragging: "I got a tape measure on my tool belt. I'll prove it!"

The Appalachian woman is vocalizing her preference for Judas over Brutus. Don Knotts's voice dissipates into a quiet, fuzzy chuckle. My life is being swallowed by Empty, Ridiculous Grandeur. I'm being absorbed into myth and reality.

Part Two: Away

1

Now I'm in bed.

Not *my* bed.

Whose bed, then? A hotel bed?

I think so, but I'm not sure. The bed keeps moving.

"Moving?" No, that's not the right word. It lacks specificity. If I say "the bed keeps moving", you might imagine the bed shaking violently, like the little girl's bed in *The Exorcist*. That would give you the wrong impression. So allow me to try again: my bed is floating and drifting and dipping in mid-air.

Yes, that's better. The room is like a swimming pool. My bed is like an inflatable raft. It floats and it drifts. It gently knocks against a wall, ricochets off, and lurches backward. Its right side dips toward the floor, and I'm fearful of falling off.

I don't fall off, however. Leather straps keep me secured to the bed.

Sometimes the bed rotates clockwise, like a screw, until it's upside-down. When that happens, I want to throw up. Sometimes, the bed rotates so it's rightside-up again. That should make me feel better, but it doesn't. It doesn't, because that's when I'm in a better position to appreciate the nightmarishness of my predicament.

You see, the bed isn't the only object in the room that's floating. A cheap widescreen television floats. A thick coat of dust adorns the back of it. Some of that dust levitates off the plastic and floats toward me. I sneeze.

The force of the sneeze propels my head and shoulders forward. The sudden movement makes my bed (my world) wobble. I feel seasick.

And if all that weren't bad enough, the sneeze ushers in further unpleasantness. Like everything else in the room, my snot floats. I don't mention this because I'm trying to shock you. I'm mentioning it because *it's happening*. It's part of my suffering. As such, I must relate it.

"What suffering could come from floating snot?" you might ask. "Aside, of course, from the aesthetic suffering endured by watching such a disgusting blob cavort unashamedly through the air. You're overreacting."

This would be a reasonable argument, were it not for the fact that one tendril of that snot remains affixed to my right nostril. In other words, the snot isn't floating free, an object in and of itself. Rather, one tendril of it won't let go. So, my snot is like a sticky, disgusting helium balloon. A string of mucous tethers it to my nose. It bobs and dips as I bob and dip. I shake my head around, trying to hurl it away into the air.

It boomerangs back toward me. It ends up plastered firmly on my upper lip; no longer drifting, but glued onto my skin. I have a mucous mustache. I crane my neck to the side, try to wipe my nose against my shoulder. I'm able to wipe away half of it. The other half is now jammed further up my nose.

The remote control floats. The alarm clock floats (although its cord keeps it anchored to the electrical outlet). A pad of Zodiac Hotel stationery floats. (Now I know for certain where I am.) Some pens float.

Coat hangers float in a cluster around the closet. A landline phone floats. (Beige, fractured plastic; a knotted cord connected to the receiver.) A hair dryer floats. Tiny shampoo bottles and soap bars float, too. Somehow, they managed to drift out of the bathroom! A roll of toilet paper floats. A Gideon's Bible floats.

Sometimes, the objects all seem to be whirling around the same fixed point. Sometimes, they seem to form constellations. For example: the television, stationery pad, bible, and telephone form something like the Big Dipper (the telephone cord and receiver form the Dipper's handle). Constellations imply patterns. Patterns imply order. Thus, I conclude there's some coherent meaning to be found. Yes, all the meaning in the universe only *seems* to be fragmented. It's actually united in a Grand design!

The exact moment I reach that conclusion, the objects start to drift apart. The constellations erode. Perhaps, I tell myself, they're just morphing into new constellations. I look for new patterns. I come up empty. The Grandeur proved to be illusory, and therefore Empty. Empty, and also Ridiculous. I can no longer lie to myself. All is chaos.

Then the bed flips upside-down again. Every time this happens, I expect my glasses to slip down my nose. They don't. So, my vision remains in focus. I see the carpet. This reassures me, because this carpet is *one object*. Some carpets are constructed from thousands of individual fibers, and the individuality of each fiber persists even into the carpet's old age. This carpet, however, was made cheaply. The individual fibers have been smooshed together by the feet of thousands of guests. *E. Pluribus Unum*. Out of many, one.

Sure, it's a humble object. Apparently unremarkable. No doubt, it has been trod upon by plenty of shady businessmen, cheating spouses, and whining toddlers over the years. None-theless, the carpet is *one single object*. Therefore, it bears within it all the meaning in the universe. What I mean is: the mean-ing isn't diluted, the way it is when I'm forced to look at dozens of dissociated floating objects. Wholeness = Holiness.

Moreover, the carpet is a *stable* object, glued so tightly onto the floor that it doesn't float. A floating carpet (or, if you pre-fer, a *flying* carpet) would be an abomination. That which is meant for the ground should never venture into the air.

A new noise: static spitting out of a public address system. Then a voice—masculine, dignified, competent.

"Welcome, Nid Cold! This is your pilot, Lieutenant Ardo, speaking. I'd like to officially welcome you aboard the *Zodiac*. This craft is a Class Nine diplomatic transport vessel, a prod-uct of the Interdim Quatros Corporation's Homerealm Ship-yard. As you surely have realized by now, we're experiencing a slight malfunction with the artificial gravity. We expect to have that resolved momentarily. In the meantime we ask that you please remain strapped down in your bed."

I close my eyes. Feel a scream claw (and Claw and *CLAW*) its way out of my throat. The scream is muffled by my mask. What comes out sounds like the cry of a hurt hawk.

Can anyone think clearly when they scream? I don't believe it's possible. I want to latch onto comfortable thoughts: *I'm in a hotel, not an interdimensional spaceship. There's no such thing as Indrid Cold. It's a Grandly Ridiculous and Empty name. I never traveled back to the year 2007. I didn't speak to my father tonight. I have an overactive imagination. I'm always making up little stories. Now I seem to have graduated to making up big stories.*

These are the thoughts I *want* to think. Unfortunately, I can only manage to *half*-think them because I'm still screaming.

No. That's not true. Now, *right now*, I can only *quarter*-think them.

Why can I only quarter-think them? Because, once again, cognitive entropy is having its way with me! Phrases drift apart from one another. Words and letters float away from their moorings even as I try to reassemble them in my head. I seem to be fainting. Yes, I'm fainting and I...

2

...come to, shivering. I'm still strapped down to the bed, but I'm not in Room 312. I'm in a meat locker.

That's wrong. I'm in...something else. Everything around me is made of steel. Steel cabinets. Steel counters. Webs of frost have been spun on all the surfaces. My teeth are chattering. I have only one consolation: the gravity has been fixed. Nothing floats.

Something walks toward me. A woman? A doctor? A nurse? She's wearing scrubs, a cap, a surgical mask, and gloves. She seems to be white, but she's not pale. She looks like the kind of white person who obsesses over tanning. Hers is not a healthy tan, but an over-tan; the type of tan that will almost certainly result in melanomas. Her skin sags, as if wanting to free itself from its tormentor.

Her eyes are dark. Her glance, intrigued. She holds a test tube in her hand. Her fingers are only half the length of ordinary fingers.

They don't seem to have been amputated. I mean, I could be wrong about that. She's wearing gloves, after all. That said, the *shape* of the fingers is ordinary. I don't get the sense that there are stumps underneath the gloves. It looks like she has rounded fingertips. Her fingers are just, well, small. *Dispropor-*

tionately small, when compared to the size of her hand. A dark blue liquid appears in the test tube. It wasn't there at first, but it's there now. My shivering worsens.

"Enough of that now," she says. "Shivering never solves anything."

Her voice is warm and soothing. Her actions, not so much. Her fingers are tiny, but strong. She whips off my mask and jerks my mouth open. I think I hear my jawbone crack. It's all I can do just to scream.

She gets all up in my face. Starts screaming back at me, matching decibel for decibel. "Stop. Being. A. BABY! Screaming. Baby. SCREAMING BABY! Screaming all the livelong day. Screaming when we got you. Screaming as we keep you. Screaming when we try to calm you down. Screaming. Never. Solves. ANYTHING!" She doesn't seem to appreciate the irony of screaming a denunciation of screaming. (Do as I say, not as I do.) She forces the test tube down my gullet. When I've swallowed it all, she puts a new mask on my face.

I don't like to have objects forced into my mouth. I mean, I suppose I'm not unique in that regard. But for me, it triggers bad memories: that night in college when I woke up...

Don't think about it...

...with a..

Don't think...

...dick in my mouth. The guy was a heavy, hairy presence. He reeked of cheap beer and b.o. His voice wasn't warm. Wasn't soothing.

Don't think about it. Don't think about it. Don't think about...

I gagged on his dick. Afterwards, I threw up. Brushed my teeth for thirty minutes straight. Stayed in bed, paralyzed with a headache, for two days.

Don't think about it. Don't think...

I tried to pretend it never happened. I think he picked my room at random. I'd fallen asleep before I had a chance to lock my door. My roommate was sleeping with her boyfriend that night.

Don't!

I never reported it. And for the last thirty years I've tried to get the image of the guy's swollen cock out of my head. I've tried to ignore the way…

Don't!

…his glob of cum clung to the insides of my throat. And most of the time I've been able to forget it, but I can't now, because this so-called medicine is globby. It, too, clings to my throat. This is the reason I never take cough syrup.

I choke, and I cough, and the Doctor/Nurse/Whatever shakes her head. Forces my mouth shut.

Don't!

"Stop it right this instant," the medical-thing says. "I can hear your thoughts, and I need to correct them: *you* weren't raped."

I struggle. Try to spit the witch's potion back in her face. Her grip on my jaws grows stronger.

"Look, I'm not saying you're lying. I'm saying that, *if* your recollection is correct, then this shadowy man raped your *human costume*. Not *you*.

"But it's understandable that you would misunderstand things. We failed you. We never told you about your costume, and about the true self who dwells *beneath* your costume, or about the true heritage from which you sprang. And, if you think about it, one's true heritage is one's destiny. It's a terrible thing to go through life with no knowledge of your origins."

The globby elixir paralyzes my vocal cords. I want to scream, but can't. My screams are now locked inside my throat, the same way my body's confined to this bed. My scream was like a fire and the medicine (if that's the right word) extinguished it.

I can't speak now, let alone scream. Can't so much as whimper.

"Much better," the medical-thing says. She nods when she says this, as if trying to convince herself of the fact.

I flail around in my restraints. Am I trying to break free, or just throwing a tantrum?

"I see you have plenty of energy. This is because you slept during the entire flight. Understandable. You needed rest. I can only imagine how exhausting it is to carry around one hundred and fifty-five pounds of costume! And, you, poor thing, have had to do it for nearly fifty years! That's why you've always been so tired, you know. That's why your head has felt like a cinder block. You're carrying two brains around in there. An outer, human, *costume* brain, and your inner, Other, *real* brain. But I'm getting ahead of myself. I haven't even told you who I am. My name is Layla Dodd, and I'm here to explain your procedure.

"Today, we begin the work of removing your costume. It's a big costume. Six feet tall! So, it will take multiple surgeries to remove. Today, the doctor will be making a vertical incision down your lower abdomen and pelvic region. He'll remove all the layers of the costume in that region. By the end of the day, you'll get your first glimpse of what you really look like. Isn't that grand?"

I want to resist Layla Dodd. I want to resist Indrid Cold, the Interdim Quatros Corporation, and the Homerealm. I want to gnaw my way through the leather restraints, throw punches, find a gun, and fight for freedom. I want to resist.

No, that's a lie. I don't want to resist. I *want* to want to resist. Just like I want to want to feel concerned about my father and his dirty adult diapers. Just like I want to want to call my hometown hospital and check on my sister. But it all seems so distant, too distant to be relevant.

"It *is* distant," The Thing Calling Itself Layla Dodd says. "It *should* be distant. *Celebrate* your distance from the human frame of reference! You have lived for too long in the remote, outer provinces of existence. Now, you're coming into The Core. Such is your birthright."

The Thing picks up an antique leatherbound book. Opens it up. The faded gold lettering on the cover tells me the book is a *Family Bible*.

She announces the reading for the day: "An excerpt from *The Book of Origins*."

3

[1] There was a world before our Homerealm: an inferior Old-realm. But let us not speak of such trivialities.

[2] From inferior to superior, the world progresses. The beginning of all beginnings was the most inferior of all times. [3] Let us speak only of *our* beginning. Let us speak only of the Homerealm's origins, the birth of the most exceptional of worlds!

[4] At *our* beginning, there was only the Sleeping Cosmic Maiden. [5] Through many dark eons she dozed happily, without suffering even a flicker of a dream. All would have been well for her, had she remained asleep forever. [6] Alas, everything that sleeps must awaken.

[7] Now, in a neighboring dimension there lived a sly god, unnamed and unnamable; a figure of twisted light. [8] Endowed, he was, with the power to see past The Walls of Heaven and the Jungles of Time. [9] Endowed, he was, with the power to pick up the scent of alluring women.

[10] And it was in this manner that he tracked down the Cosmic Maiden.

[11] He found a way into our Realm, from his own Realm of Twisted Light. [12] How he got in remains unsolved, and unsolvable. [13] He found a way into our dimension, and he found a way into the Maiden. [14] She awoke to find him inside her. And, upon awakening, she screamed. [15] The sly god found a way into the Maiden and a way out again. In and out, in and out, in and out! Then out of our dimension he went, never to be seen again. [16] How he left, no one knows. Where he went, no one knows. Such matters are unknowable. [17] We only know this: the goddess was broken in the aftermath.

[18] And so it came to pass that the Sleeping Cosmic Maiden no longer slept. For sleeping now brought forth nightmares of this sly god, known also as the Beast of Light. [19] And so it came to pass that the Sleeping Cosmic Maiden became the Awakened Cosmic Mother, for the sly god had sowed one thousand seeds inside her.

[20] The Cosmic Mother only held five hundred eggs. And of these five hundred eggs, only three hundred and twelve were fertilized. The Number of Conception is three hundred and twelve. It is also The Number of Birth, and of Pain.

[21] These were uncommon offspring, all of them male, and all so intelligent that they spoke while still in the womb. And they spoke not as young offspring speak to their mothers—with tantrums and whining. No, they spoke calmly, clearly, and cruelly, with deep voices. They spoke as though they were their mother's superiors, for theirs was a regal bearing.

[22] They harassed her with unanswerable questions. "Where is our father, wench?" they asked. [23] They asked this because, even in their fetal state, they knew the sly god had been there. And likewise they knew he had left. With their half-grown eyes

and noses, they detected certain signs which led them to that conclusion: a few sparks left behind in the sly god's wake, a lingering scent of ambrosia. [24] The Goddess's womb, her skin and muscle, posed no obstacle to their senses. They could see and smell the scene that existed outside of it. Just as the father could see and smell through barriers, so could the offspring.

[25] Yea, verily, they took after their father. They were his boys, in heart and mind; in viciousness, most of all. [26] "You were but a ditch for spilling seed," they told their mother. "Our father is divine! What have you done to make him abandon you? Why is he not by your side?"

[27] "I did nothing to him," the Cosmic Mother said. "Where he has gone, I cannot say."

[28] "Tell us our father's name!" they demanded. In unison they spoke, but with different accents, trills, and rhythms. [29] For, unbeknownst to the Cosmic Mother, they possessed a multitude of forms. (For the Beast of Light holds within him many aspects.) [30] In the voices of fetal fish-gods and foul-gods and ape-gods, they asked. In the voices of fetal worm-gods and ghost-gods, too.

[31] The Cosmic Mother did not answer.

[32] "Who is our father? Tell us his name!"

[33] Loudly, without ceasing, the voices in her womb repeated their questions. The Cosmic Mother gritted her teeth and said nothing. She could not bring herself to say: "Your father is a sly god. That is all I know."

[34] "Speak to us!" the fetal gods demanded. "Who is our father? Tell us, so that we might go to him when we are born, and address him properly, and be recognized as his heirs."

[35] But would a sly god, even if located, accept his children as heirs? This is not the way of sly gods. [36] The Cosmic Mother pondered how best to explain this to the children. She could

not find the right words. She could not even search for the right words. [37] The noise of children blocks all concentration.

[38] "Who is our father? Where is our father? How long ago were we conceived? How long until we are born? We will find our father. We will not be denied our inheritance!"

[39] The Cosmic Mother moaned and wept, and cursed the day of her Awakening. [40] She wished the fetal gods would die, but instead her belly swelled. To the point of resembling a boulder, it swelled. And, like a boulder, it weighed her down so that she could not get up off of her back. [41] And the rage of the fetal gods swelled also. Day and night, the choir grew ever louder. Soon it came to pass that they were no longer content to simply scream. For screaming had done nothing to satisfy their demands.

[42] And so it was that they began to chew and scratch and kick the womb, to force themselves out into the world prematurely. They would go out into this universe, they thought, and find their father on their own.

[43] From the inside to the outside they traveled. Through the amniotic sac they clawed. Through the birth canal, they marched. Through the Goddess's belly they gnawed. Through her rectum they slithered with hate, trailing filth and blood in their wake, and the Goddess howled and wept.

[44] And up her esophagus a hundred ran. Out of her mouth, they sped. They forced her jaws open and dashed away. [45] Is it not understandable that she turned against them? Is it not laudable that she found the strength and will to close her teeth upon their necks? That she devoured them and despised them and smote others with her fists?

[46] So the melee had begun. Mother slew offspring to quell their rebellion. Offspring slew offspring to gain a greater share of the inheritance. Offspring slew Mother to escape into the

world. Blood and sinew festooned the fight. [47] Ugly are all origins, and ours is no exception.

[48] In the end, only two fetal gods survived: The Raven and The Ghost. [49] The former survived by flying away from the fight, and then scavenging the meat of his mother. The latter escaped death because she had never been truly alive.

[50] Together these gods founded our Homerealm. From the bones and gristle of their mother and siblings, they built a multitude of worlds. Like *nests*, they assembled these planets; one piece at a time.

[51] And when some years had passed, The Ghost and The Raven did mate. [52] And the first offspring The Ghost gave birth to was The Land, which covered the planets with soil and vegetation. [53] And the second offspring The Ghost gave birth to was The Sea, which clung to The Land of each and every world in an eternal embrace. [54] And the third offspring The Ghost gave birth to was a male slave, a hairless biped. And the fourth offspring The Ghost gave birth to was his female counterpart. And The Raven flew these slaves to a planet all their own, so that they might grow, mature, and mate. For The Raven and The Ghost were in need of a star to heat their worlds. [55] The flesh of slaves makes excellent star-fuel.

[56] In the dark and the cold, these slaves did pass their days. [57] And The Raven did appear to them at regular intervals, to let them feed on the remaining scraps of his fallen siblings, the fish-gods and worm-gods and ape-gods. On their knees, the slaves fell, for their feeding. And The Raven slipped the food from its beak into their mouths.

[58] In time, the slaves did mate.

[59] When it came to pass that the population of the slave planet had grown to ten, The Raven swooped down and slew five. [60] And he flew them out into the void, and he set the corpses

in the proper arrangement, the feet of all five bound together in the middle, with the heads radiating out at equal distances. [61] For when corpses are arranged in such a manner, they will begin to smolder of their own accord.

[62] By this magick, the flame was lit! And these five were the first kindling of our star.

[63] After twenty years, the Raven slew five more slaves and threw them on the pyre. And after forty years, five more. [64] So it was, over the course of a million millennia, that the fires grew. [65] And when the Homerealm Star had grown warm enough, The Raven and The Ghost mated once more. And the Ghost did give birth to The First Free Homerealmer, an entity who was neither male nor female, nor Raven nor Ghost, but rather both, or neither. And the Ghost did give birth to The Second Free Homerealmer, a male who was a Ghost like unto her. And the Ghost did give birth to The Third Free Homerealmer, a female who was a Raven. And it is from these three beings that all Free Homerealmers are descended.

[66] And to this day there are some Free Homerealmers who seem more The Ghost, and others more The Raven. And still others seem to be equally both. And there are some Free Homerealmers who are male, and some who are female, and still others who are equal parts both.

4

The Thing closes the family bible.

"You, Nid, are a Red-Eyed Ghost Raven. Your father, Indrid, comes from a long, slightly peculiar line of Ghosts; a line that, for eons, had never mated with a Raven. He broke with tradition when he impregnated your mother."

I want to know her name.

Then, I don't want to know her name.

Why the flip-flop?

Well, I'm wary of taking any of this too seriously. Don't get me wrong, I want to take it seriously. Despite all its oddity, it seems to carry weight and truth. Part of me likes the idea that my name is actually Nid Cold, and that my father is a cosmic Ghost named Indrid Cold, and that my mother was a sentient Raven. If these claims are true, they might change my life for the better.

But they probably aren't true. It's all too silly.

Then again, the *whole world* is silly, these days! We elected an orange toad president! Moreover, I have witnessed the *reality* of this silliness with my own eyes! I've *experienced* weightlessness! I've seen the medical staff's deformities!

Floating objects, floating objects, and short fingers! Short fingers grasping a Family Bible. Cosmic Maiden, Beast of Light, and Rapacious Creation. Rapacious Creation, Insolent Offspring, and Swollen Funeral Pyres. Rough, angular, yellow blobs overhead and HELL IS...

...real?

Layla Dodd speaks.

"Perhaps you'll stop doubting when I explain the details of your birth. Or I suppose I should call it your *pseudo*-birth. The year was 1973. Our fleet was exploring the East Coast of the United States. Your mother insisted on following your father on the mission. She sat atop your egg, breathing deeply in and out, letting all thoughts of the past and future burn off like fog so she could focus exclusively on the present. This is how all mothers in the Homerealm occupy themselves while sitting atop eggs. It's an ancient practice, one which we brought to your planet many thousands of years ago. Yes, that which you call 'meditation' has its roots in the Homerealm. We gifted it to the Hindus. Even though your species need not sit on eggs, it was appropriate to teach the technique to the Hindus because they were *metaphorically* incubating the birth of a New Age. The Hindus in turn gifted it to the Buddhists and Gnostics."

Layla Dodd has not convinced me. In fact, her strange claims only increase my doubt.

They smack of "ancient aliens" bullshit.

"Doubting never solves anything," she says. Then she continues her story.

"Your mother fell into a deep trance during her egg-sitting. So deep, in fact, that she didn't even notice when the artificial gravity failed.

"Yes, the struggle to maintain artificial gravity has long plagued our voyages. Believe me, it was even worse back in 1973! As a result of this difficulty, and her obliviousness to it, your egg drifted into a wall and cracked. Thus, you were born prematurely.

"Indrid never forgave her for this, by the way. It was her second such transgression. Your brother's egg had cracked as a result of this very same type of mishap! After your egg cracked and you were born prematurely, Indrid went to the Interdim Quatros board meeting and proposed a measure to ban expectant mothers from their vessels. The directors took his side. In fact, your name appears in all our history books, as the board's ruling came to be known as 'The Nid Cold Decision'. Never again would eggs shatter against a ship's hull!"

A dubious honor. My name was used to promote interdimensional sexism.

"Without a doubt, an honor," Layla Dodd corrected. "You must understand, you nearly died. Hatchlings who emerge prematurely don't live long. This is especially true of those, like you, who emerged at an extremely early stage of fetal development. The only reason you didn't die right then and there is that we performed a radical experiment to save you. It had only been attempted once before: with your brother.

"One night, we sneaked into a house in that place you call 'Maryland', and we performed a certain operation. We implanted your fetus into the body of a human newborn. Your Raven Ghost brain was implanted into her brain, and, in fact, took it over. Your Raven Ghost bones were implanted inside her bones. And so on."

Implanting bones *inside of* bones? I'm pretty sure that's not how surgery works.

"It's how *our* surgery works. We implanted you inside of the human infant, and now it's time to extract you from the human adult. Actually, you would be better off if we could keep you in there a while longer. You're not quite sufficiently incubated. You may find this surprising, but you're still a fetus. Viable outside the womb now, but still a fetus! This goes to show you how far advanced the Homerealm Race is compared to Earthlings. Our fetuses possess cognitive and linguistic abilities superior to those of the average human adult. This is why you've struggled to fit into Earth culture. This is also why your parents never understood you. You're a foreigner, a citizen of another dimension.

"Ideally, you should have been incubated for exactly fifty Earth years. That's how long Homerealm Ravens sit atop their eggs. However, recent events on Earth have introduced certain risks we're not willing to take. I refer, of course, to this virus. Even we do not yet fully understand it! What if your human costume succumbed to this illness? Then your incubator would be shut off, and you might die. Or you might survive the death of your costume, and find yourself buried alive. Or, even worse, *cremated* alive. We could not allow you to come to such a shameful end. In our culture, cremation is only for slaves!"

"This is why Commander Cold went looking for you. All parents want the best for their offspring."

Layla Dodd then shoves her tiny fingers into the back pocket of her scrubs. Fishes out a white handkerchief. Places it into her mouth.

I want to laugh, but I can't. Besides, laughing never solves anything.

Layla Dodd starts chewing the hanky. There's suddenly a hint of honeysuckle in the air.

Now she's gagging on the hanky.

Now she's coughing it out.

Now the handkerchief is purple. She wipes purple, honey-suckle-scented drool from her lips and smiles. "My salivary glands have been altered. At the appointed time, they secrete this liquid. It's like ether, but far more powerful." She rips off my mask and replaces it with the handkerchief.

I wish I were back in my gross, cluttered house. (At least then I wasn't assaulted with purple saliva!) I wish I were back under my unwashed sheets, looking up at the dust-laden ceiling fan. I wish, even, that I were back in Room 312, floating upside-down and gazing at the carpet with adoration.

Or, at least, I *half*-wish these things. That's the best I can do, because I'm now only *half-conscious*. My brain fails. Cognitive entropy. Phrases drift apart. Words get jumbled up. *Dust-laden Car Pet. Floating ceiling. A door's elation.*

I'm woven within layers of fuzziness. By the time sounds reach my ears, they're nearly dead. "I believe that's sufficient," something seems to whisper, "yes, Nurse Dodd, that's enough anesthesia. I've got the knives. Let's do some cutting."

5

I awaken in a state of confused pain, surprised to hear myself grunt. Has the globby vocal cord paralyzer worn off? Was it really in my system to begin with? There's nothing worse than distrusting your own brain.

I'm in bed. At first I think I'm wearing an adult diaper. Then I realize I'm wearing bandages over my entire belly and pelvis. Wire coat hangers cover my upper arms and boobs.

A *mess* of wire coat hangers, to be precise, covering my *naked* upper arms and boobs.

Freeing myself from the coat hangers' thrall isn't easy, because they're all knotted up with each other. I'm not strong enough to heave them to the floor. My brain's too muddled to heave them to the floor. I want to get up out of bed, but even the slightest movement proves exhausting.

I think I'm back in Room 312. Somewhere around here, a landline telephone is off the hook. Maybe it's been off the hook for a while, but I'm just now noticing it. The persistent busy signal (*BUH! BUUUHHHH! BUUUHHHH! BUUUUHH-HH!*) distracts me. The stinging in my stomach distracts me.

No, "stinging" isn't the right word. Or at least it's not the *only* word. There's also a snapping sensation. In fact, the snapping sensation comes first. First the snap, then the sting. Over and over and over. It's like ten little boys have taken up residence in my belly, each of them armed with a rubber band. *Tormenting* little boys, *snapping, snapping, snapping* their rubber bands against my insides.

Only, I no longer feel like I *have* insides. At least not in the traditional sense. Honestly, I was wrong when I said the pain was like ten little boys snapping their rubber bands *against my insides*. It's more like the ten little boys *are* my insides. I suppose what I mean is, I don't think I have a stomach anymore. I still have a heart and lungs and neck and brain and hamstrings and leg muscles and feet, but the center of me is no more. My belly and loins have been removed. Before the surgery, I had a stomach and a cervix, intestines and a uterus, ovaries and a rectum. I had a spleen, a lower spine, a pancreas and hip bones. All of these have been carved out. I only have the little boys and their rubber bands.

Screaming solves nothing, so I grunt like a sow instead. Then I wince. Then I whimper. I groan and toss my head around and take in more of my surroundings. (Someone, it seems, made sure I had my glasses on when I came to.)

The landline phone lies on the carpet like a murder victim in need of a chalk outline. *BUH! BUUUHHHH! BUUUHHHH! BUUUUHHHH!* —sonic blood gushing out a punctured artery. Broken glass litters the dresser (the corpse of a little coffee pot). The nightstand has collapsed onto its side. The lamp is nowhere to be seen. However, a bathroom light has been left on, allowing me to take in the carnage.

Outside the room, a man's voice. (Muffled, the way voices always are when heard through doors.) "You got your badge?" he asks.

I hope he's not expecting an answer from me.

BUUUHHHH! BUUUHHHH! BUUUUHHHH! goes the busy signal.

Snap-STING! *Snap*-STING! *Snap*-STING! go the little boys squatting where my guts used to be.

The man in the hallway is not expecting an answer from me. He's talking to another man in the hallway. I know this because I can hear the other man's reply. "Yeah, I registered last night."

"You still remember last night?" Man #1 says.

Man #2 laughs. It's not a natural laugh. It's a forced laugh. It's the laugh of someone who feels pressure to have a good time. "I remember drinking bourbon with Lymon Zinn. That was after you went to bed."

Man #1: "Starfucker!"

BUUUHHHH! BUUUHHHH! BUUUUHHHH!

Snap-STING! *Snap*-STING! *Snap*-STING!

Metal coat hangers and bandages. Bandages and talk of badges. Metal coat hangers. Talk of badges. *BUUUHHHH! BUUUHHHH! BUUUUHHHH! BADGES!*

Then, the voice of a third man. "Heads up, my friends. Coming through."

Man #1 and Man #2 (collectively): "Oh, sorry dude."

A clicking sound. My door opens. The first thing I see is a wheelchair. The second thing I see is the strong, athletic, cleancut frat boy type pushing it.

"Oh, dear. Too much sensation!" the frat boy says, glancing around the room.

BUUUHHHH! BUUUHHHH! BUUUUHHHH!

"You must be annoyed by that repetitive noise," he says. He pushes the wheelchair aside, leans down, and places the receiver back on the cradle. No more busy signal.

Well, no more busy signal *for two seconds*. Then...

BUUUHHHH! BUUUHHHH! BUUUUHHHH!

"How alarming," the frat boy says. "The phone isn't acting the way a phone should act. It must be disciplined." He yanks the phone cord out of its jack.

It still doesn't take its cue! *BUUUHHHH! BUUUHHHH! BUUUUHHHH!* it babbles. (Technology is a staged spectacle, featuring actors not quite up to their parts.) The frat boy refuses to give up. He sits in the wheelchair and (with some difficulty) rolls over the phone (over, over, over the phone). After a few minutes, it's smashed to bits.

Its death wail (*BU-BU-BU-BU-WHAHRW!*) sounds like an incredulous stutter ("B-b-b-b-but why?"). The air smells like ozone in the aftermath.

"Now let's get these coat hangers off of you," the frat boy says. He doesn't even try to disentangle them. His tiny fingers are able to grab onto the collective mass and toss it aside like a bale of hay.

Now, my boobs are exposed. The frat boy pays them no attention.

"I'm pretty sure you're aware, by now, that the gravity is on the fritz," he says by way of explanation. "On and off, on and off, on and off it goes. After your surgery, we brought you back here. The gravity was working at the time. But it seems as though it went off again while you were sleeping. Objects floated through the air, drifted around willy-nilly. As it so happened, the coat hangers drifted until they hovered right over you. Then, *ker-plop!* gravity came back on. So, they fell atop your chest. What goes up, must come down. But at least you slept through the whole ordeal.

"Fortunately, I foresaw this possibility. Foresight is the best sight, I think you'll agree. Last night, shortly after you arrived here, I applied an adhesive to your spectacles to make them stick to your nose. That way, they wouldn't get lost in Zero G. No floating eyes on my watch!

"Now, for your pain medicine." He walks to the bathroom and comes out with a test tube full of steaming, fizzing red liquid. "This will help your adjustment."

His fingers are tiny, but strong. Almost as strong as Layla Dodd's. He starts to pry my mouth open, but soon realizes he doesn't have to pry my mouth open. I want the pain to go away. I accept the medicine willingly, like a communicant accepting the blood of Christ.

The medicine starts to work immediately. I can't say that it removes the pain (*Snap*-STING!). Rather, it incites a pins-and-needles sensation throughout my remaining human flesh, so that the *Snap*-STING! sensation in my nonhuman belly no longer seems quite so weird. The effect is to flood the body with discomfort, and to make the discomfort relatively uniform throughout the body, so that the phantom-belly discomfort ceases to feel remarkable.

"Next, I'm going to introduce myself. My name is Whitey Mare, and I'm your assigned liaison for MothCon 2020. To begin with, I must educate you about certain grave, mysterious matters." He removes a device from his front pocket, a smart phone of some kind. Slides and stabs his little fingers over the glass surface. Begins to read a prepared statement, presumably sent to him via email or text.

"In late October of 1966, a Red-Eyed Raven-Ghost was being retrieved from an incubator in Parkersburg, West Virginia. His egg had cracked open prematurely in 1916, so he had been implanted in a human incubator. He was the first to undergo such an operation!

"His fifty-year gestation period was up. The time had come for him to be reunited with his family. Unfortunately, the retrieval team was not as careful as they could have been. For example, they did not bother to tell the hatchling about his origin, and the origin of the Homerealm. As a result, they enabled the hatchling to over-identify with his human costume. Furthermore, they failed to explain to him why surgery was the only alternative. This was, perhaps, their greatest blunder of all. Out of context, surgery can be mistaken for torture, and medicine mistaken for poison. Thus, it is of no surprise that this hatchling went batty and flew away!

"Nid, this particular Red-Eyed Raven-Ghost was your brother. His name is S'Indrid Cold. S'Indrid, of course, is a contraction of 'Son of Indrid'.

"When High Command notified Indrid that the retrieval process had gone awry, he did all he could to track down his son. In his fervor he was careless and exposed himself to public scrutiny. Is the name 'Woodrow Derenberger' familiar to you?"

It's not.

Whitey Mare can read my mind. I don't say a word, but he answers as if I've given him a verbal reply. "No matter. You'll find out quite a bit about Woodrow Derenberger during MothCon. We want you to learn all you can about the events of November 2, 1966. That's the day your father made the mistake of initiating contact with Mr. Derenberger. Mind you, I don't mean to disrespect your father. Even he would admit he erred.

"You see, he cared. About your brother. Then he erred. By making contact with Woodrow Dereberger. The relationship between your father and Mr. Derenberger was analogous to the relationship between Dracula and Renfield, in the elderly Universe film."

I think Whitey Mare means "the old Universal (Studios) film".

"Just as the former needed the latter to make certain arrangements on his behalf by daylight, so your father needed someone to search for S'Indrid freely, unrestrained by the need for subterfuge. And, believe you me, there *is* a need for subterfuge. If we're too straightforward in our approach we could give the humans clues as to what's really going on. They would resent us if they found out we'd used two of their species as incubators.

"But I digress. The point is: your father recruited Mr. Derenberger into the search. He thought Derenberger was smart enough to perform the task, but not smart enough to figure out The Secret of Incubation. Your father took this risk because he cared about your brother. To care is to err, to neglect benign! That was, indeed, his original 'S'in'. I know it's traditional in your language to say 'no pun intended', but in this case it was."

Whitey Mare is a frat boy, but he's not a frat boy. No frat boy speaks like this. Is he wearing a human costume, too? Or, is he some oddly tangible ghost from the Homerealm? Perhaps he's a Renfield, himself, driven crazy by his commerce with entities from another dimension.

Or does he just *think* he's a Renfield? Maybe he hasn't been *driven* crazy. Maybe he's always been crazy. Maybe the woman calling herself Layla Dodd is his mother. Maybe she passed down to him a strange genetic trait: extremely short fingers. Maybe they sneaked into my room while I was asleep, trashed it, and have made up this 'artificial gravity on the fritz' story to cover their tracks. How can a hotel (firmly tethered to the ground by three dozen steep granite steps) simultaneously exist as an interdimensional spaceship? It can't!

But I saw objects floating. I heard the pilot's announcement. I felt (no, not just "felt", I *feel*, right this very moment) the *Snap*-STINGS!

Maybe I'm mad, too.

"You're not mad, I'm not mad," Whitey says. Then he starts rambling about "quantum consciousness" and "quantum entanglement" and "queer location". (I think he means "bilocation".) He's talking like some stoned grandmother just off the plane from Sedona.

Maybe I'm hallucinating him. Maybe I came down with the virus, and I'm actually still in my cluttered house in Indiana.

Earlier I decided this experience wasn't a dream, but can I say for sure it's not a *fever* dream?

"I understand this is a lot of information to crap on you at once…"

I'm pretty sure Whitey Mare means "*dump* on you at once…"

"…but this 'novel coronavirus' on your planet has forced us to rush the acculturation process. We had hoped to slowly and steadily reveal the truth to you. Perhaps perform the surgeries over a series of months. Obviously, that plan went up in a puff of gas."

Smoke. A puff of *smoke*. Whitey has trouble with English idioms, it seems. Layla Dodd did not. It seems Homerealm citizens have varying degrees of fluency in English.

"I am not a citizen of the Homerealm. I am a kind of… well…*guest worker* for the Homerealm. I was born on Kipple, the sixth planet in orbit around the star Radeen. The Homerealm is the fourth planet. Once there was a war between the two planets and the Homerealm emerged victorious. You are most fortunate. You were born into the winning team! You enjoy all the benefits of Homerealm citizenship. Homerealm Command will brave the most remote stretches of the Interdim Tunnel to bring you back. We Kippleodians, on the other hand, are quite disposable."

I suppose I should feel bad about the Kippleodians' plight, but I'm more concerned by Whitey Mare's ability to read my thoughts! I'm used to owning an opaque mind. An opaque mind is an okay mind. But now my mind is transparent, and it's not fair. My thoughts can be read, but I can't read Whitey's thoughts.

"You'll learn, soon enough, how to read them," Whitey Mare says. "Before long you might even learn how to bleed them. By which I mean, of course, you'll be able to cure them from any malfunction, the way your people cure ailments with leeches."

Yes, Whitey Merry may very well be mad. Mad *and* ill-informed about modern medicine. Then again, he could actually be from another dimension. After all, a being from another dimension wouldn't think the same way we do. Their speech would operate under a different syntax. They might teach themselves to mimic the syntax of the more commonly-spoken Earth languages, but they wouldn't quite nail it.

Moreover, their assumptions about social interactions would be nothing like our own. They would have different obsessions. Their knowledge of our medical practices would be centuries out of date, because they travel *rapidly* through time. From their perspective, our centuries would blur together the way individual trees blur together when seen out a car window. Their consciousness would transcend our own, and any sufficiently transcendent consciousness is indistinguishable from madness.

But is the reverse also true? What I mean is, can we say that any sufficiently mad consciousness is indistinguishable from transcendence? Yes, I believe we can say that. Transcendence and madness are forever entangled in each other, like wire coat hangers or chains of DNA.

No, strike those statements from the record. I was wrong. Or, at least, I implied something that's mistaken. I'm making it sound like transcendence *is synonymous with* madness. But they're not the same thing. Anyone who has looked an untreated schizophrenic in the eye can attest to that. Sometimes, a madman is *just* a madman. Sometimes, there are no holy fools—just fools. The nasty funk of a ranting homeless guy is a far cry from incense.

But Whitey Mare isn't homeless. He doesn't smell. *I* smell. My armpits reek. If I could take a shower, I would. But none has been offered to me. Perhaps I should ask for one.

I don't have a chance to ask for one. Whitey Mare starts jabbering again. Actually, "jabbering" isn't the correct verb. It implies rapid speech. Whitey's conversation has a measured, scripted feel to it. He's enthusiastic, but only in the performative way a museum docent or tour guide is enthusiastic. Whitey offers up *canned* enthusiasm.

"November 2, 1966. Today marks the fifty-fourth anniversary! A lifetime ago! And yet, despite the passage of time, there are still those on your planet who know about the day your father met Woodrow Derenberger. Not the common herd of people. Only those whose consciousness has some plasticity, and who know the consciousness *of the universe* has some plasticity. In fact this event, this so-called 'MothCon', exists in no small part to celebrate your family's legacy. For the Earthlings call your brother S'Indrid 'The Mothman'. They have built a statue of him, where worshippers can pay homage. They have made a film about him, starring their greatest living actor. His story is told over and over. He is famous, in the sense that his image is legend. He is unknown, in that his true identity escapes even the most diligent Earthling researchers."

Oh dear. This is more fucked up than I imagined!

I want to laugh and sob and groan. My vertigo worsens. My heart wobbles in my chest. The *Snap*-STING! sensation worsens. Whitey Mare's words corrode the nerves connecting my ears to my brain, corrode the brain, itself. Sicken my soul.

Of course, I've heard about Mothman. I know he's a kitschy cryptozoological entity, Bigfoot's avian kin, the subject of credulous History Channel documentaries. Whitey Mare and Layla Dodd and Indrid Cold are all trying to perpetrate a moderately funny, extremely cruel practical joke at my expense. Who knows? Maybe Giuseppe the Puppeteer is in on it, too!

A joke. At my expense. Haven't I suffered enough? I've traveled hundreds of miles so far. I've tripped over multiple curbs. I've suffered under the baleful eyes of a Mysterious Starer. I've read a Mysterious Message. I've watched a poodle die. I've been forced to contemplate the paradox of blue grass. I've been forced to look upon a sharp, angular, blobby landscape. Smokestacks and smokestacks and asphalt and toad signs. I've ruminated on Hell's nursing home. I've imagined demonic finger painting. I've considered the role such artistic endeavors may have had in the origins of West Virginia.

I've seen Mysterious Breath. I've fucked up my air compressor while trying to fix a flat. I've traveled back to the year 2007. I've been forced to accept the reality that my father has *always* been a ventriloquist's dummy.

I've suffered the tyranny of objects! I've found myself floating in a cocoon of hotel-junk. I've had creatures with short fingers strap me down to a bed. And why, *why* have I undergone all these tribulations?

So that I could end up at a fucking *Mothman* convention.

I feel cheated. I obviously didn't know what all this was leading up to, but I had assumed I was experiencing a *personal, idiosyncratic* revelation of unreality. Instead I find out I'm caught up in cheap, collective folklore. *West Virginia* folklore! This Grand Strangeness has plunged me into a labyrinth of kitsch! It's as if I had been promised a meeting with a shaman, only to be brought to the tent of a tacky carnival illusionist. It's as if I were rowing down some remote, exotic river of consciousness, admiring the haunted flowers and poisonous toads along the shore (flowers and toads I believed no other human being had ever witnessed), only to find out I was in a theme park ride all along. The moment I disembark from the rowboat and step onto the pier, I find a gift shop selling T-shirts adorned with cartoony, anthropomorphic flowers and toads.

Mothman: the ironic obsession of hipsters, the *un*ironic obsession of the gullible!

Who actually believes in Mothman? The same people who spend hard-earned money on ghost hunting equipment, that's who! The same people who waste their time posting theories about Atlantis on Facebook.

Whitey Mare clears his throat. Glares at me. Whispers some more. "Enough! You must disentangle your mind from the human frame of reference. Let your brain out of its cocoon, Nid. Burst out of the costume brain!

"In the *Book of Vertigo*, chapter seven, verse thirteen, it is written: 'Do not reject the reality of unreality because you see it wrapped in absurdity. Take the time to unwrap the gift, and accept it with a humble heart.' In all honesty, I didn't expect you to greet this disclosure with such cynicism. Anyone who has watched *The Mothman Prophecies* should know that your brother isn't merely, as you might say, a 'cheesy urban legend'."

The Mothman Prophecies. I've heard of it, but haven't seen it. I think it came out in the early 2000s. I was a horrible drunk, back then. I didn't get out much. I didn't watch movies at home, either. It was all too much to keep up with. It still is. Even to this day, I generally don't watch movies. I got out of the habit during those years of drinking, and have never felt compelled to pick it up again.

I have no idea who starred in it, but I'm pretty sure it wasn't "the greatest living actor". Even to this day, I'm so estranged from pop culture that I wouldn't even have a clue who that would be! George C. Scott is dead, right?

Whitey Mare once again clears his throat. I stop thinking about George C. Scott and listen to this frat boy who is not a frat boy: "Another thing you must remember: your brother is not, in fact, a 'cryptozoological' creature. That implies a terrestrial origin. You and him are both entities from another *dimension*, just as I am. That said, I think you should attend this morning's plenary session, a lecture titled 'Mothman: The Thinking Man's Cryptid'. Although the title makes use of a misnomer and the speaker has many mistaken notions, he approaches the topic with respect and imbues it with gravitas. You should find his overall thrust quite helpful in dispelling your misconceptions.

"This is not to say there's no basis for your concerns. In years past, MothCon has attracted the sort of novices and nobodies you have mentioned; humans who can boast only average intelligence, whose thinking suffers under the influence of popular culture and the internet. They think they're searching for answers to profound questions. All they really seek is a shortcut to transcendence.

"But that is the glorious thing about the year 2020. These 'dum-dums' (as I believe the idiom goes) won't be in attendance this year. The virus has scared them away. This year, only the purest pursuers of knowledge will be in attendance, the people willing to *risk death* to learn more about your brother."

I think attending a Mothman convention during a pandemic is actually the "dum-dum" move.

Whitey Mare sighs. Fidgets. Raises his hand up, as though he'd like to slap me. Then his eyes light up with panic (with *recognition*, perhaps, that it would be a mistake to strike the daughter of Indrid Cold). He takes a deep breath. Counts to twelve. Then, he continues.

"This year the convention was going to be canceled due to the novel coronavirus. As you might imagine, registrations had decreased considerably and hotels were not in the mood to offer a discounted room rate for only thirty-six guests.

"That's where we stepped in. In our guise as 'The Zodiac Hotel' (a struggling, dilapidated operation in need of business), we offered rooms at fifty dollars a night, cheap catering for two meals a day, and threw the conference meeting rooms in for free! Now, please understand, we Otherdimensional beings have *always* attended MothCon. But this year, thanks to Covid-19, we have swallowed it whole! To borrow an example from your ancient folklore: we are the whale and MothCon is Jonah!

"We chose this particular tactic because it seemed to be the *most efficient* way to find out exactly what the Earthlings know about our operations, and what they *want* to know, and what puzzles they've tried but failed to solve. Not only do we hear what they say during the panel discussions, but all the rooms are equipped with listening devices. So, we can hear what they *really* think. Moreover, by hosting the event we have control over the milieu. We assign the rooms in which everyone sleeps. If we desire to have one of our spies near a too-astute researcher, we can arrange it. If someone in a panel gets a little too close to the truth, we can make it seem as though his microphone is failing. We have also produced a series of fake Mothman documentaries, which will appear on the televisions in their rooms. This is how we will sow the seeds of disinformation. It is most important to control the narra-."

A series of muffled blurping, bleeping sounds interrupt Whitey's Empty, Grand, Ridiculous speech. It would seem my cell phone is somewhere in the room. Under the bed? Yes, I believe it to be under the bed.

"I hate to interrupt, but do you mind getting that for me?"

Whitey Mare scowls. "You understand what I've just told you, correct? About your family?"

I nod.

"And what Nurse Dodd told you? About the Homerealm?"
I nod.

"Then you know that any incoming messages from that device are not intended for you, but for *your costume*. I know it will be difficult, but you must learn to differentiate between the two. You don't want to end up like your brother, do you?"

"I don't know. What happened to him?"

"I told you. He went batty. But allow me to be more specific. He's a vagrant, Nid. A cosmic hobo, ricocheting from one dimension to another. Instead of living under a bridge he lives under an ice volcano on Titan. Then he might take shelter in a black hole, or in some remote stretch of rain forest, or in the unmapped outer reaches of Mammoth Cave, or in an abandoned warehouse in Cairo, Illinois.

"He's homeless, lost in spacetime, and mentally ill. Even now, he doesn't quite grasp who he is. He doesn't know *where* he is. Or, if by some chance he *does* know where he is, he's unable to find his way back to us. For that matter, he's unable to communicate his needs or wants. All he can do is shriek or groan. That's the other reason we have always kept a close eye on MothCon. Every year, humans come to the convention and claim to have seen him. While the vast majority of these sightings are misidentified cranes and owls, we have reason to suspect ten percent are legitimate. These are some of the best leads we've had."

I don't want to be the Mothman's sister. I don't want to be a ventriloquist dummy's daughter. I don't want to be snared in the tangle of heredity. (Four family trees. Human costume mother's side. Human costume father's side. Ghost side. Raven side. Every single branch and leaf afflicted with the blight of madness.)

Lovecraft gave hereditary madness a veneer of ancient Grandeur in "The Rats in the Walls". Jack Hill made hereditary madness seem ridiculous in *Spider Baby*. In my experience, hereditary madness feels Empty. Empty, like the crib purchased for a stillbirth.

I just want to be back in my house, in Indiana, resting in bed and looking up at my dust-laden ceiling fan. I want to savor the smell of my neglected house. (After all, "to care is to err, to neglect benign".) I don't want to scream, because a wise woman once told me that screaming doesn't solve anything. I just want to be alone.

Instead, I'm at a convention.

But I'm going off on a tangent. I can't afford to do that. While I've been waxing philosophical, Whitey Mare has started dressing me up in a pink T-shirt adorned with the logo of the Cracker Barrel restaurant chain. As he maneuvers my arms into the sleeves, I get a whiff of my own b.o. He then covers the rest of me with pink terry cloth sweatpants and pink hospital socks.

This is every bit as embarrassing as being forced to wear a jester's costume. I've been made to look like a rube! A stinky, *braless* rube whose breasts droop and flop about like fleshy beanbags.

"It's regrettable that we didn't have someone available to give you a scrubbing down," he says. "But at least you have clean clothes to wear. Yes, you stink—but your apparel does not. Freshly laundered cloth, such as that which now adorns you, provides a buffer that prevents the full magnitude of your stench from being discovered."

He has a point. The clothes I wore yesterday were far too sweaty to wear today. This pink ensemble must have been the only outfit available in my size. Yes, it's a ridiculous outfit, but maybe that's not such a bad thing. It can be healthy to laugh at oneself.

Then again, maybe it's *not* the only outfit available in my size. Maybe all of this is a cruel joke. Maybe the aliens have a sadistic streak. Maybe they abduct humans because they need court jesters. Maybe all of this is being captured by a hidden camera and beamed into the throne room of the Homerealm King. Maybe I'm being subjected to this mire of existential slapstick so an alien monarch can derive a few chuckles from my plight!

I have no evidence that this is the case. Nonetheless, I take the hypothesis seriously. The very concept of evidence has no place in the twenty-first century. It's too boring.

6

And now Whitey Mare has decided the time for talk has ended. He huffs and puffs and grunts and pulls me out of bed. Plops me into his wheelchair. The seat creaks and squeaks. One of the spokes snaps. My weight should not have broken the chair. Not only have I always been skinny, I've also just had a good chunk of my human flesh and bone removed! Nevertheless, the empirical evidence abounds: the chair is broken. Broken, but not entirely useless, it would seem. I'm in motion now, rolling out into the hallway!

Sort of.

Whitey has to huff and sweat and grunt just to get the chair to lurch forward two feet. It rattles the whole time. I'm half-afraid it will fall apart. After getting it to move two feet, Whitey stops to catch his breath. Then, when he's good and ready, he huffs and sweats and grunts some more. This time, it goes three feet.

As it turns out, the wheelchair isn't merely broken, it has two flat tires. It rattles when Whitey pushes me. I did not break the chair. How could my weight result in two flat tires? No, as it turns out the wheelchair was already in a state of disrepair when Whitey brought it to my room.

The ancients thought there were four basic elements which served as the building blocks of the universe: Earth, Air, Fire, and Water. This belief was, of course, mistaken. The four elements are actually Annoyance, Tragedy, Abnormality, and Brokenness.

Emptiness is the Brokenness taken to the extreme. Grandeur is Abnormality taken to the extreme. Ridiculousness is an especially perverse alloy of Annoyance and Abnormality. And so on, and so on, for every last thing in the universe.

Broken spokes, flat tires, and a creaking, squeaking seat. Tangled coat hangers, jaundiced bullies, and half-real neighbors who prefer Judas over Brutus. Madmen, madwomen, Russian novels and *Jerry Springer*. Other Dimensions and Don Knotts and road trips. Blurry asphalt and toad-men and spaceships and surgeries and badges and smokestacks and busy signals and tractor trailers and stomach bandages and HELL IS REAL.

Ka-lunk, ka-lunk, ka-lunk goes the wheelchair as Whitey forces it into unnatural motion. Why doesn't he realize the futility of pushing a wheelchair with two flat tires? Surely, there's more than one wheelchair aboard the *Zodiac*. Why doesn't he just stop and call for another orderly to bring a new one down for me?

Whitey Mare answers. "Because there's no time for that! We have less than an hour until the opening ceremonies!"

Would it really take that long to find another wheelchair and bring it down here? No. I think he's just trying to maximize my discomfort. It's true that I don't feel any pain in my butt, because my butt no longer exists. And I don't feel the jostling too badly because all the rest of my body has been rendered all tingle-tingle-tingly from the pain medicine. But the abrupt motion makes me car sick. Whitey strains and grunts. Even with his great finger strength, I barely move an inch. And then he strains some more, and I don't move *even* an inch. And finally, on the third or eighth or nineteenth try, the wheelchair goes *ka-lunk*ing forward. I move a half dozen feet and nearly topple out! This is hardly the way to treat someone who has just undergone surgery.

Yet my fate is in his hands. He could shove this wheelchair down a stairwell and cackle as I plummet on the landing. He could then gallop down the stairs, pointing and laughing at my broken neck. I don't trust him, but I must trust him. Or, at least, I can't make too much of a fuss. I have a feeling that I'd get into some sort of terrible trouble, if I made too much of a fuss.

Now Whitey Mare is giggling. He's not *pointing at me*, but he's giggling. No doubt, he has read my thoughts and my fear of breaking my neck amuses him!

Again, the question arises: am I in the thrall of a madman? Whitey Mare is talking about the kinds of things madmen talk about, using the stilted, awkward manner typical of a certain variety of madman. He giggles like a madman. An outside observer would say this is the most likely scenario.

Then again, an outside observer might say I have gone mad, too.

They'd say I've gone mad and Whitey Mare (if that is his real name) has gone mad, and Layla Dodd has gone mad, and that there's no such place as The Zodiac Hotel, and that my Raven/ Ghost hybridization genealogy seems like an awkward, overly-complicated imposition of madness. (For madness, true madness, is always awkward. There's no such a thing as an organic, naturally flowing experience with madness. The madman is always trying to shoehorn his particular obsession into reality, even when it doesn't fit.)

Physical reality interrupts my philosophizing. A shaggy-headed twentysomething in a black T-shirt, blue jeans, and brown leather boots (with fringe!) needs to pass us. He tries to squeeze past the right side of the wheelchair. He ends up sideswiping me. The sudden clatter makes me dizzy and panicky.

"Oh, sorry dude," he says.

Dude. *Dude!* I'm wearing all pink, and still: "Dude!"

The offender is wearing a red bandanna as a face mask. This makes him look like an Old West train robber. I can't imagine this red bandanna does much to rein in the spread of Covid, but what can I do? He has met the minimum standard.

In other respects, he has failed to meet the minimum standard. I speak, of course, of his sideswiping my wheelchair! This fails to meet the minimum standard of hallway courtesy.

If this happened on the Interstate, I could try to catch up with him and take a picture of his license plate and report the incident to the police. If this happened in an elementary school, a hall monitor would take note of the incident and report it to the principal. But it happened in a hotel hallway, and the only harm it caused was dizziness and nausea of the (presumably) temporary kind. Thus, I have no legal recourse.

Whitey Mare seems taken aback by the sideswiping. He stops pushing me. He leans down and whispers in my ear. I'm expecting him to offer a few words of encouragement: perhaps confide that he stared at the sideswiper and committed his appearance to memory, perhaps promise to track this callous train robber down and give him a tongue lashing. Maybe he'll even promise to report him to Indrid Cold.

Instead, he stops to catch his breath in the middle of the hallway. Leans down. Adds insult to injury by whispering horse shit in my ear. "Soon you'll be completely out of your costume, revealed in all your majesty. No one will dare side-swipe you then!"

Then he huffs and grunts and pushes the wheelchair some more. "I promise this won't take much longer," he says between frantic breaths. His mask goes concave when he inhales, convex when he breathes out. "The elevator is right around the corner."

7

And so it is. He stabs the down button with a stubby finger. As we wait, I feel something light and airy land atop the pins and needles of my right hand. A promotional poster, for a film titled *The Virgil Falls Zoo*. It's a poorly designed advertisement. Cheap paper. Smudged black print, apparently applied via a magic marker. ALL CAPS. Exclamation points!!! The ink smears onto my hand as I read it. It offers no information on where or when, exactly, one can view the film. It merely says:

THE VIRGL (sic) FALLS ZOO!!!

WORLD PREMIERE AT MOTHCON 2020!!

Then it goes on to list a series of laudatory quotes. The first is from a website called ParaDocsFilmReviews.com. The whole blurb consists of a single word: "…interesting…"

I don't bother reading the rest.

"My company is involved in this release," a weary male voice says. I jerk my head upwards, expecting to see him looming over me. He's not there.

The man lets out a raspy chuckle. "Down here, silly." He taps my hand with a finger so dry and brittle I expect to find crumbled bits left behind in its wake.

I lower my glance and see an emaciated bald man in a motorized scooter.

On second thought, he's not a *bald* man. He's simply a man who has shaved his head. There's a difference, you know. This man has stubble all over his head. Truly bald men boast no such abundance.

"Two o'clock in Canis Minor," the film's producer says. Of course he's wearing a mask, so everything he says is muffled. "It's a hoot, isn't it," he says. (At first I think he's said "hoop", but then I figure it out.) "I mean, the way all the meeting rooms in The Zodiac Hotel are named after constellations!"

I feign a polite chuckle.

"I mean, think of it: 'two o'clock in Canis Minor'. That sounds like I'm telling you when and where to find a meteor shower! And you know what, that's only fitting. Because *The Virgil Falls Zoo* is destined for meteoric fame!"

I'm a bit confused. Is meteoric fame a good thing? Doesn't it refer to the kind of fame that, although intense, burns out quickly? Moreover, *The Virgil Falls Zoo* doesn't sound like it has anything to do with the Mothman. Judging from the title alone, it would seem to be a documentary about a plucky Mom and Pop tourist attraction that brings camels to Appalachia.

I don't have time to dwell on such concerns, however, because The Producer has moved on to another subject. "By the way, I'm pretty sure the location is tentative. I mean, yes, *do* show up at Canis Minor at two p.m. But just be aware they will probably move us to Canis Major when they see the size of our crowd."

Mercifully, the elevator chimes. It has reached our floor. Soon, its doors will open.

Soon...

Soon…

Wait for it…

Something goes wrong. The elevator ascends. We've been forsaken.

The Producer, of course, keeps on talking.

"David said he might be swinging by here on his way to New York, just to take in the opening. We've been friends since his days in Philly, you know. He'll probably be incognito, because he doesn't want people to hound him with questions about a possible Season Four of *Twin Peaks*. But we might be able to persuade him to do a lecture on Transcendental Meditation. He's very into it, you know. He'd have to disguise his voice, to make that work. But you do realize that his trademark voice, that nasal thing, that's not his real voice anyway. You knew that, right? When he's just being himself, not talking in front of a camera, he actually sounds a lot like Wilford Brimley. I mean, think about it. He's originally from Montana! He only assumed that nasally voice to try to fit in on the East Coast.

"But my point is, he'd have to revert to his real voice, to pull off a lecture. At least, if he wanted to stay incognito. That's his thing, you know. Transcendental Meditation. T.M., for short. Tom, of course, is all about Scientology. Not T.M. That's ironic, if you think about it, because you can't spell "Tom" without "T.M." But David is all about T.M., not Tom.

"That's why you'll never see Tom in one of David's projects. There's no room for a meeting of the minds. It's a shame, though, because I really think Tom could have raised the profile of David's little art films. Little, I mean, in the commercial sense. Which, if you think about it, is the only sense that makes c-e-n-t-s, and hopefully a few dollars, too!"

And now The Producer's giggling. His mask is fluttering around his mouth. He seems to think he has told a particularly witty joke.

To be polite, I offer a chuckle. The Producer seems to think it's genuine. Or perhaps he knows it's not genuine, but doesn't care. Maybe his primary goal is *to be memorable*. He wants to make an impression. He doesn't care if I find him distasteful, as long as his schtick has put him on my radar!

Now he and Whitey have moved on to a new topic. Whitey's explaining why I'll be unable to attend the screening. It's not an honest explanation. He's weaving a tale, making an excuse. Pointing to me, Whitey says: "She's a good friend of Jeff's, so she wants to go to his screening instead."

I have no good friends, let alone good *male* friends, let alone good male *filmmaker* friends named Jeff.

"Jeff has friends?" The Producer raises an eyebrow. "A *lady* friend, no less?" He's skeptical.

I try to make it convincing. "Strictly platonic."

"Very commendable, to support one's friends. I can't argue with that." Then he turns back to Whitey Mare. "So, she can't make it. But what about you?"

"I'm her valet. Where she goes, I go."

The Producer nods gravely. "Hmm…I see. Well, in any case, it was very nice to meet you." The scooter's motor whines as he nudges even closer to me. He scratches behind his ear, then takes my right hand in his. Clasps it tight.

Odd. His hand is no longer desiccated. It's suddenly *moist*. It's slathered with a glob of translucent, quivering gel. And so my hand is now moist, from the gel. And now the gel is shapeshifting. Coalescing. It's no longer just a *glob* of gel. It's worm-shaped.

No, "worm-shaped" isn't quite right. Worms don't have dozens of little feet. It's more appropriate to say it's "centipede-shaped". Yes, my hand is now the home of a translucent, gelatinous centipede. Little translucent, gelatinous feet skitter over my flesh.

Then, the sting!

The centipede has some sort of pincers or teeth. Not at all gelatinous, but hard and sharp and vicious. A spot on my hand turns bright red, hot to the touch. The centipede has opened up a tiny, stigmatic hole in my hand. Yes, it has opened up that hole and it's tunneling into it. I see the translucent gel-worm disappearing down into the wound it has just made. There it is, making itself at home inside my body, without my consent.

I try flailing my hand around, in the hope of flinging it away. No luck. It has already submerged completely under the skin. I'm tempted to say "no trace of it remains", but that's not quite true.

I can see it just underneath my skin. It looks as if an inch-long segment of vein has declared a revolution from its kin, grown feet, and decided to march toward cleaner pastures. It crawls up my arm quickly, covering about two inches per second. It leaves a bright red trail of inflammation in its wake.

If it had occurred to me, while still in Indiana, that such a fate might befall me, I would have never left my house. If this had occurred prior to my arrival at The Zodiac Hotel, I would have screamed and shook and wept. But I've developed a tolerance to these sorts of things. Don't get me wrong: I'm upset. I'm just not *screaming*. A barely-audible, high-pitched moan escapes my lips. It's the same sort of moan I make when I barely avoid a collision on the highway. (Tractor trailers, tractor trailers, and moaning. Moaning and moaning and horn blasts.)

Up my arm it goes, stinging all the way. It disappears under the sleeve of my Cracker Barrel T-shirt. I think it's heading for my skull. I wonder if it has the strength to crack it open and invade my brain. Judging by the muffled crunching sound coming from my temple, it does.

It's magickal gel.

Or a topically-delivered hallucinogen.

Or a gel that is both genuinely magickal and artificially hallucinogenic.

Why do I make such claims?

Because I suddenly feel flush. My eyes...they're fizzing. Yes, they're swollen and fizzing like soda. They're changing, somehow. My brain's changing, too. I feel something up there break apart. But it's a *pleasant* breaking apart, if that makes any sense. The breaking apart of chains.

The Producer smiles. Talks about me as though I'm not there. "Well, perhaps if the little lady takes a closer look at my poster, she'll change her mind. Guillermo has some fine things to say about this project. Says it will do for Mothman documentaries what *Pan's Labyrinth* did for Spanish Civil War films!"

I take a second look at the poster. I doubt The Producer secured such a promotional blurb honestly, but a lie that outrageous merits a glance!

Only one problem: the poster is no longer a poster.

What I mean is: it's still a piece of paper, but it no longer promotes a film called *The Virgil Falls Zoo*. Instead, it bears a message written in black fingerpaint against a white background:

I HAVE A HUGE DOLLOP OF GEL HIDDEN BEHIND MY EAR.

THE GEL MAKES IT SO THEY CAN'T READ YOUR THOUGHTS.

THEY'LL *THINK* THEY CAN READ YOUR THOUGHTS, BUT THEY'LL ACTUALLY BE READING *DECOY* THOUGHTS GENERATED BY THE GEL,

"THOUGHTS GENERATED BY A GEL?", YOU ASK. "THAT MAKES NO SENSE."

ALLOW ME TO EXPLAIN: THE GEL CONTAINS A SENTIENT LIFEFORM THAT ONLY THINKS ABOUT EATING AND FUCKING. IT BURROWS UNDER YOUR SKIN AND BECOMES A PART OF YOU, BECAUSE ITS THOUGHTS ARE SO OBSESSIVE, NOT EVEN WANDERING FOR A MOMENT FROM ITS DUAL FIXATIONS, THE PATTERNS SHOW UP MORE DISTINCTLY ON THE ALIENS' THOUGHT-READING "RADAR".

SO BE PREPARED: YOUR CAPTORS WILL THINK *YOU'VE* BECOME OBSESSED WITH EATING AND FUCKING.

LET THEM KEEP THINKING THAT.

THE EATING AND FUCKING THOUGHTS ARE THE DECOY THOUGHTS.

YOUR TRUE THOUGHTS WILL REMAIN UN-READ.

FURTHERMORE, THE GEL CONTAINS A CHEMICAL, ABSORBED INTO YOUR NERVE ENDINGS, THAT ALTERS YOUR BRAIN CHEMISTRY AND OPTIC SYSTEM SO YOUR EYES CAN READ THIS MESSAGE.

NO ONE ELSE CAN READ IT.

AND NOW, THE MOST IMPORTANT PART OF THIS MESSAGE:

I KNOW ALL ABOUT YOUR CAPTORS.

I KNOW YOU ARE HERE AGAINST YOUR WILL.

I HAVE BEEN SENT TO RESCUE YOU.

NOW IS NOT THE OPPORTUNE TIME FOR ME TO ACT. BUT I CAN TELL YOU THAT, THIS VERY AFTERNOON, I WILL TAKE YOU FROM THIS PLACE.

THE SENTIENT LIFE FORM IN THE GEL HAS HAD A NANOTECH TRACKING DEVICE IMPLANTED JUST

BENEATH ITS SKIN.

SO I WILL BE ABLE TO USE THAT TO LOCATE YOU, NO MATTER WHERE YOU ARE.

THEY WILL HAVE YOU HIDDEN AWAY IN A PLACE LIKE UNTO A DUNGEON,

BUT IT WILL AVAIL THEM NAUGHT.

I CAN TELL YOU THIS BECAUSE I AM A PROPHET, BLESSED WITH NO SMALL AMOUNT OF PSYCHIC ABILITY.

A ridiculous message, I think you'll agree. Empty to the brim. Yet, simultaneously, larger than life. Grand.

I believe in psychic ability. That is, *sometimes* I believe in psychic ability. For example, the Homerealmers have it. Otherwise, how could they read my thoughts? Other times, I don't believe in it. For example, when I have been driving around southern Indiana, and spotted a sign advertising the services of a local psychic, I've mourned for all the desperate people who've wasted their cash on such a huckster. I feel the same way when I pass churches and payday loan establishments.

So much depends on the context. Paranormal events always sound goofy, until they happen to you. I have sensed, in my own mind, the telepathic answers Indrid Cold has offered to my unspoken questions. I have seen, with my own eyes, how an unimpressive homemade film poster was actually a secret message. I don't believe there is any way a switcheroo could have been done via sleight of hand. Thus, The Producer seems legit.

On the other hand, The Producer gives off skeevy vibes. He boasts that he's a

...PROPHET, BLESSED WITH NO SMALL AMOUNT OF PSYCHIC ABILITY,

which seems gauche, right? Gauche and tawdry and hucksterish. Moreover, even before he presented himself as a psychic, he revealed himself to be a name-dropper and crass self-promoter. Thus, The Producer is a con man.

However, he's not charging me for his services. If he were a con man, there would be some financial angle to all this. But I see no angle. He seems to be genuinely interested in my welfare. Maybe he's a *loveable* con man, a con man with a heart of gold.

So, as you can see, this is not as simple as it seems. To navigate all these contexts, one needs to appreciate nuance. Context and context and nuance.

Existence *equals* nuance! (Nuance and nuance and suspicions of insanity—a gray maze under a gray sky.)

Maybe I have never left my house. Maybe I'm still in my bedroom, staring up at the ceiling fan! Maybe I didn't buy Mircea Eliade's *Myth and Reality* at a secondhand bookstore. Maybe *I* am the awkward college girl who kept it around for decades as proof of her education. Maybe I'm older and grayer and more wrinkled than I'd like to admit.

Maybe I wasn't laid off from work. Maybe I'm permanently disabled. Maybe I only read it because I was incredibly bored and incredibly sad and needed an activity I could do while bed-bound. Maybe the illustration of the alien on the cover triggered a series of daydreams.

It would be deeply unsatisfying, if all of this were happening in my head. I mean, I suppose I could cope with it, because it would at least mean I had my freedom (i.e., it would mean I wasn't being held captive by aliens). That, I suppose, would be a pro. The cons, however, are numerous and far outweigh that single consideration.

For example, it would also mean that I'm not particularly special. That is to say, it would mean that I'm just an ordinary human being, not a fetal mothwoman wearing a human body as a costume. It would mean my life was far less grand than I had been led to believe. It would mean I was far more ridiculous than I had been led to believe. It would mean my life was achingly empty.

I would no longer have a convenient excuse for my alienation from my family. I would no longer be able to say to myself: *I'm alienated because I'm a fucking* alien. I would have to accept that there's no real reason for my alienation. It just *is*.

Or maybe I'm dead and HELL IS REAL.

But enough self-pity. It's unattractive. Let me show some regard for you, the mysterious entity privy to these thoughts of mine. You, who have somehow been able to read my mind even before Indrid Cold arrived on the scene. You, who can no doubt still read my thoughts even now that the gelatinous centipede is in my brain.

Yes, I sense your presence in my head. I know you're still here.

It would be unsatisfying for *you* if all of this turned out to be in my head. After all, you've probably become a little invested in the outcome. Will I make it "home" to help my Earthly family in Maryland? Will I end up in the "Homerealm" dimension, instead? Will I retreat back to my "home" in Indiana? Will I live or will I die? Will I cross paths with my more famous brother? What will *he* be like?

You want answers to these questions, and you'll feel cheated if all of this turns out to be nothing but a whirlwind of hallucinations and delusions. In fact, you would probably feel more cheated than I would.

Are you worried about this possibility? If so, consider this: so-called "reality" only happens in our heads. The eyes (which, you may have noticed, reside *in our heads*) have limits; there are certain wavelengths of light they cannot see. Thus, they essentially *filter out* some stimuli so they can focus on others. An irrefutable fact: evolution has decided there are certain things we are better off not seeing.

In any event, these flawed organs of visual perception send tiny bursts of electric nerve signals up to our brains (which, you may have noticed, reside *in our heads*). Our brains interpret these signals, to the best of their ability, according to the dictates of the cultural context in which we've been raised. I look up at the night sky and see Orion the Hunter. If I had been born in Bronze Age Babylon, I would have looked up at the same stars and seen The Heavenly Shepherd. Thus, reality is formed in our heads.

Of course, that's not exactly correct. What I mean is, such a statement opens the door to many gross misunderstandings. Whether I believe in gravity or not, I'll plunge to my death if I walk off a cliff! Thus reality is not entirely subjective.

But it is *partially* subjective, and therefore we must employ nuance to understand it. Even an astrophysicist would say so! String theory (or something like it) tells us there are an infinite number of universes, a "multiverse". Therefore, in one of those universes, I will not plunge to my death if I walk off a cliff. And in another of those universes, I'll only plunge to my death if I happen to look down. (Such a universe would operate like a Warner Brothers cartoon. Wile E. Coyote would be that universe's Stephen Hawking.) And in a third universe hippos would grow beards and shit diamonds.

Infinite, after all, means *infinite*. If you say bearded, diamond-shitting hippos are impossible, then you're putting a limit on the number of universes that may exist. How unscientific of you!

If you believe in science, you must admit that a universe

exists in which I *really am* sitting in a wheelchair outside an elevator at The Zodiac Hotel. And if you believe in science, you must admit there is a universe in which all of this is in my head; a universe in which I'm still in Indiana, staring at the cover of *Myth and Reality*. If you believe in science, you must believe both are true simultaneously.

As I have said before: existence equals nuance. Vertiginous nuance. Layer after layer of nuance. Blinding shades of gray. Just thinking about it makes my head pound. So I stop thinking about it.

I think, instead, about the note in my hand. Will The Producer actually be able to pull off a rescue? Whitey Mare (or Layla Dodd, or Indrid Cold) will be keeping watch. They'll make sure I'm under lock and key! The Producer looks frail. If he truly is my rescuer, there must be more to him than meets the eye. Can his motorized scooter transform into a small aircraft? Can it shoot missiles or laser beams at Indrid Cold? Will it deploy its tractor beam and tow me with it, into the sky?

According to string theory, at least one universe exists in which I'm rescued this afternoon. Likewise, at least one universe exists in which the attempt fails. Soon, I'll find out if I reside in the former or the latter.

Part of me doesn't want to find out. Part of me wants to just linger here, at this crossroads of possibilities.

But then the elevator chimes.

Time insists on moving forward. I've never been a fan of motion of any sort. I've always been quite happy lying in bed, staring up at the ceiling, caught in a spiderweb of stillness.

Scratch that. I'm mistaken. That is, *slightly* mistaken. I can't honestly say that I've been "quite happy", under any circumstances. It's more accurate to say that I was "content" with lying in bed, or better still, to say I "had few, if any, reservations about" lying in bed.

Stillness and tightness and fan dust.

Fan dust and fan blades and wind.

Wind and pseudo-wind and Giuseppe the Puppeteer.

I suppose I like the ceiling fan because it always moves in the same, predictable way. Circles and circles and circles. The only sound it makes is a gentle whirring. Well, there's also that persistent rattling sound. (My landlord didn't do a good job of mooring the fan to the ceiling. That's why it rattles.)

No, that's not the reason it rattles. It rattles because there's a loose lightbulb, barely clinging to its socket. Whatever. The point is that the rattling noise is always the *same* rattling noise. And the whirring noise is always the same whirring noise. And the predictability of such noises comforts me.

The elevator dings a second time. The doors open. I see five people inside that little ascension chamber.

Dinging and motion and *co*-motion and busy-ness.

Five people, that is to say, five objects. They are, in fact, five *sacks* of objects (each person holding within them organ-objects and tendon-objects and fecal-objects). Also, multiple objects rest atop of these objects: black T-shirts, shoes, caps. Many of them cover their skin with tattoos, their shirts with printed slogans, and their caps with sports logos. Such adornments add yet another layer of gratuitous nonsense to the tableau. Some have lanyards around their neck-objects, some neck-objects remain bare. They're all wearing mask-objects over their lip objects over their gullet objects over their stomach objects.

The lone female object in the group looks young. It has adorned its face with three layers of makeup. It wears no lanyard, but has adorned itself with two separate necklaces (both the shade of bubblegum). It also wears bracelets around one wrist and one ankle.

How odd, that I have slipped into referring to the young woman as "it".

It seems rude to *objectify* another woman, so I stop thinking of her in those terms. This is not to say that I stop *staring* at her, however. I just change the lens through which I view her. She's a person, not a thing. She's a *she*, not an it.

I stare at her because she interests me. My interest is purely recreational: I would like to tell myself a little story, and she seems like good fodder. How old is she? Thirty? Nineteen? Could be either. I'm terrible at guessing ages. Anyone under forty is young. Anyone forty to sixty is middle-aged. Anyone older than sixty is old.

She has purple hair and big boobs. Even in high heels, she's a tiny woman. Her crop top reveals a pale, pierced belly. She's wearing a short jean skirt and fishnets. She has her youth and knows how to use it.

I envy her.

She hasn't noticed that the door has opened. She's oblivious to the fact that two passengers with mobility devices need to get on. She has her arms wrapped around a tall, ape-like man whose cowboy hat scrapes against the elevator's ceiling. They're swaying back and forth, almost slow dancing.

Three shorter dudes surround them. They haven't gotten out of the elevator either. Their eyeballs sag in their sockets. Dark circles adorn the area beneath their lower lids. They lean against the elevator. They sigh. I get the impression that they're annoyed by the public display of affection. (Not because they're uptight about such matters, but because they're jealous.) One of them lowers his mask for a moment to take a hit off a flask. The smell of vodka varnishes the air.

For a moment, I feel a surge of inexplicable guilt. I don't feel like I'm simply trying to get onto an elevator, I feel like these five people are engaged in some momentous ritual. I feel like I've interrupted them.

Then I realize the irrationality of such thoughts. "Hey," I bellow, "I need to get on." The couple stops their swaying, the lonely hearts stop their pouting, and they all leak out into the hallway.

Finally, there's room for me!

Whitey Mare rubs his hands together, braces himself, and starts to push the chair toward the door. At the same time, The Producer zooms ahead in his scooter.

There's not enough room for both of us!

The Producer sideswipes my chair. The collision lifts my right tire off the floor. Everything's askew. I'm tilted at an angle. I'm dizzy again, panicky again. I let out a high-pitched moan.

I've only been in this wheelchair for a very short time, and already I've been sideswiped twice. What the Hell, people!

The Producer puts his scooter in reverse. It beeps, just like a tractor trailer. My right wheel clatters back to the ground. (Tractor trailers, tractor trailers, and clattering.) Another spoke has broken.

"Please forgive me," he says. "I'll catch the next one. I'm in no hurry. The longer I can hang out by the elevator, the more people I can get to my screening! Besides, I'm already registered." He shows off his lanyard and name tag. There's no *name* on The Producer's *name tag*. No personal name, that is. It is, instead, emblazoned with the putative name of his supposed film company. It merely reads: Nevada Studio Alliance.

"Thanks," Whitey Mare replies. Then he huffs and sweats and grunts. Pushes my flat tires a few feet forward. Wipes his brow with his forearm. Stumbles in after me.

Elevator thoughts: *I want to go to sleep. I want to be alone. I want to get back on the road. Back to Maryland, to see my parents. (Even if they are, in fact, my pseudo-parents, the parents of my costume, and not truly mine.)*

Crowded hallway thoughts: *At least they're predictable. Familiar, if not exactly family. That's not so bad, given the alternative. I hope I'm rescued. I hope I see Maryland again. But my highest of hopes is to return to my bed, back in Indiana, and stare at the dust-slathered ceiling fan. That would be Heaven.*

Instead, I now find myself in the registration line. Instead, my head's pounding again. Instead, I have to decide if I should permit myself to be rescued. It seems at first to be a no-brainer, but maybe it is, in fact, a brainer. I'm in no condition to change adult diapers.

Perhaps I should let Indrid Cold's surgeons perform more operations. Then I can fly around the cosmos and look for my missing brother. (The brother who I've never met. The brother who might not exist, because he's the fucking *Mothman*!)

Russian novels, *Jerry Springer* and the History Channel.

Surgeries and a costume and the cosmos.

Brothers and sisters and finger painting demons and blobby stars. Blobby stars and Producers and dead poodles and asphalt and flat tires.

We've been in the registration line for a long time. We're made to feel like livestock. Or maybe we have always felt like livestock and are just now realizing it. I find myself scanning the ceiling. I'm looking for ceiling fans. Life is always better when I find four blades that go round, round, round. Ceiling fans are your best entertainment value.

I find no ceiling fans. I *do*, however, see tiles. White squares. Textured paint. I start to count them. When I get to ninety, I feel something draped over my neck. A lanyard. A name badge.

It says I'm a V.I.P. I look up at Whitey Mare and smile. "This is the closest I've ever come to winning a gold medal."

Whitey Mare's scolding me for some reason. "Keep that mask over your nose! Your father will kill me if he sees it out of place." He gets all in my face. Apparently, when I craned my neck up, my mask dipped under my nose. So, now he tucks my nose in, like a baby under a blanket. "I know you're hungry, but you won't be getting anything to eat if you don't shape up!"

He's reading my decoy thoughts. He thinks I'm hungry, so he's using the threat of starvation to goad me into compliance with the mask policy. The gelatinous centipede works!

Please note: I'm not trying to be gratuitously weird. I wish I could tell you something mundane, but even the mundane parts of my life have always been odd (Russian novels, Jerry Springer, My Mother the Ventriloquist, My Father the Dummy). Current events have washed me in a second wave of oddity. (President Toad, Governor Toad, Covid-19.) The Homerealmers toppled my brain over with a third wave (Mothwoman, Mind-reading, Costumes, Surgeries). Then, just when I thought my brain might be steadying itself, The Producer nearly drowned me in a fourth. (Mind-jamming, the gelatinous centipede, Decoy Thoughts, Rescue Mission.)

Before, I had a sense of being at one with The Strange. Now, I realize this is a poor way of describing the relationship. "Being at one" with something implies that you peacefully coexist with it. Clearly, The Strange is at war with me. "Being at one" implies that there are two discrete entities joined together in harmony. I, on the other hand, struggle with this imposition of weirdness. I want to live a normal life, but have never been granted the courtesy. If I were to say: "I am at one with the universe," I would mean I'm *communing* with the universe, that a state of interbeing exists between us. But what I'm experiencing isn't communion. It's colonization. The Strange is in charge.

Now Whitey Mare is grunting again. This means my chair will soon lurch forward. It will shake and rumble beneath me. I'm being pushed around because I can't walk under my own power. I can't walk under my own power because I had surgery. I had surgery because my costume needs to be removed. My costume needs to be removed because Indrid Cold says so.

8

The Orion Ballroom is a nightmare. A black smudge covers the full length of the ceiling. Could be oil or mold or soot. On top of this background, someone has spray painted a monstrous excess of pentagrams. A *chorus line* of pentagrams. *Gold* pentagrams. Row after row of them. Sixty-six, by my reckoning. The Homerealmers are sending a message: "The trail ends here."

It all looks hastily done. None of the pentagrams were painted with geometric precision. Not a single equilateral polygon in the mix! They look like the sort of pentagrams I drew when I was a little girl.

(Well, I didn't exactly draw pentagrams as a child. I drew *stars*. What I mean is, I didn't set out to draw pentagrams. I set out to draw stars. It just so happened that the only way I could depict stars was to draw *pentagrams*! In fact, even to this day, if you were to ask me to draw a star I would crank out a sloppy pentagram.)

I have just come up with a theory that may explain the aliens' artistic failure: to the Homerealmers, a black, starlit sky holds no beauty. No more, at least, than a black asphalt road with a yellow stripe painted down the middle. Spacetime is simply the road on which they travel. To them, the night sky possesses no grandeur, no aspect of the transcendent. Thus, they put little effort into its depiction.

That is clearly the truth.

Well, actually, it might *not* be true. It's only true if I'm correct in my assumption that the Orion Ceiling depicts the night sky. I mean, it would only be logical for that to be the case. But I suppose they could just be *pentagrams* (by which I mean devil signs, not stars). Remember, there are *sixty-six* pentagrams. I can't believe that's a coincidence! Yes, the black background might have been intended to darken the room and convey a sense of foreboding. The gold paint might be meant to convey the *preciousness* of Satan.

But aliens can't be Satanists, right? They wouldn't decorate with occult symbols, would they? I just don't know.

And yet, a ceiling connoisseur *should* know. A ceiling connoisseur only has one job: to critique the aesthetic value of ceilings. To perform this job, she must first have a general idea of the ceiling-painter's intent. How embarrassing, to be puzzled in this case! I must reach a state of clarity on the matter. So, I nudge Whitey Mare with my elbow. Direct his attention to the object of my obsession. Whisper my question, so I don't draw attention. "Are those supposed to be occult symbols, or are they just poorly-rendered stars?"

Whitey Mare rolls his eyes. "You're *weird*," he says. He sounds a lot like my mother when he says this. My Earthly Mother, I mean. He hasn't sounded old before. He hasn't sounded like a woman before. But when he says that phrase he sounds exactly like my mom.

Then his voice returns to normal. "Time to pay attention, Nid. Stop talking about stars and stop thinking about food!

It's time for MothCon's opening ceremonies. The start of the whole shebang."

At first I'm confused. "Opening ceremonies" conjures up images of Olympic pageantry. At the very least, a ceremonial gong should be rung. And yet, as I scan the dais, I find no gong. I find no shaman in ritual garb, nor even an emcee in a tuxedo. I find, instead, a pear-shaped man wearing black slacks and a teal sweater. The sweater has a hole in the upper right arm, revealing a dingy white T-shirt underneath.

His white hair is dingier still. Unkempt and greasy. He wears a face mask, as we all do. But it doesn't hide the tight, contorted anguish stamped upon his face. He's shaking his head and muttering to himself. He's close to the microphone stand, so I can pick up some of what he's saying. He speaks with a high-pitched Appalachian accent.

"Not enough volunteers at registration…folks are still in line, gonna trickle in late. Gonna trickle…for the ceremonies. The *ceremonies*!" He makes it seem like an unpardonable offense, for folks to trickle in late; an unprecedented breach of etiquette.

But is a bottleneck at registration the true reason for the empty ballroom? You may recall that, this morning, I overheard a man in the hallway say he had registered the previous evening. He would be unaffected by today's bottleneck. If he wanted to be here, he would be here. However, as I scan the room, I find that Whitey Mare and I are the only ones in attendance.

Whitey has parked my wheelchair in an aisle on the right hand side of the ballroom. There are dozens upon dozens of empty seats all around me. Whitey could have his pick of chairs, if he wanted one. Instead, he stands behind me.

In the dim light of the ballroom, he looks *just a little* like a doll. It's hard to describe exactly *how* he's changed, but I'll try. His brow (once so strong and protruding) looks slightly shrunken or melted. When I first met him, his brow had a very distinctive, masculine contour. Now it's less distinctive. More generic. His eyes have grown glassy and unfocused.

I suppose nothing about Whitey Mare should surprise me, but this transformation defies reality.

But then again, it might not be a genuine transformation. What I mean is, everyone's appearance is mutable. No doubt, *I* look slightly different now, under the ballroom's dim chandeliers, than I did in Room 312. And certainly I looked different under the bright lamps of the operating room than I did in Room 312. Every room has its own light. Every *day* has its own light, a unique stew of sun and clouds, moon and shadows, incandescence and fluorescence. Every hour and minute and second have their own light, as the stew stirs itself up in new combinations. Under a full moon, I look like a dead girl. Under a blazing, boiling, cloudless sky, I look like a homeless junkie. Inside my house, under the kitchen's fluorescent lights, I look like an Impressionist painting.

Perhaps this is what Walt Whitman meant when he said "I contain multitudes."

I look up at Whitey Mare again, just to double check my assessment. Has he really started to resemble a doll?

Whitey leans down and whispers in my ear. "Please stop staring at me. I'm incapable of copulating with you."

Ah yes, he thinks I'm obsessed with fucking. He thinks he knows what I'm thinking, but he doesn't know what I'm thinking. I'm embarrassed to be called out in this way, but heartened to know the gel is still protecting me. Thanks be to gel!

A loud clicking, clanging, thumping noise interrupts my thoughts. It's the door opening.

The pear-shaped man's voice booms from the microphone. No longer frightful, but exuberant. "C'mon in, folks! You're in the right place. Uh-huh. Opening ceremonies. *The ceremonies!*" I look up, expecting to see hundreds of people streaming into the room. (Why else would the pear-shaped man's mood undergo such an abrupt reversal?)

As it turns out, he's greeting only two people. One is a chubby young woman with long blond hair. She wears a camouflage sweatshirt, a pink mask, hoop earrings, and jeans. Her walk isn't really a walk, it's a *wobble*. No, not a wobble. It's more of a penguin-like movement. A *waddle*. The other is a skinny old lady in an ill-fitting mask. (Too loose. She constantly has to fix it so it's back in place over her nose.) There's something striking about the way she shuffles into the room. I can't quite grasp why it's striking, but it is. I feel like I've seen that shuffle before.

The loud clicking, clanging, thumping noise once again interrupts my thoughts. The door to the ballroom has closed. It makes the same noise when it closes as it does when it opens. Is this normal?

Alas, there's no time for such trivial considerations. Voices at the front of the ballroom capture my attention. "You need any help getting on the stage?" the young woman asks. "I don't need you breakin' a hip all this way from home."

The old woman waves the young woman off. It's a dismissive, feisty gesture. "I don't need *you* making a fuss over me in front of these people. You can have a seat in the audience. My place is up here!"

The pear-shaped man doesn't know quite what to make of the old woman. "Beg pardon, ma'am. The dais is for our guests of honor. This is opening ceremonies."

"Mister, I *am* a guest of honor!" She grabs her name badge

and thrusts it up for the pear-shaped man's inspection. As she does this, I notice she's wearing a red lanyard. My lanyard, on the other hand, is black. Whitey Mare's is black, too. Perhaps the red lanyard is meant to denote her elevated status at Moth-Con.

The pear-shaped man reads the old woman's name badge. He nods. Chuckles. "Well, it does seem that someone has given you a guest of honor badge. But I don't know…" His voice trails off.

"Evelyn Carter!" the old woman bellows. "I *saw* the thing."

"Ohhh. So you're our *Eyewitness* Guest of Honor! My mistake! I forgot that we had one this year." He runs a trembling hand through his hair.

The old woman lets out a harumph. Shuffles over to an empty plastic chair that's been left at the rear of the dais, behind the nervous man. It's the first in a row of empty plastic chairs, six altogether. So we seem to be waiting for five additional guests of honor.

And an audience.

A cruel silence looms over the ballroom. How long does it linger? A minute? Three minutes? I don't know.

Mercifully, it ends with another round of clicking, clanging, and thumping. (The door again.)

Two more people show up. A young, geeky, hand-holding lesbian couple. Both have shaved heads. One, a white woman, wears a Godzilla T-shirt. The other, a black woman, wears a T-shirt bearing an image from some anime or manga cover. (The image depicts a schoolgirl with long hair and a short skirt cuddling a blobby pink unicorn.) Their face masks are made to resemble dragon snouts. They take their seats.

While the door is still open, I hear a couple of Appalachian accents clinking and clanking against each other in the hallway. A man and a woman. The voices are getting louder. Closer. "That malted sure was swell," the woman says. "Thanks ever so much for the evening out."

"Oh, we're not done yet, honey. The night's still young!"

"But Father said…"

"Your father said he trusted me to be your escort for the night. He won't mind if we take the scenic route home."

How odd, that these people seem to think they're out on an evening date. Unless I've gone mad, it's still morning. Therefore, *they* must be mad. Even so, the pear-shaped man will no doubt be thrilled to see them enter. Sanity isn't a prerequisite for admission to the opening ceremonies. Based on what I've seen thus far, it might even be an impediment.

This chronologically-confused straight couple squeezes through the door just before it closes. The man is short and husky, crowned with shaggy salt-and-pepper hair. His gut hangs over his belt. He has attempted to squeeze himself into an old high school letterman's jacket, adorned with the initials "P.P." He wears bluejeans. When he isn't speaking, his mouth twitches. A thin trail of slobber dribbles down his fat lower lip. The woman has long blond hair. She's wearing a bullet bra under a tight sweater. She's wearing red lipstick. How do I know the man's mouth is twitching and slobbering? How do I know the woman is wearing red lipstick?

Because they aren't wearing masks.

Their masklessness horrifies me. It's incredibly selfish to put others at risk. Moreover, the man's twitching and drooling disgusts me. And yet, despite the physical and aesthetic danger presented by these oddities, I must admit that it's refreshing to see people with their entire face unveiled. I have spent the last seven months looking at nothing but half-faces. I have almost forgotten that other people have mouths.

But enough about mouths. I should mention some additional aspects of the woman's appearance. At first glance, she seems much younger than the man. However, upon further examination, one notices crow's feet around her eyes. One notices how the skin in her cheeks has grown loose. Makeup can only hide so much. *Trendy clothes* can only hide so much. Snug slacks encase her saggy, rotten apple-shaped behind. (All fruit goes bad, eventually.) What a couple of characters! Perhaps I could cast them in one of my little stories.

It's been a while since I've told myself a little story. This is because I've been swallowed by a Big Story. Yes, my entire being has been swallowed by the Mothman Myth. (And by "Myth", I mean a Big Story that's empty, grand, ridiculous and true.)

Big Stories are clever predators. One moment we're strolling along, minding our own business. The next moment, the ground gives way and we're plunging down the proverbial rabbithole.

Only, the rabbithole isn't a rabbithole. It's something far worse: the gullet of the Big Story. Before we even know we're falling, its digestive juices scald us. And as peristalsis drags us inexorably towards the Beast's stomach, we have good reason to despair. For we are bound to lose ourselves in the process. Big Stories devour the individual. *Digest* the individual.

The Big Story is the collective story. The cultural (or counter-cultural) story. The story that makes its *hearers* into *adherents*.

Little stories, on the other hand, offer an oasis. Diversion. The joy of idiosyncratic speculation. A little story is a plaything that sprouts in my brain, a toy for my amusement. It starts with a chance discovery. (I *just happened* to stumble across *Myth and Reality* in a secondhand bookstore.) Then my brain starts to play with the discovery. (I noticed the book was old, but unread. Why would someone hold onto it for a long time, but leave it unread? Why didn't they just toss it in the trash?) Then my brain thinks up an answer. (A lonely girl had no interest in reading it, but kept it around for decades as proof of her education.)

There's a thrill in coming up with little stories. A light, frothy thrill. Little stories are insubstantial. There's little effort required for their construction. This enables me to adopt an "easy come, easy go" mentality with them. I can abandon them at will, anytime I please. (When was the last time you heard me refer to Giuseppe the Puppeteer?) I feel no pressure to make people believe them, let alone turn hearers into *adherents*.

Big Stories (Myths, Dogmas, Party Lines) control people. Little stories serve them.

I am in dire need of a light, frothy thrill. Both members of the straight couple are walking collisions of age and youth. How charming! I've never seen another couple quite like them. I've seen eighty-year-old women dye their hair and wear clothes better suited to thirty-year-olds. I've seen middle-aged men wear hipster fedoras to cover up their bald spots. But this couple isn't just wanting to look young. Based on everything they've said so far, they're *pretending* to be young. They're *performing* a skit. A little, meaningless skit that would make good fodder for a little, meaningless story.

Why are they performing this skit? Perhaps they're members of a community theater troupe. Yes, they're members of a community theater troupe and they're performing a skit to promote their most recent production: a redneck adaptation of *High School Musical*. Perhaps the director has made the whimsical decision to cast adults in the teen roles and teens in the adult roles. Perhaps the director thinks the only way to put butts in seats is to indulge in such hijinks.

No, that doesn't ring true.

Perhaps these roles were originally to be played by teenagers, but none came out to audition. (They're all hooked on opiates and video games. The arts mean nothing to them.) So, a couple of middle-aged hams grabbed the roles for themselves.

Yes, that seems more accurate. No director would, of his own volition, cast the slobbering middle-aged fellow as the male lead in *High School Musical*. Such casting was a necessity, a desperation move.

But I can no longer focus on my little story. Another round of loud clicking, clanging, and thumping erupts as the door opens again. At first, all I see is a black blur. It takes me a moment to realize the middle-aged thespians are under attack from a gang of swollen, jaundiced, well-dressed men who have sprinted into the ballroom. Note: by "well-dressed", I mean they're well-dressed according to the standards of the 1950s. They're all wearing shiny black leather shoes, black suits, white shirts, black neckties, black masks, black sunglasses and—most striking of all—black fedoras. They look like a gang of swollen, jaundiced Blues Brothers impersonators.

One of them pulls out a bullhorn. "Hey man, no one may enter The Zodiac without a mask. You ignored this rule, so we must eject you from the event."

The middle-aged man wrestles the bullhorn away. Shouts into it. "You just lighten up now, buddy. We're historical re-enactors, here to educate the audience about the teenagers who first discovered the Mothman back in 1966. We were told to appear at opening ceremonies and perform a little skit about that fateful night. That's all we was doing!"

My little story missed the mark. Can I be blamed for getting things wrong? I didn't know re-enactors bothered themselves with great moments in *cryptid* history.

The woman squirms away from her captor and leans in toward the bullhorn so she can get her two cents in. "Our costumes have gotta be *period authentic*. You wouldn't ask a Civil War reenactor to wear a mask, right? It would compromise their educational mission. You'd have kids thinking there was Covid back in the eighteen hundreds! Well, the same principle applies! The same princ-".

One of the well-dressed men wrestles the bullhorn back into his possession. Cracks it over the woman's skull. Sends her collapsing onto the floor. The middle-aged man screams. "Linddaaaaa!" His voice is so fierce and guttural and desperate that he needs no bullhorn to be heard.

Soon enough, he's tackled. Five of the well-dressed men succeed in handcuffing him. The entangled throng flows toward the exit. Two of them carry the dazed woman on their shoulders. The others push the man out.

The pear-shaped man doesn't like the way this is shaping up. He wails into the microphone. "Woah! Hold your horses, gentlemen. Do you have to eject them? What if they promise to be good and wear a mask? Then they can watch the ceremonies...the *ceremonies*!"

The swollen men ignore him. The ballroom door closes. The loud clicking, clanging, thumping noise is the only answer he'll get.

I feel sorry for the guy. More than anything in the world, he wants a crowd for the opening ceremonies. And he was right on the cusp of getting a couple of extra bodies into the room when the swollen men ejected them. Obviously, the security guards were right to address the issue. It really isn't safe to have people cavorting around unmasked, just for the sake of historical accuracy. Nonetheless, I feel sorry for the pear-shaped man.

I suppose I feel a little disappointed in myself, as well. My little story turned out to be completely off the mark. Usually, my little stories are unfalsifiable. For example, I can't *prove* a socially-awkward college graduate kept *Myth and Reality* around as a conversation piece, but you can't *disprove* it, either. Yes, I've suggested that I might have been that college girl, but that was just another little story! The same goes for Giuseppe and the infernal nursing home. They're all unfalsifiable fun! But here, for the first time, I've seen one of my little stories fall to pieces under the weight of cold hard facts.

Well, I say *fuck* facts! They have no place in little stories. They have no place in Big Stories. Nobody wants them. We should let them go.

9

More of the loud clicking, clanging, and thumping. (Why must convention organizers keep the doors to meeting rooms closed? People inevitably arrive late and the *clicking-clanging-thumping* sound proves more distracting than any conversation from the hallway would be!)

Sadly, the new arrivals aren't convention-goers. They're a fresh detachment of black-clad swollen men, armed with cans of Lysol. One hops onto the dais, as graceful as Nureyev in his prime, and sprays Lysol all over the pear-shaped man and Evelyn Carter. They burst out into a duet of coughing fits. Another slinks over to the lesbians. He whips out two cans, one in each hand. He's posing like an old west gunfighter. He empties a can on each woman. A third gets Evelyn's granddaughter. "Fuck off!" she screams. Evelyn gasps.

A swollen man is about to give me the same treatment, but Whitey Mare reaches out a doll-like hand and mutters something in the security guard's ear. I only catch a couple of words ("...the daughter....show some respect...").

The black-clad men stop in their tracks. Pause. One sprays two gentle little puffs of Lysol a few feet away from me. I can smell it, but I don't choke on it. Then one of them pulls out a chrome whistle. Blows a shrill note. They all retreat to the door.

Clink-clank-THUMP!

Whitey Mare whispers in my ear. "Don't worry, Nid. That should kill the virus. Even if it doesn't, you were wearing a mask at the time of the possible exposure. Furthermore, the re-enactors were on the other side of the room. But here is the most important reason you should feel reassured: let's say, just for the sake of argument, that you *have* just been infected by the virus. It's unlikely to present difficulties. After all, it takes a few days for it to incubate inside your human costume. And by tomorrow, you will finally be released from *your own incubator*, your human costume."

The pear-shaped man is pacing the dais, choking and wringing his hands and itching himself all over his torso. "Damn those Men in Black!" he says. "I mean, they're not real Men in Black. The hotel just thought it would be fun to dress their security guards up as Men in Black, for MothCon. We usually have our own security staff, you know. But this place required us to use theirs. And boy, they just pulled off some *sinister* crap, don'tcha think? Ladies and gentlemen, of course we need to go along with the hotel's mask policy. I mean, that's the only way we can have a convention this year. But Good Lord, there's a right way and a wrong way to enforce the rules. Those folks could have been given masks and told to settle down and then they could've enjoyed the ceremonies. But them daggum Men in Black interfered!"

And now the Orion Ballroom is utterly exhausted. Any sense of giddy anticipation has been flogged out of it by the preceding ruckus and subsequent rant. As a result, the air has grown too heavy to bear. We're overwhelmed by the bombardment of strong odors and emotions. We're lost in a fog of kooky references.

An example of the latter: I don't understand why the pear-shaped man finds it necessary to mention a Will Smith film in his rant. The lesbians seem equally confused. Only Evelyn Carter appears to understand. I see her up on the dais, nodding grimly.

There's a moment of awkward silence.

A *minute* of *agonizing* silence.

The pear-shaped man is out of breath.

Whitey Mare hands me a convention schedule, points to the grid. Something's wrong. His stubby finger looks like raw cookie dough. When he whispers in my ear he sounds like he's underwater. "It's already 10:15, and these 'ceremonies' are supposed to end at 10:30. If these are the best and brightest of the so-called cryptozoologists, I think our secret is safe. They can't even get their attendees to show up for the start of their event!"

I look up and around at him. I realize he's not turning into a doll. In fact, it wouldn't quite be correct to say he's turning into *anything*. He's not transforming from one shape to another. He's losing shape. He's not an artificial man. He's not a man at all. He's sentient *goo* that has been placed into a man-shaped mold. And that mold was able to keep him in a convincingly humanoid shape for a while, but now he's reverting to his true cookie dough form!

Why, then, is he gloating? Why isn't he oozing his way toward the nearest exit? Perhaps he doesn't know he's losing shape. Perhaps he knows that everyone in the ballroom is busy staring at the pear-shaped man. After all, the pear-shaped man is the featured speaker. He's up on the dais. Whitey Mare is lingering behind me. No one is looking at him. Reason enough to feel unthreatened. Perhaps he suspects that, if by some chance, one of the lesbians did look back toward him, they wouldn't believe what they saw. They'd discount it as a trick of light.

Thus, the literal melting down of Whitey Mare goes largely unnoticed while the metaphorical meltdown of the pear-shaped man takes center stage. I can understand why the latter holds the lesbians' attention. It's not every day that you see a grown man fall to pieces.

Those parts of his face which are visible above his mask have turned beet red. Upon closer examination, I notice he's shaking. His powder blue surgical mask is now closer to navy blue. It's absorbing his tears.

Something inside him has broken. He's now wobbling down the stairs of the dais. He's trying to get words out of his mouth, some explanation for his departure. In fact, no verbal explanation is necessary. Everyone knows he's leaving because he's been humiliated. The opening ceremonies were the pear-shaped man's child, so to speak, and every father mourns a stillbirth.

He's staggering down the middle aisle. All eyes remain on him. The lesbians still don't seem to notice the cookie dough entity standing behind me. Surely they must see it, now that their glance is directed backward.

They don't.

A thought occurs to me. Perhaps *I* was mistaken. After all, I've been through a major surgery: the excision of one-third of my human costume. I've been given a test tube full of steaming, fizzing red analgesic. Maybe I'm loopy on pain meds! Maybe the pins-and-needles sensation throughout my body is a kind of nerve stimulation. Maybe certain optic nerves in my brain are being stimulated, resulting in hallucinations.

New evidence presents itself that seems, at first, to support this conclusion. Whitey Mare's hand grabs the schedule again. It's no longer a cookie dough hand. It's once again made of human flesh. Order has been restored!

No, it hasn't.

It's not the same hand I saw before. It's a smaller, more graceful hand. A woman's voice is whispering in my ear. "My name is Mary White, and I am your new Kippleodian liaison. With my male counterpart gone, you should be less distracted by lust. The repetition of sexual thoughts prevents us from engaging in any real dialogue."

And so, he *was* actually shifting from one shape to another. The "sentient goo" appearance was an intermediate state. I take a glance up at my new (?) caregiver. She's young and pretty, with long blond hair and adorable cheekbones. She looks more normal than I do.

10

Now the pear-shaped man crosses the threshold out of the ballroom. The loud *click-clang-THUMP!* of the closing door adds a sonic punctuation mark to the scene.

The lesbian couple erupts in nervous giggles.

No one seems quite sure how to proceed.

The time is now 10:17 a.m.

The lesbians look restless. Perhaps they'll leave and take a pee break before Lymon Zinn's keynote address at 10:30.

Evelyn Carter shifts nervously in her chair, muttering to herself. The microphone picks up a word here and there: "… spectacle of himself… go home… Kick myself for even…."

The chubby young woman who had accompanied Evelyn

into the ballroom waddles up the dais, grunting all the way. Grabs the microphone off its stand. "Hey, y'all. Don't leave yet. My grandmaw drove seven hours, all on her own, to get here. She was supposed to say something during this ceremony. Now she might not get a chance to say anything at all on account of all the bullcrap that just went down."

Evelyn Carter shakes her head. Says something. The microphone picks up a single phrase. ("…raised better than that…")

The granddaughter giggles. "Grandmaw don't like it when I say f-u-c-k-o-f-f or b-u-l-l-c-r-a-p. Anyway, I know we only have a little bit of time left until some professor comes in and talks your ear off. But would you like to hear from someone who learned about Mothman from *seeing* him? I mean, Grandmaw didn't learn about him from reading books. She saw him. Would you like to hear about what she saw?"

The lesbians pound their hands together and cheer. Mary White and I offer token applause. The granddaughter gives the microphone over to Evelyn. In a dry, crinkled voice she tells her story.

"Well, it was night, when I saw it. It was when I was working at the Quarter-Cleaner Laundromat. It was an awful windy night in March. It was like a hurricane, but it wasn't raining. Just all that wind. A lot of bad things happened that night. It was the same night the screen at the drive-in theater fell down, on account of all that wind, and it was the night the McKinney girl…Audrey? Audrey McKinney?" Evelyn pauses. Looks at her granddaughter for confirmation. It seems important for her to get this name right.

The granddaughter shrugs.

"Well, it was the night the McKinney girl drowned. Her name was either Audrey or Andrea. Started with an 'A', Lord Rest Her Soul. She was the mayor's niece. Afterwards, some folks tried to connect what I saw with what happened to her. You know, they tried to say *the thing* hurt her. But I don't believe it. I know it's not right to speak ill of the dead, especially of a young dead girl, but I suppose enough time has gone by and it's okay to tell you that she was already an awful drunk. Put her mother through Hell, even before she drowned. Mayor's niece or not, she was a wild one. The thing didn't kill her, she passed out in the water after drinking a whole bottle of Boone's Farm!"

The granddaughter motions for Evelyn to give her the microphone.

"What?" Evelyn says. Her voice cracks, so it comes out as two syllables. "Wha-uht?" She's reluctant to yield the floor. She seems annoyed to even be *asked* to do so. Clearly, she feels like she's just now hitting her stride.

The granddaughter leans her head toward the microphone. Speaks into it. "These people don't know the McKinneys. They just want to hear about the *thing*. Tell them what it looked like."

"Well, I was getting to that. The first time I saw it I thought it was some big old trash bag flapping around in the wind. Or maybe a kite, because kites sometimes flap around in the same way. And that's what got me looking up in the sky, because I had to wonder who on Earth would be flying a kite at night?"

The granddaughter speaks into the microphone again. "And you saw it after you got off work, right?"

"That's right. I was the night manager for Quarter-Cleaner. Each night I got off work at ten o'clock. To be honest, I probably shut it down a little early that night, on account of the way that wind was whistling out there. Right around March is when tornadoes can start up, and the news said one might be coming. The only place I could've taken cover at the Quarter-

Cleaner was inside one of the dryers! So after I locked up I got a move on. I had parked out back, in the little parking lot set up for folks who worked at those businesses on Rouse Street, and that's when I first heard the flapping.

"Like I said, I thought it was plastic at first. Maybe a kite or a trash bag. But I suppose even then I knew it wasn't plastic, because I heard these other noises. It called out, you see, like a hawk. But it didn't sound like a normal hawk. It sounded like a hawk that had pneumonia or something like that. It's like it wanted to let out a big mighty 'Cawwwwww!' sound, but it was too sick to do it. Imagine if a hawk had a death rattle. That's what it sounded like.

"I had buried my mom two weeks before, and I was there to hear her death rattle, so I guess that sound was fresh in my mind. Some people say that's why I saw the thing. They think that Mom dying made me go off my rocker. It really hurts my heart when they say things like that. Lots of people lose their mom, and they don't see things like what I saw. The only crazy idea that's *ever* gotten into my head was the notion that Nixon deserved a second term!"

The lesbians are too young to get the reference. I get it and let out a polite chuckle, just so Evelyn doesn't think her joke fell flat.

The granddaughter is losing patience. "You still haven't told 'em what it looked like, Grandmaw."

"I haven't?"

The granddaughter shakes her head.

"Oh. I guess that's because, at this point of the story, I'd only heard it. I hadn't yet seen it. I wish I never did see it. I wish I had just heard it. Then I could've pretended it was just a trash bag or a kite or a hawk with pneumonia. But it wasn't any of those things. It was…"

All of a sudden, her dry, crinkled voice becomes high-pitched. She's whimpering, weeping.

"It was scratching the roof of my car! I was driving home from work that night, and I kept hearing the flapping. And I knew then it wasn't a kite or a trash bag. I heard the flapping, and I heard something go wrong with the roof of the car. And I was thinking maybe a heavy branch fell down on it, and I was worried that I'd have to make an insurance claim. But then I heard that sick cry, that gurgly screech, right over top of me. And I suppose what really got to me was that it wasn't a violent sound. Or at least, not *mostly* a violent sound. It was the sound of a sick toddler. It's like this thing was sick, and wanted to get better, but didn't know how, and had run out of patience."

"But what did it look like, Grandmaw? Tell these folks what you told me."

"Can you get me a tissue?"

The granddaughter reaches into her purse and pulls out several.

Evelyn dabs her eyes. Blows her nose. Turns to her granddaughter. "Did I get it all?"

The granddaughter nods.

"So, you just asked, I think, what it looked like. Well, I didn't see it until I got home. When I first pulled in the driveway, I knew it was on top of my car. It was staring at me. I didn't see it staring, but I just kind of knew it, the way people do when they're being stared at. And I just wanted to forget it. Whatever it was, I didn't want to see it. I just ran inside.

"I got in the door, and I slammed it shut, and I locked it. And I guess I looked like I'd seen a ghost, because Charlie got up off the couch to see what was the matter. He had a bad back, so it wasn't easy for him to just spring up onto his feet, but that's exactly what he did. And he ran over to me and I guess I was hyperventilating because he said, 'Take deep breaths, girl, or else you're gonna faint.'

"But I couldn't take deep breaths. Because right then is when I heard…S-sammy barking out in the yard."

And now I know why Evelyn Carter's shuffle seemed familiar. I saw her at the rest stop. With her poodle. My face flushes. My heart gallops. I want to leave.

"Charlie had let Sammy out to do his business. So he was out there with that thing. And I could hear him out there barking and growling like he never barked and growled before. And I knew he was out there with that thing so I rushed back out and tried to find him. Sammy, I mean. To bring him in. I wasn't worried the thing was going to attack me, but I just didn't know how it would react to Sammy going after it.

"So when I got out there, the security light flicked on, and that's how I saw it. And it was standing there, on top of my car, still as a statue. But then it stretched its wings out real broad, like birds do when they want to make themselves look big, you know, to show off and scare away anything that's giving them a problem. And it was a huge bird, but it wasn't *just* a bird. It had a pale blue patch of skin on its face, too. Like, a blue *person's* face. And sometimes the skin was on top of the feathers and sometimes it was underneath, but I somehow saw both the skin *and* the feathers, and there were little speckles on its belly that weren't just speckles, but they were drifting in the air, like mist. It's hard to explain, but there was flesh and feathers and mist all dancing around each other. It was kind of like there were holes in its belly, and the holes were filled with fog. But I *knew* that he didn't have holes in him. He was standing up too straight to be wounded. He wasn't injured, exactly. Just *sick*. Somehow the fog was *a part of him*. Maybe the *diseased* part of him, but a part of him.

"But the eyes were probably the scariest thing. They weren't solid flesh, like human eyes. They were a thick liquid, like lava. Not that they were hot and burning or anything like that, but they were thick and red and it looked like they sloshed around in its eye sockets. They never oozed out like lava, though. They stayed in the sockets. But I'm not sure how they stayed in the sockets. They were liquid, but they somehow didn't drip out.

"And Sammy, he just collapsed and started having fits. I took him to the vet right afterwards, and the vet couldn't find anything wrong with him. Somehow, *that thing* gave him fits."

"Seizures," the granddaughter corrected. "And you don't have to talk about that part, Grandmaw."

"Honey, *I do* have to talk about that part. I...." She can't finish the sentence. She's shaking too much. It's almost like she's imitating Sammy's death throes. But she's not having seizures. She's just falling apart. For the second time in less than an hour, the microphone in the Orion Ballroom is being held by a bawling, red-faced elder. This cannot bode well.

She wipes her eyes against her sleeves, wipes her nose with her kleenex and perseveres. "I *do* have to talk about that part, on account of people won't believe me unless I give them all the details. Now, I saw the thing in 2010. Or maybe 2011? I can't remember. Sammy was only two or three years old. He lived until..."

She's about to utterly collapse into sobs, but bites her lip and moves on. I get the impression that Evelyn is a woman who is used to tears, and used to forcing her way through them. "He lived...until yesterday. You see, I don't go anywhere without him. He was my traveling buddy. He was going to stay here in The Zodiac and everything, on account of they're pet friendly. But we got out at a rest stop in Kentucky and it happened again. The seizures, I mean. He never had them before, other than that time he saw the thing. And that was in a little town up around Vincennes, Indiana, by the way. That's where I've always lived.

"I've taken Sammy down to Gulf Shores, Destin, on vacation every year or two. So traveling in the car didn't trigger these new seizures. But we were on the way to this big meeting here in West Virginia, to talk about the thing, and we stopped off in Kentucky so Sammy could do his business. And Sammy starts going into seizures just like he did that night, only this time he was too old and weak to go through them. And I had to stop off and find an animal hospital that would cremate him. Thank the Lord my granddaughter lives in Lexington. She's been my anchor, through all this mess. I was able to stop off and she found a place that would take Sammy. Anyway, that's why I just now got here, you know. I thought about turning around and going back home. But if I did that, Sammy's death would be in vain. And it shouldn't be. Other dog owners need to know about my story. They need to know to keep their dogs away from this thing.

"Don't get me wrong. I don't think it *means* to hurt animals. But there's something about it that messes with the heads of little dogs. Like, gives them an aneurysm or epilepsy or a stroke or something. That thing must have been hanging around the rest stop. I didn't see it. Didn't even hear it. But it must've been around there. That's the only thing I can think of. That's why Sammy had seizures again. Somehow, that thing knew we were coming here, and it hung out at that rest stop so it could see us again. I know it sounds crazy, but how else can you explain what happened to Sammy? Like I said, I don't think it *means* to hurt animals. If I had to hazard a guess, I'd say it was just lonesome and wanted to see a familiar face. It doesn't realize the effect it has on some animals' brains. Some animals aren't able to take it all in. Their brains overheat when they see it. That's what I think, anyway."

The lesbians are whispering to each other. No doubt, they're relishing the absurdity of it all: the Mothman loitering around a Kentucky rest stop! They'd probably laugh out loud if they knew the truth: the Mothman's *half-sister* inflicted the mortal blow to Sammy the poodle, and her actual name is Nid Cold.

11

Of course the lesbians *don't* laugh out loud. That would be cruel. But *someone* is laughing out loud. It's not the lesbians. It's not me. It's not Mary White. It's not Evelyn Carter's granddaughter. And, of course, it's not Evelyn, herself.

It's a group of young men in the hallway.

Theirs is a dude-bro, frat boy sort of laughter. *Annoying* laughter! That said, I don't think the dude-bros are mocking Evelyn's story. There's no way they could have heard it.

Wait, that's not true.

It's *possible* they heard it. If the hallway was quiet and Evelyn's amplified voice carried out into the hallway, they may have heard it. This is a small convention. Barely even a convention. It would be unusual for a hallway to remain quiet during a typical convention. But MothCon 2020 is no typical convention. If I recall correctly, they sold only a few dozen memberships. Not a thousand. Not even a hundred.

So, maybe these dude-bros in the hallway *are* laughing at Evelyn Carter. However, they could also be laughing because one of them ripped a loud fart. For that matter, they might be laughing for no good reason at all. They could be performing the sort of *forced* laughter I heard in the hallway outside of Room 312 this morning, the laughter of people trying to convince themselves they're having a good time. Perhaps one of them told a joke that isn't funny, but they're laughing anyway, and laughing *heartily*, because they're at a convention, and they feel compelled to have a good time.

The longer I hear this laughter, the more I want to scream. Whether the dude-bros are laughing at Evelyn Carter or not, it *feels* as if they are. Yes, it feels like Evelyn is the wacky neighbor in a '70s sitcom recorded before a live studio audience of dude-bros.

And now the laughter gets louder.

And now, *click-clang-THUMP!*

And now, the laughter's inside the ballroom.

And all of us in the audience (all five of us, that is) twist our necks and torsos back to catch a glimpse of The Laughers. It's as if we're at a wedding, and the music has just started, and we're all looking back to catch a glimpse of the bride.

As fate would have it, The Laughers are unusual. Of course, *most people I meet* are unusual. But, as I get a chance to size them up, I realize the Laughers are *particularly* unusual.

Why do I say they're particularly unusual? Well, they are—in a sense—reverse Whitey Mares.

By this I mean that Whitey Mare looked like a frat boy but didn't sound like one. The Laughers, on the other hand, *sound* like frat boys but don't look like them. (They look, instead, like the 1980s stereotype of a nerd. Thick glasses. Unfashionable hairstyles. Pimples all over their foreheads.)

Even worse, they're wearing ill-fitting, polyester, gray-pinstripe business suits. Neckties, too. *Polyester maroon* neckties. I can't say for sure, but I would guess they're clip-on ties. Their (polyester) masks are yellow. A smiley face has been printed on each one.

Another odd detail: the Laughers are all very short.

To clarify, they are not "little people" (in the medical sense of the phrase). It's just that none of them can be more than 5'6". However, they're not children or adolescents. They seem to be college age. And yet, they still find themselves afflicted with pimples!

There are seven of them. Ordinarily, seven is considered a lucky number. In this context, however, it bodes ill; there are seven of them and only six of us Non-Laughers (four in the audience, two on the dais). Suddenly The Laughers have taken over the ballroom!

I call them Laughers, but once they cross the threshold of the ballroom they make an impressive attempt to minimize their laughter. They quiet themselves and stride toward the dais in unison.

No, "stride" is not the correct word. As the seconds tick forward it becomes clear their movements are all part of a dance. Yes, they're dancing in unison, like a street gang in *West Side Story*. But this choreography is far too strange for Broadway or Hollywood.

The first movement of the dance: an exaggerated lifting of the right arm into the air, followed by a downright melodramatic use of the right hand to wipe tears from their eyes (they have been laughing so hard they have cried). Now is an inopportune time to use one's hands to wipe tears from one's eyes. You can get Covid that way. Perhaps the dancers have given some thought to this. Perhaps, if I had the chance to get close to them, I'd see that their hands never actually make contact with their eyes. It would not surprise me. Everything about them seems to be an affectation.

The second movement of the dance: they take a step forward with their right foot. Most of them thrust their hips forward when they make this move. Some do not.

The third movement: they tilt their necks backward, in an exaggerated fashion.

The fourth movement is subtle. They make their cheeks bulge out. I only notice this movement because I'm fascinated by their smiley face masks. They're slack, ordinarily. But all of a sudden they bulge out and tighten around the wearer's face. At the same time, the Laughers make snickering noises (in unison, in an affected fashion). Clearly, this part of the performance is meant to convey their inability to fully restrain their Laughter, despite their best efforts.

The fifth movement is quite inventive: the Laughers become completely quiet, let their cheeks grow slack again, halt their progress toward the dais, ball up their fists, stiffen their arms and legs, and stand almost perfectly still. I say "almost", because their arms and legs quiver, just a little. Most people wouldn't notice this quivering, but then again most people are too shy to stare at the Laughers. I, on the other hand, feel increasingly comfortable with staring. Hence, my ability to give a real time report of the dance.

What are we to make of this Grand, Ridiculous dance move? Is it Empty of all meaning? I don't think so. Although there may be room for multiple interpretations, I see it as their way of demonstrating how difficult it is to go through the world without Laughing. It takes effort, both physical and mental, to restrain a laugh. In my own experience, holding in a laugh can be every bit as strenuous as holding in urine while on a frantic search for a bathroom. Hence the quivering. It serves to convey the strain put on all the body's muscles. If the Laughers let *any* muscle relax, the Laugh might escape as a chaotic guffaw.

That said, they can't linger, stiff and awkward in the middle aisle forever. And so, in the sixth movement of their dance, they try to walk forward once again. Only this time, they keep

their muscles stiff as they walk. The result is an awkward, wob-
bly, zombie-like shuffle.

Evelyn Carter looks at them all wide-eyed. It's confusing
enough to see these young nerds in cheap suits *dancing up the
aisle*. It must be downright *perplexing* to see them stiffly wobbling *toward you*.

At this point, the choreography ends. Most of the Laughers take seats in the front row. (Oh what a racket it is, to hear
their chairs collide against one another as they all rush to grab
a seat.)

One of them (the lad at the front of the procession) does not
grab a seat in the front row. Instead, he leaps onto the dais and
grabs the microphone out of Evelyn's gnarled hand.

"Time's up, Granny," he barks.

This is too much for his brethren in the front row. They
crack up.

I gasp at the rudeness of it all. "Time's up, Granny" sounds
like the sort of thing the Grim Reaper would say to his next
victim. Such phrases should be avoided when talking to senior
citizens.

The lesbians gasp, too. I'm not sure if they're gasping at the
Reaper-esque qualities of the nerd-bro's statement, or at the
rude way he wrestled the microphone out of Evelyn's hands.
Mary White however, doesn't gasp. I suppose Kippleodians
have a limited understanding of human etiquette. As a result,
they can't be shocked.

The nerd-bro with the microphone starts yelling into it.
He hops around as he yells. He looks and sounds like an old
school professional wrestling manager hyping up his star. His
brethren are still goofing off. They put each other in head-
locks, give each other noogies, flick each others' ears, and in
general act like boys.

The Microphone-Bearing Nerd-Bro speaks. "Mr. Zinn ran into some fans outside of the elevator and he's still signing books for them, so he may be a few minutes late. In fact, I think he signed some girl's tits, too, so he might be a few *hours* late!"

The Laughers in the front row hoot and howl. "OOoooooooOo." Several rise to their feet and thrust out their hips in a pantomime of intercourse. Some giggle.

Microphone Nerd-Bro smiles. Offers a fake-sounding chuckle. "No, I'm just joking. Mr. Zinn has actually shaken off the crowd, but he's now performing his pre-lecture meditation. He meditates before every public speaking event. In fact, he uses the same guided meditation that he sells online! He meditates to the sound of his own voice reading a guided meditation. I can assure you this is the closest he's ever come to masturbation."

This just makes the Laughers laugh some more. You would think the masks would muffle their laughter. Nope. Through some sort of miracle, perhaps attributable to the hitherto-unknown acoustic properties of polyester, the laughs sound every bit as loud and clear as the laughs of Bedlam.

The same Laughers who pantomimed intercourse a moment ago rise to their feet again, this time to pantomime jerking off. Knowing this to be a particularly crude gesture, they turn around to display it to the rest of the audience.

The lesbians get up to leave. Microphone Nerd-Bro taunts them on their way out. "That's right, ladies, head on back to the kitchen and make me a sammich!" The Laughers laugh.

Click-clang-THUMP! goes the door as it closes.

Click-clang-THUMP! goes the door as it opens again.

About a dozen men walk in, each and every one looking as peppy and wide-eyed as kids on Christmas morning. Scruffy beards lurk under their masks. They wear black T-shirts and blue jeans and boots. The older ones wear trucker ball caps, presumably to cover their bald spots. They all have tattoos on their arms.

Evelyn Carter's forehead turns bright red. She seems to be trembling. Her granddaughter glares at Microphone Nerd-Bro and escorts her off the dais.

Microphone Nerd-Bro isn't done chirping at her. "Go back to your knitting, Granny, and when you're done make me some bacon from that hog trotting alongside you!"

All the men in the ballroom cackle. Something like a sob erupts from Evelyn Carter's granddaughter. I predict that Evelyn will never attend a cryptid convention again.

"Let's see…that makes four gyno-Americans down and two to go!" He glares at me and Mary White. "Are you two dykes, like those other two? I can see why the cripple might want to just lie back and get her pussy licked. That's probably all she can handle. But what about you, Blondie? Don't you miss cock? There's plenty here, you know, and I can tell by the way you're staring at me that you want it. But if you want cock, why did you bother bringing the ball and chain along with you? The whole point of breaking your girlfriend's legs is to keep her at home in bed while you go play the field!"

The Laughers in the front row all say "OOoooOOOOOoooOOO." The rest of the men in the audience follow suit.

I look up at Mary White. Mary White looks down at me. Rolls her eyes. Whispers in my ear. "Feel free to laugh back at him, Nid. He is nothing more than a whining mosquito. Not even as troublesome as a mosquito, actually. They make annoying sounds *and bite*, whereas this cretin troubles the ears alone. And his insults need not even trouble *those*. He mocks

your human costume, and the human form I have just now tak-
en. He maligns the coat, not the wearer."

I want to believe what Mary says. I want to brush off the
words of this would-be insult comedian. I want to say "sticks
and stones might break my bones, but words will never hurt
me."

But words hurt me.

Even though Mary White isn't my girlfriend, and even
though my legs aren't broken, and even though I know full
well I'm only a temporary occupant of this wheelchair, the
words cover me in their stench. And you can't reason away a
stench, nor can you minimize it through logic. Microphone
Nerd-Bro is like a man who drops trou and shits in public. The
irrationality of the act doesn't negate its offense.

Microphone Nerd-Bro hops and saunters around the stage,
aggravated and delighted to see me and Mary stay put. "Oh
dear, we have suffragettes in our midst. They insist on infect-
ing our space. Very well, let's see how they deal with the Red
Pill Lymon Zinn's about to…SHOVE…DOWN…THEIR…
THROATS!"

The Laughers in the front row join in with Microphone
Nerd-Bro's shouting. "SHOVE…DOWN…THEIR…
THROATS!" is apparently a communal chant, a popular
catchphrase among Zinnites. They jab their fingers in the air,
pantomiming the act of shoving Red Pills down throats. One
of them turns around and tells me and Mary to "choke on a
dick". What does any of this have to do with the Mothman? I
suppose Lymon Zinn will soon tell us.

"So, anyway, where was I?" Microphone Nerd-Bro asks.

"Zinn and meditation," a dude yells.

"Oh yeah, like I said, Mr. Zinn is using his own guided
meditation to prepare for his keynote address. He'll be in the

Dealer's Room later today. If you want to buy a whole CD chock full of his guided meditations, I'm sure he'll be happy to sign them for you. You can buy digital downloads, too.

"But for right now, he's meditating, and as a result the keynote will be delayed a few minutes. He asked me to go ahead and start his introduction, though, because it will take *at least* five minutes. I mean, that's how much the man has accomplished."

Microphone Dude-Bro clears his throat. Starts reading from prepared notes. "Lymon Zinn is *everywhere*. His debut book *Moth* MAN: *Cryptids and the Crisis of Imperiled Masculinity* has stayed atop Amazon's Cultural Cryptozoology bestseller list since its 2015 debut and is currently being adapted into a News Max documentary series. His YouTube channel *Zinn and the Art of Motorcycle Maintenance* gives Lymon a weekly platform on which to share the knowledge he's acquired as a longtime Harley-Davidson owner. But he's perhaps best known for his occasional guest appearances on the *Joe Rogan Experience*, which rank among the most popular in the show's history.

"And yet, when Mr. Zinn was born on August 24, 1958, few would have predicted such astonishing success. His father, Rudolph, was a humble shopkeeper in Cumberland, Maryland; a hard-working immigrant who brought his pious Catholic faith and Austrian work ethic with him to Ellis Island. Lymon's mother, the former Gerda Müeller, was a waitress in Bavaria before meeting Rudolf in a postwar refugee camp. Soon after their arrival they learned English. In fact, Rudolph and Gerda burned all of their German books, correspondence, and photographs on a bonfire so they could truly leave behind the Old World and embrace the New. Even Goethe's *Faust* caught fire on that propitious night. More than anything, they wanted to assimilate. Through rigorous effort, they did. In fact, both of Lyman's parents lost their accents before he was even born!

"As a boy, Lyman took to badminton. As a teenager he was on track to compete at the Olympic level. However, a knee injury sustained while thwarting a robbery at his father's store ended that aspiration."

The Nerd-Bro looks up from his script and directly addresses the audience (now numbering around twenty, all male except for Mary and me). "I think," he says, "you'll agree that badminton's loss was our gain."

The Laughers applaud and laugh. The men in the audience applaud and laugh. Mary White offers a golf clap. I refuse to go along.

"The damage done to Mr. Zinn's body led him to focus on the cultivation of his mind. While continuing to work in his father's store, he began a rigorous program of self-education. Through the mail order purchase of various books, pamphlets, and audio cassettes, Mr. Zinn was able to obtain the equivalent of a college education without taking on the burdens of radical leftist ideology and student debt.

"Mr. Zinn never took an interest in cryptids until cryptids took an interest in him. Over a span of several days in late June, 1981, he was visited by the figure popularly known as the Mothman. Although, as he will soon explain, that is not the entity's true name.

"Although most of these visitations took place in the evening or late at night, two happened in broad daylight. During these encounters, the entity revealed his reasons for visiting Point Pleasant, West Virginia in 1966. He revealed the message he was trying, in vain, to pass on. He revealed the reason why the town suffered great calamity in December of 1967. He also revealed the true meaning of Indrid Cold's words to Woodrow

Derenberger. Other paranormal investigators won fame for raising questions, but only Mr. Zinn was given the answers. Yes, answers, *and a mission*: the entity told Mr. Zinn to pass on these communications to all mankind!

"Despite the magnitude of the entity's revelations, you will never hear them articulated on any mainstream paranormal cable show. The woke SJWs at the History Channel are too scared to interview Mr. Zinn for their cryptid documentaries, because their corporate masters at Disney fear the truth. No doubt they're jealous of the fact that the entity chose *him* as his human ambassador and *not them*. The most important truths of this world are never detected through investigation, but are obtained, instead, by revelation. Revelation, specifically, to *Lymon Zinn*!

All the dudes give this line a standing ovation. I have never heard a standing ovation for an introduction before. Microphone Nerd-Bro seems aware of this. His role is to be a dutiful John the Baptist. He is not Christ. He *foretells* the coming of the Messiah. He, himself, is not the Savior. He motions for the crowd to settle down. "Thank you, I appreciate the applause, but save the standing ovations for Mr. Zinn!"

Some men in the crowd chuckle, even though Microphone Nerd-Bro hasn't really said anything funny. They obey and take their seats. Satisfied with their compliance, Microphone Nerd-Bro continues.

"Now, MothCon is not a perfect event. The mask policy is appalling."

The Laughers get riled up. Mindful of the directions that have been given them, they don't rise to their feet. But they *do* applaud and holler. "Hell yeah," one of them shouts. "Trump train!" shouts another. The Microphone Nerd-Bro nods, raises his right arm, and balls his right hand into a fist. The gesture, it seems, is meant to convey his solidarity with the president's admirer.

"Let it be known to one and all," the Microphone Nerd-Bro announces, "that Mr. Zinn is only wearing a face mask here under great duress, at the insistence of the hotel staff who will not let the matter go. "

Microphone Nerd-Bro looks up from his prepared text. Ad libs. "Although, rest assured that when he unwinds tonight for a little R&R in his room, he won't be wearing a face diaper. And if a few friends just happen to stop by his room for some free drinks, well, that should be well within the rules, I believe."

Laughter, applause, hooting, hollering. The Zodiac ballroom is now a gathering of cavemen. I can't speak for Mary White, but I feel like an intruder. Perhaps I should ask to be wheeled out of here.

On second thought, that would be a terrible idea. I couldn't stand all the ridicule. Can you imagine Mary White doing her best to get the wheelchair moving, amidst the cat calls of the men? Can you imagine all their jokes? I can. "The wheels aren't the only thing on that chair that's flat," they'd say. And then they'd point and laugh at my B cups.

No, far better to stay put until the end of Lymon Zinn's speech. Then, when he and his minions leave, I'll ask Mary to push me back up to my room. I need some quiet time. More than anything, I want to lie in bed. I want to look up at a blurry ceiling fan. I want to feel the kiss of its breeze on my skin.

But instead, I'm forced to listen to the ravings of Microphone Nerd-Bro. Did he just insinuate that Zinn will be hosting a mask-free room party tonight? I can't imagine the Men in Black will permit such festivities! At the same time, I can't believe Lymon and the Laughers would yield as easily as the historical re-enactors did. The irresistible force will meet the immovable object.

Click-clang-THUMP!

The ballroom comes to a hush. The men twist their necks back to see if it's Lymon Zinn. With some chagrin, I find *myself* twisting my neck back to see if it's Lymon Zinn.

I've never seen Lymon Zinn. Prior to this morning, I'd never even heard of the man. I know he's not a celebrity. He's merely a big fish in a small pond. And yet, my brain is powerless against the *collective sentiment* of the assembled audience. I have no choice but to absorb their sense of anticipation. My heart may not be racing, but it's power walking.

And now the moment arrives. I see neatly curled salt-and-pepper hair edge past the threshold. Not a face. Not yet, at least. Just hair. Based on the thunderous applause, I assume I'm gazing upon the hair of Lymon Zinn. He's poking his head into the threshold, but only allowing his hair to be seen by those inside.

Perhaps his hair is his trademark. Perhaps, by letting his hair (and only his hair) appear through the cracked door, he's trying to milk a dramatic entrance for all it's worth. Is it naturally curly, or did he have it permed? It would be quite unusual for a misogynist to have his hair permed, but the curls are too tight and symmetrical to be acts of nature. Yes, empirical study of the hairdo suggests it may very well be a perm.

For a few seconds, the hair just lingers in the threshold, and I wonder if Lymon Zinn might not be a sentient ball of hair. Yes, that would be a fine little story to ruminate on. His misogyny could be traced to hatred of his mother. She abused all sorts of terrible drugs while he was in her womb, and as a result he never developed all the organs possessed by an ordinary human being. His neurons, stomach, and heart are somehow braided into his curls. He feeds on the flies and gnats that crawl into his curls. If you were able to observe him eating, you would be reminded of a venus fly trap. As soon as the insects land on his hair, the curls tighten around their bodies. Like tiny pythons, they squeeze the life out of their prey.

But how, exactly, does he move about? He has no legs! He must slither around, like a snake.

No, that can't be right. After all, the curls are lingering about five feet in the air. (That's roughly the height at which I see them sticking through the threshold.) Perhaps they have thousands of microscopic suction cups, enabling him to scale doors and walls with aplomb. Perhaps his hair-brain (hah! harebrained!) is blessed with mystical powers of levitation. Yes, that makes sense. Sentient hair would need to levitate so it could capture insects in its venus fly trap curls!

No, that makes no sense. None of this is the case. I'm telling myself one of my fanciful little stories. It's all impossible.

But who am I to say what's possible or impossible? A day ago, I would have told you it was impossible for me to end up at a Mothman convention. A year ago, I would have told you it was impossible for the world to be seized by a hitherto-unknown plague. A decade ago, I would have said the U.S. would never elect an exotically-colored amphibian as its president. And yet, here we are.

The ballroom erupts in applause. I imagine everyone can read my thoughts, and they're applauding the cleverness of my observations. But then I remember the crowd is full of humans, not Homerealmers, and I remember that even if they *were* Homerealmers, the gelatinous centipede shields my brain from spying. Anyone who tries to read my thoughts will think I want to eat and fuck all day.

The irony, of course, is that I seldom eat well and never get laid. I might find potato chips tasty, but I've never obsessed over eating them. I might let my eye linger here and there, but I've never truly *lusted* after anyone. This leads me to think Layla Dodd might have been right about my origins. Maybe the real me, underneath the costume, isn't human at all.

Or maybe I'm just asexual. Or depressed. Or both.

12

At least one thing becomes certain: they aren't applauding the candor of my thoughts. They're applauding Lymon Zinn. He's up on the dais now. He's not sentient hair. He's a human being, remarkably short of stature (though not, it seems, quite as short as his followers). The part of his face that's visible looks bumpy and sunburned, like a bust sculpted from Martian stone.

"Thank you….thank you so much…thank you…" he says. He nods. He smiles. He's trying to drop a hint that he's had enough applause. The crowd picks this up. Grows quiet.

At first, I assume that he's acknowledging the same round of applause that greeted him when he stuck his perm through the threshold. Applause directed at his mere *presence in the room.* But I soon gather this is not the case. While I was daydreaming about sentient hair, a Powerpoint presentation was set up on the dais. While I was telling myself a little story, the presentation advanced past the title slide.

Yes, the more I observe the scene, the more I realize the audience is applauding one of Zinn's talking points. That's what his body language suggests. That's what the beads of sweat on his stony red forehead seem to indicate too. He's been talking for a while now. He's fired up.

Like The Laughers, Lymon Zinn wears a gray pinstripe suit,

maroon tie, and yellow smiley face mask (although his appear to be made of silk, rather than polyester). Like Microphone Nerd-Bro, he skips and saunters around the dais. He makes sweeping gestures with his stony red hands.

On the left side of his Powerpoint, I see a stylized drawing of a falcon in profile. The caption underneath tells me it's no mere drawing, but rather "The name of Horus as represented in ancient Egyptian hiroglyphs (sic)". On the right side, I see a simple, stylized drawing of the Mothman. It has been rendered in profile, to make it resemble the name of Horus. In fact, the only resemblance I can see is that they both have long wings wrapped around them like a cloak.

When the applause recedes, Zinn picks up where he left off. "Yes, Horus! *That* Horus: the sky-god of ancient Egypt, the god who flew over the pyramids! In days of old it was said that his right eye was the sun and his left, the moon. *That* is the entity who visited Point Pleasant, West Virginia in 1966." He gestures to a table that has been set up alongside him. Microphone Nerd-Bro sits at this table with a laptop in front of him.

"Next slide, Jeremy."

So, Microphone Nerd-Bro he has a name. Nonetheless, I suspect I will always think of him as Microphone Nerd-Bro.

No, on second thought I realize this isn't true. I want to continue to think of Zinn's slide operator as "Microphone Nerd-Bro", because it captures some of my disdain for him. But "Microphone Nerd-Bro" requires five syllables whereas "Jeremy" requires only three. We live in an era which insists on truncation whenever possible. Pabst Blue Ribbon becomes "PBR": even though only one syllable is saved in the abbreviation. We live in the era of TL;DR. And, as much as I am an outsider to this era, I can't help but swim in the same thought-ocean. Thus, I find myself reacting to the same currents. I end up thinking of him as Jeremy.

Jeremy responds to Zinn's request with alacrity. The next slide appears. The Horus hieroglyphic appears at the top center of the screen. Below that, I see a half-dozen vintage news headlines.

From a grease-stained front page of the *Point Pleasant Register* (Wednesday November 16, 1966): COUPLES SEE MAN-SIZED BIRD…CREATURE…SOMETHING

From the tattered front page of the *Athens* (Ohio) *Messenger* (Friday November 18): MONSTER NO JOKE FOR THOSE WHO SAW IT

From page 19 of the *Athens Messenger* (Thursday, April 13, 1967): UFO's (sic) SIGHTED AGAIN AT CAMP CONLEY, MASON.

From page 5 of the *Messenger* (Tuesday April 18, 1967): UFOs OUT IN FORCE ACROSS MASON SKIES

From the front page of the *Raleigh* (West Virginia) *Register* (November 4, 1966): PARKERSBURG SALESMAN SPEAKS TO SPACEMAN

From the front page of the *Point Pleasant Register* (Saturday, December 16, 1967): SILVER BRIDGE TUMBLES, TOLL, 7 DEAD 41 MISSING

Lymon Zinn speaks. "Having established the uncanny resemblance this so-called 'Mothman' bears to Horus, we are left with several perplexing questions. Why would an ancient Egyptian sky-god appear in West Virginia? In 1966?

"What connections might we draw between Horus and the UFOs reported around Point Pleasant? How do Woodrow Derenberger and Indrid Cold fit into all this? What about the Silver Bridge disaster? Was Horus, in some way, responsible?

"These are, of course, weighty questions. Yes, weighty questions made *all the weightier* by the fact that no other investigator has asked them! This may be the first time many of you are hearing about the Horus Connection.

"You may only know about the events in Point Pleasant because you've seen the film, *The Mothman Prophecies*. If so, you're probably asking yourself why the Horus Connection was never explained therein.

"A smaller number of you may have taken the time to read the book that inspired the film, written by the so-called 'Fortean investigator' John A. Keel. If so, you're probably asking yourself why *Keel* never made the Horus Connection. After all, he was open-minded. Indeed, possibly too open-minded! He thought the entity in Point Pleasant could be the ancient Hindu Garuda. He believed this, despite the fact that the former looked nothing like the latter!"

I have never seen "the ancient Hindu Garuda". I can't attest to its resemblance (or lack thereof) to my brother, the Mothman. But I *do* know that the Horus hieroglyph showed only the most superficial resemblance to him. Therefore, I know Lymon Zinn is a poor judge of such matters.

"It's possible that a few of you are unfamiliar with the film *and* the book. You may have only heard the story told on podcasts. Or, Heaven forbid, you might have only heard about it from the so-called 'documentaries' on the subject. These poorly-produced works reveal nothing but the madness of their filmmakers. We have one such psycho here this weekend, the fool who made the 'Zoo' movie."

The Laughers in the front row elbow each other. Gasp. Let out "OooooOooooOOO"s and "Ahhhhhaaahh"s. Zinn has called out a fellow convention guest, and his followers love it. They love it, because (like many other young men in the early twenty-first century) they confuse rudeness with charisma.

"Yes, I know, I know. I should try to play nice with the other guests, right? Oh no, my friends. I never play nice. When I know someone is propagating a lie, I have no choice but to grab a big hunk of truth to SHOVE...DOWN...THEIR... THROATS!"

Jeremy joins in with the familiar chant. So do all the other Laughers. A handful of dudes in the audience start to pick up on the game, joining in as well. It occurs to me that I'm not merely living in a world colonized by the Strange. I'm living in a world colonized by the *Masculine* Strange. (My alien father, my alien brother, and Lymon Zinn. Lymon Zinn, and Laughing Men and The Producer. The Producer, The Hallway Sideswiper, and Giuseppe the Puppeteer. Giuseppe the Puppeteer and Swollen Men and the Men in Black and Horus the Sky-God and...)

I feel dizzy. I'm weepy. My heart is racing, probably because it wants to escape from my ribcage. My temples ache, probably because my brain is ricocheting from one side of my skull to the other. It probably wants to shake loose the gelatinous centipede.

I want my mother, my *Earthly* mother. Yes, it's true, she's kooky. But she's not Strange. Her kookiness is grounding, because it's always focused on the mundane. She has kooky suspicions about my sister. She's kookily domineering over my father. She's a ventriloquist. She's always been a ventriloquist. But her kookiness, in and of itself, has never led me to question reality. Now, more than ever, I need an unshakeable foundation of fact. As much as I'm loath to admit it, I *need* my mother. My Earthly Mother.

I suppose I want my Homerealm mother, too. It's possible she would love me far more than my Earthly mother ever did, because I'm actually hers. My Earthly mother must have suspected my presence in the family was a mistake. She could never have guessed the role aliens, incubation, and Indrid Cold had to play. She just knew I was *weird*. But, to my Homerealm mother, my birth mother, I wouldn't be weird.

I might consider *her* weird, though. I've never met a sentient Raven before. Would she respond to all my questions with a simple "Nevermore"?

I want to fall asleep. Then I wouldn't have to deal with any of this. For that matter, I wouldn't mind leaving Lymon Zinn's presentation and starting my second round of surgery. It's going to happen anyway. Why not go ahead and get it over with!

No, on second thought I don't want to have surgery. I want to go back home to Indiana. But is Indiana truly home? What is home? Is it the place where your life crash landed? Or, is it the place of your origins? Maybe I should try to find a way back to Maryland. The Producer says he wants to rescue me, but what does that mean? Does he plan to take me back to Indiana or take me on to Maryland? Or, does he plan to simply check me out of The Zodiac Hotel and check me into the closest Econo Lodge?

And speaking of The Producer, Lymon Zinn is now going off on him. "Do you want to know the hypothesis pushed by this *Virginia* (sic) *Falls Zoo* documentary? I'll tell you right here and now, so you don't have to bother seeing it later today. It argues that in the late 1960s a group of sadomasochists bought a two-hundred-acre farm near Point Pleasant, on the site of the abandoned Virgil Mill, so they could act out their sex games in the open. It states that the dominatrix who ran the place, the aptly-named 'Lady Circe', had a very peculiar fetish. Like her ancient Greek namesake, she wanted to turn men into animals. However, she lacked genuine magickal powers. So she had to make do with the tools of the theater and the methods of the rabble, instead.

"For example, when she was possessed by a whim to make a man into a bird, she procured tar and feathers, and with the man's own consent subjected him to scalding humiliation! She also used a stage harness and fake wings, such as those used to portray Mephistopheles in productions of Goethe's *Faust*, and tarred and feathered *the wings* with matching plumage.

"She then had her on-site leathersmith construct a bird mask. Bright red eyes were painted onto the mask, for dramatic effect. But the mask itself had no eye openings, thus blindfolding the poor submissive fool. Furthermore, a red ball gag had been strapped over the mask, so the bird-man couldn't talk. He could only make muffled, gurgly sounds; sounds eerily reminiscent of a bird cry!

"And, according to this so-called 'documentary', a crane would lift the man up by the harness to make it seem like he was flying. Of course, much vertigo and vomiting ensued. The ball gag blocked the puke's exit. The man choked and died. Then, on the first anniversary of his death, he came back to Point Pleasant in the form of a *ghostly birdman* and moped around for a little over a year.

"Now friends, if this were just another crackpot theory about the Point Pleasant entity's origins, I wouldn't single it out for condemnation. My time is too precious to debunk the work of well-meaning, but kooky, investigators. No, I'm singling out *The Virgil Falls Zoo* because it is a work of radical feminist propaganda! It would have us believe the Point Pleasant entity *is not* The Great and Immortal Sky God, but a sniveling weakling slain by a powerful woman.

"I'm singling out *The Virgil Falls Zoo* because it offends Horus! In the course of my meditations, I have communed with him. He has appointed me to be his messenger to all *man*kind. And here is the message he has shared with me: it

wasn't a coincidence that he happened to arrive in Point Pleasant *in 1966*. He chose that year because it was a pivotal one
for young American men. It was the year when more and more
of them started to wear their hair down to their shoulders, like
women. It was the year right before the so-called 'Summer of
Love', when boys traveled out to Sodom-Cisco to wear flowers
in their hair. It was an era when American girls were becoming
more masculine.

"Horus visited Point Pleasant because he knew West Virginia was a bastion of masculinity! Where better to make his
stand? Hounded out of decadent Egypt, he traveled to the
place where he felt he could make a difference. He was trying
to prevent the feminization of American men. He was trying
to prevent Helen Reddy from singing 'I Am Woman, Hear Me
Roar'. He was trying to prevent the rise of working women,
latchkey kids, TV dinners, and other assaults on civilization.

"Allow me to turn your attention once again to the slide.
Let's examine these headlines through the lens of what I've
just shared with you. First: 'COUPLES SEE MAN-SIZED
BIRD…CREATURE…SOMETHING'. This is exactly how
the uninitiated would describe Horus! Think about it. In this
headline, we see a reference to Horus as both a concrete form
(a 'man-sized bird') and an uncanny abstraction ('something').
He is also described here as a 'creature'. An interesting word,
I think you'll agree; suggestive of something in between the
well-defined and the purely abstract. Horus came back to the
world to save masculinity from its own suicide. He connects
men to our rightful place in the sky. He connects the body,
that is, his material aspect, to the world of the spirit, i.e., the
indescribable 'something'. If we strive to achieve communion
with him, we too can thrive in the synergy of body and spirit,
immanence and transcendence."

The Laughers, for once, aren't laughing. They let out reverent gasps and groans. They're dramatically placing their hands to their chests. One even throws his hands up in the air and sways back and forth, as if he were at a Baptist revival. This can't be the first time they've heard Zinn's spiel, but they act as if it were. They act as if they were having a conversion experience.

I believe they're putting on a show. They know such melodramatic actions can be contagious. They know some awkward, alienated man in the audience will see this group, this community, in the front row and envy their enthusiasm and mutual connection. They know this man will eventually throw his arms in the air and sway back and forth, too. They know he'll approach the dais after Zinn's talk and try to have a moment with him. They know he'll go to the dealer's room and buy all of Zinn's books. Perhaps he'll even ask how he, too, might one day be allowed to don a gray pinstripe suit and join the Laughers.

Or maybe they know none of this. How do *I know* what *they know*? I can't read minds.

Then again, maybe my Homerealm brain is maturing in its abilities. Maybe I'm developing the ability to read minds, like all the other aliens can.

No, that's a foolish thought. None of this can be true. The man calling himself "Indrid Cold" is just some sicko trying to brainwash me into joining his little cult. Otherworldly creatures such as the Mothman do not exist. The Zodiac Hotel is just an old, abandoned hotel. I didn't set my GPS to arrive here, someone else did. They broke into my house and drugged me. Gave me something that made me dissociate, but still kept me alert enough to drive. Are there any such drugs in existence? If I had my phone I could do a Google search and find out. Google would tell me the truth. It always does.

Maybe I'm being recruited into a cult. Or maybe it's something less serious than that. Maybe I'm being recruited into a live action role play. Yes, it's quite possible that I've been kidnapped, but only so I can play the role of the Mothwoman in a LARP. The person running the simulation (perhaps "Indrid Cold", himself) created my character and needed someone to play the role. With Covid and everything, volunteers were few and far between. So they shanghaied me.

But why me? Perhaps the role requires a woman of a certain height. Yes, they have a Mothwoman costume for me to wear. They say that I'm wearing a human costume, but in fact they plan to put me in a Mothwoman costume. They plan to fool me into believing I really am the Mothwoman, because they know I would never actually join a LARP. Or perhaps they think I *would* join a LARP, but wouldn't do a good job of acting the role. So, they need to make me believe I am the Mothwoman. That's the only way I'll put on a good show. Maybe they've seen the videotape of my performance in a college production of *Macbeth*, and know I suck as an actress.

No, that makes no sense. For that to be the case, they would have had to monitor me since 1995! No, it has nothing to do with a LARP. It has to do with Giuseppe. Yes, Giuseppe the Puppeteer wasn't content to make the trees move in the absence of wind. Or, perhaps, *he* would have been content to leave it at that, but he was hired *by a third party* to play additional pranks. Hence the Staring, and the message on my window, and MothCon.

And now I hear Zinn again. He's pointing to the second headline.

"MONSTER NO JOKE FOR THOSE WHO SAW IT. That headline is entirely consistent with what I've just shared.

Horus wasn't here to fool around. He was there to make a serious impression."

I want to leave. No, I *need* to leave. But I can't move on my own volition. I nudge Mary White with my elbow. She whispers in my ear. "No, I'm not going to sleep with you. Nor am I going to feed you. Stop thinking with your orifices and start paying attention!"

And my hopes for escape are dashed by the too-effective thought-masking of the gelatinous centipede. I'm still pretty weak from the surgery, but not quite so weak as I was immediately post-op. I can raise my arm up slightly. I can smack myself about the head, first with one hand, then with another, in the hope of dislodging its pincers from my brain. If successful, Mary White won't think I'm obsessed with my orifices. She might begin to take me seriously. But then she would also know about The Producer's plan to rescue me this afternoon.

And Lymon Zinn is now rambling on about how most of the UFOs in the skies over West Virginia during the Mothman flap weren't spacecraft at all, but rather Horus's "spectral sperm" that wriggled through the air and landed in the Ohio River, where they would somehow plant "the seed of true manhood" into America's water supply. (The Ohio flows into the Mississippi, which flows into the Gulf of Mexico, which flows into the Atlantic.)

"In addition," Zinn says, "these 'strange lights' (finger quotes) drew worshipful glances up to the sky. That is, up to *masculinity*. Up to Horus. He fertilized the Ohio River, and he fertilized the eyes of countless West Virginians. He prepared them to see what the feminazis didn't want them to see."

I have no idea what it means to "fertilize" eyes. I'm not sure Zinn knows, either. Perhaps, if he were pressed on the matter, he would improvise an answer acceptable to his minions.

Something about "the implantation of a new way of seeing", "a seminal red pill" (or red eye drops, as the case may be).

And I have to wonder what would happen if I just started to scream, long and loud. I've been led to believe such behavior solves nothing. In the context of the Homerealmers' operating room, I'm sure it wouldn't. But I'm not in the operating room now. I'm in the Orion Ballroom (the ballroom in which Orion is nowhere to be seen). I'm listening to a misogynist crackpot shoehorning his ideology into the Mothman myth. Screaming might solve *this* problem. It might lead the Men in Black to take me away. Perhaps they would torture me, but listening to Lymon Zinn is torture too. I've never been tortured by Men in Black before. The novelty of the situation would deliver some relief.

So I decide to scream. Lymon Zinn deserves to have someone scream at him. I start to clear my throat, so I can give it my all.

Then I choke on my own spit. Or I suppose I should say that *my costume* chokes on *its* spit.

Zinn notices my coughing. "Gargle with cum. That will clear up the congestion."

The Laughers laugh. The other men in the audience laugh. I feel my muscles tighten, my heart gallop. I can't stop coughing.

Zinn raises his voice, moves on to his next subject: time travel. I have experienced time travel (only one short trip back to 2007, but that's more than most people). I suspect Zinn has never time traveled. I suspect he never will. I suspect his take on it will be utter nonsense. And yet, even as I'm coughing up a lung, something compels me to listen. I'm annoyed with myself for wanting to listen, but I do.

He's directing his laser pointer to the headline PARKERS-

BURG SALESMAN SPEAKS TO SPACEMAN. "Now, as you can see from the date of the article, this incident occurred shortly before the first 'Mothman' sighting, However, the two are clearly related. As many of you may know, the 'PARKERS-BURG SALESMAN' was none other than Woodrow Deren-berger. An army veteran. A man's man. Nothing effeminate about him.

"The so-called 'SPACEMAN' introduced himself as 'Cold'. I say 'so-called', because he was not an extraterrestrial. He was a time traveler from an emasculated future! At least, that's what we can infer from Derenberger's recounting of his experience. He describes Cold's clothes as being 'reflective', which implies excessive adornment. Mr. Cold told Derenberger that he came from a place 'less powerful' than Derenberger's West Virginia. Clearly he's saying his culture, the future American culture, had been emascul—"

My coughing gets even worse. It again disrupts Zinn's momentum. He pauses and glares at me. Points at me. "Hey, look. I'm shoving so much truth down *that* bitch's throat that she's choking on it." Then he addresses me directly. "Don't spit the truth back up, baby. Swallow it!"

The Laughers laugh. And laugh. And laugh.

And I feel something happening. I'm no longer choking. I'm hyperventilating. I'm hyperventilating, and I'm flopping around in my wheelchair. I feel like the ghost of Sammy the Poodle is getting his revenge. I seem to be having a seizure. Yes, some kind of *panic-induced* seizure.

Mary White gasps. Screams. "Get the M.i.B. in here, stat."

M.i.B. STAT. Truncation, abbreviation. Flailing. Choking. Sammy's Ghost. The ceiling. Spray painted pentagrams going in and out of focus.

A catalog of sensations: I'm feeling the omnipresent pins-

and-needles sensation, but now another sensation *displaces* the pins-and-needles sensation. The pins-and-needles sensation doesn't go away, but it's *eclipsed* by this new sensation: a new stinging sensation. Not the *snap*-STING! sensation. It's more like I have paper cuts on both hips.

Actually, it's not just in my hips. The sensation starts there, but moves up my sides all the way to my armpits, and down again to my hands. It's like my surgical incisions weren't sewn up properly. The seizure is making my stitches come undone, and the incisions are spreading from my hips up along the flank of my torso. My human costume is coming undone, like a zipper. In public. This could end badly.

More twitching and jerking. Do I see what I think I'm seeing? Lymon Zinn is galloping down the dais. Far from being repulsed by my fit, he's entranced by it.

"Please leave her alone," Mary White says. "She's having a seizure."

"Seizure?" Zinn asks. "I barely knew her!" Even though it's an unfunny joke, the Laughers laugh and laugh and laugh. Zinn, too, laughs at his own joke.

At least, he does until I take action to shut him up.

Or, maybe I don't take action. "Take action" makes it sound like I've consciously decided to act. This doesn't feel like a conscious decision. It just happens. I see my fingertips split open, like blooming flowers. The zipper around my fingers has come undone. A couple of teaspoons of human blood splatters out when this happens. Black talons shoot forth from the ruined stumps. *My first sight of the real me!*

These talons rip open Lymon Zinn's face. The sight of his blood thrills me. His whiny little howls amuse me. The whole experience grounds me. I spend too much time in my head. The physicality of this act feels good.

So, I don't mind it when the Laughers come to the defense of their guru. It means even more physicality is on its way. Three of them start shoving Mary White. The rest pile onto me. Jeremy picks up the microphone and thrashes me about the head with it. At first, I think it hurts. Then I remember it's only hurting my human costume.

Moreover, there are certain benefits that come with being thrashed over the head. At least, there are for an incubated Mothwoman. The thrashing further loosens the hold of my human costume. When Jeremy clobbers me over the nose, it cracks open. Like an egg. This allows the tip of my beak to escape. When he leans in close to strangle me, I whip off my Covid mask and peck away at his face. (At this point, the mask is unnecessary. I'm no longer dependent on the human respiratory system.)

I get two or three pecks in. I'm not accustomed to using my beak. The first two are little more than pinches. The third one, though, is delicious. It cuts into the little prick's neck. For Jeremy there are no benefits to bodily harm. He's just an ordinary human. There's nothing magickal or alien incubating under his skin: he's just meat and bone and tendon.

I let out a croaking, cawing laugh as his blood spurts through the air. One part of me feels guilty for laughing, as the wound I've inflicted might require stitches. Another part of me feels proud. I've stood up for myself.

The Men in Black disagree with my assessment. They topple my wheelchair and dogpile onto me. I feel the sleek fabric of their suits on my skin. One of their neckties flops against my cheek. Their hands are warm and rough. I loathe their touch. I want them to get off of me.

They won't get off of me.

Thus, I'm again reminded of how I'm enveloped by objects.

(Men, suits, ties, hands.) And I'm reminded that all of us in the ballroom are, in turn, enveloped by a spray painted ceiling (which could be seen as a cheap facsimile of the night sky). And I know that if the ceiling of the Orion Ballroom had windows, we could see the autumn grayness that passes for daylight, and we would know the natural, daytime sky is no more impressive than this facsimile of night, and we would cringe at our awareness of being wrapped in both.

Only one fact offers solace: I'm not in contact with the floor. I'm levitating off of it. To be clear, I'm not levitating *much*. Just a half inch or so. I doubt if anyone in the audience notices it. But *I* notice it, and it feels good to know that at least some part of my body is left untouched.

Just a minute ago I craved physicality. Now, I find it hideous. I don't want my body to touch anything, even the ground!

As I'm carried out of the ballroom, one of the Men in Black whispers in my ear. "Hey man, you're revealing too many of your powers in front of the humans. Show some modesty!"

The Men in Black carry me out into the corridor. Passersby gasp, take cell phone pictures, mutter words like "abduction". Some redneck who thinks he's Billy Bob Badass starts railing against the government.

"CIA's done raided MothCon!" he shouts.

One of his friends disagrees. "Nah. The CIA ain't *raided* MothCon. They're *running* MothCon. Maybe they always have."

"What they do to her? Her face looks all fucked up."

"Well, genius, if her face looks all fucked up I reckon it's on account of they fucked it up."

"She's got a beak!"

"That ain't a beak. Her nose is just all black an' blue."

The Man Who Knows I Have A Beak says something I can't

hear. He runs up to my captors. A tussle ensues. His cell phone makes a sound that indicates he's taking a picture. It's the sound old film cameras used to make, a crisp whirring sound, the sound of a captured moment. Two of the Men in Black let go of me (leaving me in the hands of three others). They perform various martial arts maneuvers to force the phone out of his hand.

"Hey man, you're interfering with a convention security matter. This constitutes a violation of MothCon's attendance agreement. I'm afraid I have to confiscate your phone and de-lete all photos that invade our privacy. After we're finished, we'll have the phone returned to you via first class mail."

The buddy of The Man Who Knows I Have a Beak speaks up. "Something's wrong. This ain't the real MothCon. This is a fake convention ran by the CIA to keep tabs on us."

His commentary draws a small crowd. One of them is a woman who, it would seem, smokes fifteen packs a day. "You sure they're with the government? Lookit their yellow skin! You sure they ain't aliens?" She's got her arm extended so her phone can record the melee. "I'm posting this on Facebook, y'all. This ain't right."

A neckbeard whips off his mask and starts screaming about the Deep State, and Q, and the "plandemic". He whips a pis-tol out from under his waistband. "They're kidnapping a little girl," he says. "Sending her off to Hillary!"

I have no idea how I'm being mistaken for a little girl. I'm middle-aged. I'm six feet tall! People see what they want to see.

This mistake is contagious. Q-Anon Neckbeard has two friends in tow. They whip off their masks, too. All three of them are unpleasant to gaze upon. Their hair is overgrown, their eyes are glassy and unfocused. Their jaws, slack. Their breathing, heavy, They look over-medicated (or not medicated enough). They look like they haven't read a book in twenty years. They look like they've never fallen in love. They look only half-alive. They look like they *know* they're only half-alive. They look like they've no idea of how to better their situation. They're armed.

They start spitting in our direction. They start chanting. "LET. HER. GO! LET. HER. GO!" One has started drinking early. He nails a Man in Black in the forehead with a half-full beer bottle. Yellow blood drips from the wound.

Another Man-in-Black whispers in my ear. "Hey man, see what you've done? Now they're onto us. You've endangered our entire mission. You're a fuck-up, just like your brother."

The words hurt, but there's no time to dwell on them. The troublemakers have discovered a heap of Budweiser bottles next to a trash can in the lobby (overflow from last night's debauches). Five fly through the air, two hit their intended targets. One smashes against the floor. Two collide with the wall.

Bystanders mistake the sound of broken bottles for gunfire. (An easy mistake to make, given that Q-Anon Neckbeard is brandishing a pistol.) "Active shooter!" one of them screams. Three more dudes whip out pistols. They call for Q-Anon Neckbeard to drop his weapon.

Q-Anon Neckbeard screams that he's trying to fight an alien/ Deep State conspiracy, not his fellow patriots.

"False flag," one of the bystanders shrieks. "You're the Deep State, not us."

The competing claims are a mess of coat hangers. Passersby can't begin to untangle them. There's a good chance someone's going to be shot. I don't want anyone to be shot. I mean, to be clear, I don't harbor any attachment to these humans. I suppose I never have. I just know that if someone gets shot, *I'll* somehow end up getting blamed for it.

The confusion gives the Men in Black enough time to whisk me away. They carry me down a hallway and stop in front of a framed copy of a Van Gogh self-portrait. One of the ones painted after he cut off his ear. One of my captors jabs his yellow fingers into Van Gogh's eyes. As it turns out, the eyes are not eyes at all! They are, rather, buttons that activate a secret entrance. A door-shaped section of wall swooshes open, just like on *Star Trek*. We all tumble inside, and the door swooshes shut. We're at the top of a stairwell. A soothing quiet replaces the sounds of rioting.

The Men in Black don't seem relaxed, though. If anything, they're handling me more roughly than before. They grab onto me too tightly, toss me about cavalierly. They resent my existence.

13

We arrive in a damp, cold room redolent of mold. This is odd, because the room doesn't look like the natural playground for mold. It looks like a clean, dry, well-maintained, recently-built office. It looks like it should smell like air freshener, or like pages just spat out of a laser printer. It should smell like a secretary's cheap perfume. It should smell like coffee and microwave popcorn. But it smells like none of those things. It smells like a flooded basement.

My sensations don't add up. First, I *see* "wind" gusting violently through trees, but don't *feel* it blow against my cheek. Now, I *feel* this room's damp chills and *smell* its mold, but *see* a clean, neat, dry, well-maintained, recently-built office. Is Giuseppe the Puppeteer responsible for this trick as well?

He can't be. He doesn't exist.

Wait. That's not quite right. He does exist. He exists in my imagination, if nowhere else. And didn't Einstein himself say imagination is more important than knowledge? (Maybe he didn't. Maybe the quote is misattributed. But a poster for sale in a used bookstore once told me he did, and that's good enough for me.)

Perhaps Giuseppe's a symbol. No, not a symbol, an *archetype*. He is a specific manifestation, in this time and place, of the archetypal Trickster, who is also the gnostic demiurge. The physical world is a jigsaw puzzle manufactured by Giuseppe. The picture on the box makes it seem like certain pieces belong next to each other, but they've been intentionally (mis) shaped so they don't fit together at all.

This is what I'm thinking about, as I'm strapped down to a gurney. It's what I'm thinking about as the lights dim, and dim, and dim, until finally the room turns black. It's what I'm thinking about as I realize the little red lights circling above me in the blackness are the glowing eyes of Men in Black. They seem to have removed their sunglasses (a costume accessory of their own) and revealed their true selves.

"We see better in the dark," one of them explains.

"Just like your father," another one says.

"The sunglasses create an artificial darkness, but we function much better in the real thing."

The door opens. (*Clink-clank-THUMP!*) I expect a little beam of light to enter the room, stray light from the hallway. This doesn't happen. I expect a lot of things. They rarely happen.

I see a puff of visible breath. I hear a nasally, high-pitched, hoarse voice. I don't see an additional pair of red eyes. Indrid Cold is similar to the Men in Black in that he sees better in the dark, but he's not identical to them. He lacks red eyes.

Father speaks: "Gentlemen, I understand we have a little

mess on our hands. To avoid it becoming a big mess, I'm invoking Containment Plan Gamma."

A Man in Black replies: "Hey man, you've got to do what you've got to do. We'll take care of it."

"Good. Now, if you'll excuse me, I need a few moments alone with my daughter."

Like a swarm of fireflies, the red eyes of the Men in Black zoom away from me. The door opens. *Clink-clank-THUMP!* This time, as the door opens, a little beam of stray light from the hallway enters the room. Only a moment before, the hallway was dark. Now, it's lit. Who turned the lights on, out there? I don't know. Maybe Giuseppe the Puppeteer. He's always playing mind games. Well, he doesn't really exist, but *in my mind* he's always playing mind games.

In any event, a beam of light invades this chamber, and I see silhouettes of fedora-wearing men in the doorway. I also see the toe of my father's boot. I see the edge of his pants. It's the most I've ever seen of him. It disappears as soon as the door closes. (*Clink-clank-THUMP!*) Then, I can only see his breath as he speaks.

"I'm concerned about you, Nid."

This sentence could have any number of meanings. Is my father genuinely concerned about my welfare? Is the concern coming from genuine paternal instinct? Then I welcome it. After all, I'm worried about myself, too. I've been worried about myself for quite some time.

And now he inserts a series of thoughts into my head.

Violence, of course, has its place. Don't misunderstand me: I'm grateful I didn't sire a pacifist! However, violence is best restricted to certain times, places, and methods. The open display of violence, in front of witnesses, is gauche. Not only is it gauche, it's careless. You blew our cover here. Our security forces, already stretched to the limit, will now have to clean up the mess you made.

Are you listening to me? I know what you're thinking and it has nothing to do with what I'm saying! Pay attention!

If you had to strike out against Lymon Zinn, you should have done it in the middle of the night. Yes, fly up to his window, burst through the glass, hover over him, smother him under a pillow, leave nothing but stray feathers as evidence, and watch the humans go mad trying to solve the crime!

Nid? Nid? Can you nod for me? Can you nod, Nid, just so I know our telepathy is working?

I nod.

Then what's with all these...strange thoughts? Thoughts that have nothing to do with the conversation? Focus!

I disapprove of your recklessness. You shouldn't have attacked Lymon Zinn in front of witnesses. What worries me more, though, is that you felt the need to strike out against Lymon Zinn at all. He vents his rage against human *females. You're not human, so you shouldn't take his rants personally. They're as meaningless as the chirping of a squirrel. And yet, they bothered you to such an extent that you burst the seams of your costume! You just* had *to attack him.*

Nid? What's wrong? Why are you going on and on about copulation and digestion? Your thoughts are unworthy of any Homerealm mind, let alone the daughter of a Mission Commander! It's bad enough that your brother has given our family a reputation for insanity. I won't allow you to shame us, as well.

What's happened to you? This fixation on the satisfaction of... orifices...wasn't present when I read your mind yesterday. Nor was this impulsive behavior. How odd. Even as your true body *begins to escape from its human costume, your thoughts become more and more human! Actually, that's giving you too much credit. Your thoughts are absolutely* subhuman. *They're more like the thoughts of one of the animals the humans have domesticated! In fact, that's paying you too much of a compliment. They're more like the thoughts of an insect! The change puzzles even me, and I'm not accustomed to being puzzled.*

I'm going to summon a specialist in these sorts of matters to perform a complete evaluation of your brain. Fortunately for you, the Kippleodians have the best psychiatrists. One in particular, Dr. Doyle Ladd, has worked on the Zodiac before. It will be a small matter to summon him. Once he receives my message, it should take only two minutes for him to arrive.

He'll bring his brain scanner with him, and we'll see what's going on up there. With any luck, the scanning will present only a minor delay. After he interprets the results, he may wish to prescribe you medication. At worst, he'll need to perform surgery, to decrease the size of your brain's pleasure centers. A smaller pleasure-brain might equate to fewer orifice obsessions. Then you wouldn't be quite so embarrassing to be around.

And that turns out to be Dad's closing line right before his dramatic exit. Soon, I hear *Clink-clank-THUMP!* The door opens. The hallway light has been turned off yet again. And then, *Clink-clank-THUMP!* The door closes.

I flail around on the gurney. Squawk and gurgle and croak. Try to escape.

I manage to levitate off the floor. Unfortunately, since I'm strapped into the gurney, it levitates *with me.* The combined weight is too much for me to manage, and the gurney crashes down onto the floor. It stays upright. It doesn't totter over. But the impact does something to my right shoulder. I think I may have broken it.

No, I didn't break it. If I had broken it, I'd be crying now—assuming, of course, that Mothwomen can cry. In any event, I didn't break it. It just feels, well...*looser* and *flimsier* than it should be.

Then another surprise: there's a large screen TV on the wall. I hadn't noticed it before, in the dark. It flickers at first (like a strobe-light). Then it shows me a movie about a riot.

No, it's not a movie. It's live footage from a high-definition security camera. Yes, I recognize the hallway outside the Zodiac Ballroom! The crowd has grown (both in numbers and in rage). The combat is hand to hand. They're all trying to perform MMA maneuvers on each other. They're all unathletic.

You might be wondering who, exactly, has joined this fracas. (Has Lymon Zinn stumbled out from his keynote address, all bloodied from my talons, to join the fray? What about the pear-shaped man? Has he brought an AR-15 to the party to mow down everyone who skipped *"the ceremonies"*?) You might be wondering about the conflicting claims of disinformation. (Do two false flags cancel each other out to make one true flag?)

For the moment, I can't shed light on any of these matters. Well, what I mean is, I *could* shed light on them. There's no biological reason why I couldn't. It's just that such topics aren't my focus. I'm fascinated by the mere fact of this television's existence.

It raises certain questions. Was it there this whole time but just turned off? Wouldn't I have noticed it when I was first carried into here?

Perhaps it was here earlier, but it was only a seed. Yes, back then it was a tiny television, about the size of a mustard seed. That's why I didn't notice it, at first.

Yes, it could be an alien, *technological* seed. My father installed (i.e., planted) it into the wall. The body heat generated by me and the Men in Black made the seed germinate and bloom. Are images its equivalent to petals? Are eyes analogous to bees? Is staring a kind of fertilization?

For some reason, I'm tickled by these ideas. I begin to wonder if all so-called "inanimate objects" grow from seeds. Maybe that's why Earth has more objects now than ever. It's not because of the development of plastics. It has nothing whatsoever to do with human ingenuity. It has to do with aliens (Homerealmers?) planting TV seeds and picture frame seeds and Halloween decoration seeds and cigarette seeds. They plant them in stores and that's where they grow.

But what about all the tractor trailers on the road (tractor trailers and tractor trailers and blurry asphalt)? Don't they deliver all these objects to the stores?

No. That's just what my father would want you to think. In fact, all the boxes being toted around by big rigs are filled with sandbags! They're an elaborate ruse. How silly it is, to think that trucks could really deliver so much freight!

You don't believe me. That's okay. String theory is on my side: there must be at least one universe in which this ruse is real. Why shouldn't it be ours?

Crack!!

Crack-crack-crack!

Blam!

And on the screen, plumes of smoke.

(Active shooter, active shooter, and HELL IS…unreal, because these sounds are coming out of speakers, and the bloodstains on the victims are just images. The victims, themselves, are just images. If I close my eyes and stick my talons in my ears, the massacre will go away.)

But I don't close my eyes, nor do I stick my talons in my ears. I don't because the smoke clears, revealing Q-Anon Neckbeard trying to poke Van Gogh's eyes out. He must have seen the M.i.B.s open the door! Soon he, too, will be *Clink-clank-*

THUMPing into here.

Yes, he'll turn on the light, and he'll see my beak, and he'll know I'm not a little girl needing to be rescued from pedophile Democrats. He'll know I'm a Mothwoman. Or, perhaps he'll misgender me and think I'm my brother. And then, he'll probably shoot me.

Yes, he'll shoot me.

Why will he shoot me? Will he think I'm part of the Deep State?

No, he'll shoot me because my corpse would bring him fame and fortune.

Clink-clank-THUMP!

I struggle against my restraints. Manage to levitate. (Not as high this time. Not for the same duration. Levitation is exhausting.) My plan is to use my powers to ram the gurney into Q-Anon Neckbeard.

Only it's not Q-Anon Neckbeard.

It's a man (or man-like thing) wearing scrubs, a cap, a surgical mask, and gloves. He seems to be white, but he's not pale. He looks like the kind of white person who obsesses over tanning. His is not a healthy tan, but an over-tan. The type of tan that will almost certainly result in melanomas. His skin sags, as if wanting to free itself from its tormentor.

His eyes are dark. His glance, nervous. His fingers are only half the length of ordinary fingers. "I'm Dr. Ladd. Your father has asked me to do some tests."

He wears a utility belt. It holds scalpels, a bonesaw, and a hypodermic.

I push my gurney toward him, using all my strength. Those little fingers are stronger! They wrestle it back to the ground.

"Levitation never solved anything," Dr. Doyle Ladd says. "Stop playing around, we need to get out of here."

And he's right. We do. Heavy footfalls echo down the stairwell. Bestial grunts, whooping sounds. Neckbeards and neckbeards and guns.

So now we're in the hallway. Dr. Ladd pushes me from behind. *Rattle-tattle-rattle* goes the gurney. Somehow, it gets a flat tire. (The front left, to be exact.) Dr. Ladd puts on the brakes. Moves to the front. Uses his stumpy, super-strong fingers to lift the gurney off the ground. Starts pushing it behind him, like a rickshaw. Now we rely solely on the intact rear tires.

Footfalls scuff the floor behind us. "Freeze, motherfucker, citizen's arrest! Get away from the girl!"

Dr. Ladd lets go of my gurney. Walks away from me, allows Q-Anon Neckbeard to approach. The neckbeard gawks, trying to take in the sight of me. The shock of gazing upon a Mothperson causes him to hesitate. That's when Dr. Ladd sends two of his scalpels racing through the air. Both find their targets, the Neckbeard's eyes. No real harm done. He was, in a sense, already blind.

More of the mob are en route, though. I can hear them coming down the stairwell. Dr. Ladd huffs and puffs and plays the rickshaw driver. We reach a framed copy of Gustave Doré's Satan. (Well, technically, not "Gustave Doré's Satan", but rather Satan as depicted *by Dante*, illustrated in an etching by Gustave Doré.)

Dr. Ladd pokes two fingers at the devil's eyes, but nothing happens. He sighs, the mob turns a corner. Spots us. Then he remembers the third eye. You see, Dante gives Satan three faces. Six eyes. A real freak show. *Weird.* Doré only etched two of the faces, though. One and a half, really. The rest are implied. Likewise, he only gives Satan three eyes. The third is hard to see, at first. It's in the background, off to the side.

Anyway, the point is, Dr. Ladd remembers the trick to open

the secret entrance we need opened. There's no reason he should know Dante. I'm assuming he doesn't even know the history of this etching, and the centuries-old tale it brings to life. Dr. Ladd doesn't know human culture the way I do. He just knows the third eye needs poking.

But enough lecturing! Once Satan's third eye has been poked, the wall slides away from itself, revealing a small chamber.

No, not a small chamber. An elevator. The mob fires gun-shots at us. I suppose they figured out we're the ones who injured Herr Neckbeard. Or maybe they just like shooting things. One of the bullets finds a way inside. It hits another of the tires, flattening it. I know this is the case because I feel the gurney sink down toward the ground. Now we have two flats.

The next thing I know, I'm floating upward. I'm floating, and I'm contemplating what the universe is trying to teach me, with so many flat tires. Maybe the universe hates me. It wants to frustrate me. It knows I want to return to the place of my origins and it wants to stymie my plans at every turn.

And so up, up, up we go. Up to Dr. Ladd's office, wherever it is. Up to the place where I shall be made sane. Dr. Ladd has already used his scalpels on the neckbeard. I suppose he'll use the bonesaw on me. I hope that hypodermic works.

My room was on the third floor. I suspect that's where the operating room is, too. I'm puzzled when the elevator passes it. We go up to the fourth floor, and the fifth, and then up beyond even that. Up to a level noted only as "R".

"I'm a friend of The Producer," Dr. Ladd says. "He's evacuat-ing us. Soon we'll be free of this whole mess."

R is for Roof.

This raises all sorts of questions. If Dr. Doyle Ladd is on my side, does this mean Layla Dodd was, too? That makes no sense. The Kippleodeans are a puzzle to me.

But now is not the time for puzzles. Now is the time for jubilation! The elevator doors open and I see a glorious sight: a black medevac helicopter with four moving blades! Tears of joy well up in my eyes. (I suppose Mothwomen *can* cry.) Of course, I'm happy I'm being delivered from the clutches of my foes. But what really pleases me is the method of my rescue. The helicopter blades remind me of my ceiling fan, back home in Indiana. This can only be a good omen.

The blades rotate slowly. Dr. Ladd pushes my gurney into the helicopter. The Producer (still wearing his mask, ever dutiful) gives us a thumbs up sign from his place in the cockpit. And the engine sounds both whiny and powerful, and the world rattles all around me, and even as the blades spin more rapidly, and get more blurry, I know they're there above me. I see their blur in the corner of my eye, out the window, and have a hunch everything will be okay.

But I can't *take it for granted* that everything will be okay. So I ask Dr. Ladd if I'm being taken home to Maryland.

He picks up a clipboard. Gives it a glance. "Yes, Maryland. That's what our orders say."

And a daydream goes through my head: a happy family reunion. Once we arrive at the airport I'll call Mom. I'll come up with some explanation for why I've been out of touch. My sister will have been discharged from the hospital. I am Dorothy. I have had my time in Oz. The technicolor world has proven too much for me. I hunger for my mundane family. Bring on the Russian novels and the Jerry Springer show (broadcast in black and white)! After all I've been through I'll revel in them.

I try to get some rest. Turn over on my side. Realize I can't.

There's a reason my shoulder felt looser and flimsier than it used to. When my levitation attempt failed and my gurney crashed to the ground, the force of impact opened up another seam in my costume. Shiny black feathers stick out from the tear. A wing is working its way out.

There's no going back to humanity.

So, there will be no family reunion. At least, no *ordinary* family reunion. I could show up at my parents' window and flap around a little. That way, I could at least see them one more time. But then, I might end up giving Dad a heart attack.

No, I don't want to do anything that could contribute to Dad's death. Mind you, I know he's not truly alive at this point. Nonetheless, I don't want to feel responsible for his death. Also, I don't want him to die of fear. I'd prefer for him to die in his sleep during a pleasant dream.

Maybe I could fly onto their roof, instead, and tap out messages in Morse code with my beak. On second thought, that would be useless. Mom doesn't know Morse code. She would think I was a demented woodpecker who had taken a liking to shingles. She'd whine about the racket.

Maybe I could use my claws to etch a message into her car hood. Yes, that's probably the best option. Of course, before I can fly to my parents' house, I'll need to finish extricating myself from this human costume. I suppose The Producer will help with that.

I wish I knew more about him. It's odd that a dude who makes Mothman documentaries has access to a medevac helicopter. It's odd for a medevac helicopter to be painted black. Then again, this journey home has been quite odd from the start. By now, I've come to accept oddity as the norm. The manner in which I fell into my "real" father's clutches was Strange. So it only makes sense that my method of escape is Strange, too. There's symmetry in all this. And, as I've said before, there's beauty in symmetry.

Actually, I don't think I *said* that. I think I only implied that

I find *dis*comfort in *a*symmetry. In any event, this thought about the aesthetics of symmetry serves as a sweet distraction from all this Strangeness. Too sweet, actually. I'm no longer sustained by an adrenaline rush. My body starts to acknowledge that it's recently undergone surgery. It begins to admit that it's worn itself out with levitation. The sweet distraction suddenly becomes a soft distraction; unfocused, vague. Words get jumbled up. *Adrenaline rush* becomes *Russian drain*. *Surgery* becomes *sugary*. *Words get jumbled up* becomes *Word up! Get humbled.*

And my brain is disintegrating under a wave of cognitive entropy. By which I mean phrases drift apart from one another. Words and letters devolve even as I'm trying to reassemble them in my head. *Russian drain* becomes *Ruh-ain. Word up! Get humbled.* Becomes *Whir Tumbled.*

And then (as if matters weren't bad enough) they devolve one more time. *Ruh-ain* becomes *Run. Whir Tumbled* becomes *Warbled.* Which is, of course, a verb describing a type of birdsong.

The arc of consciousness is long but bends towards meaning. There's the meaning of hypnagogic premonitions. The meaning of prophetic dreams. Sleep is an altered state. It opens one's mind to the warnings of gods and the wisdom of monsters. It's a grand state, not at all empty or ridiculous.

Part Three:

Home Away from Home

1

I wake up during a bumpy descent. I want to get up and look out the window. I remember once, when I had a little money and flights were cheap, I flew back home instead of making the road trip. I remember sighing wistfully at the rich blues of Maryland's rivers and the great green soup that is Chesapeake Bay. The Bay is my birthright, as it is for anyone born and bred in the state. For almost twenty years I've lived in a landlocked state. I miss it. I'd love to see it from the air again.

I raise my head up to see the water, but the windows are small and too far away. So, there is no Chesapeake. There's only the metal and plastic cabin of this well-identified flying object. There's plastic doodads. There are stickers affixed atop the doodads, meant to explain their purpose and how they are to be used. The stickers explain nothing to me, because they make use of technical jargon. "Q to 54C," one of them says. "Stream clearance," says another.

In addition, every piece of equipment bears a sticker that says: "Property of D.o.D." This confuses me. Is there a typo on the sticker? Should it actually read "Dodd", as in Layla? Or, should it actually read "Dad"? (As in, this is *Dad's* helicopter that The Producer has stolen for his daring rescue mission?)

I'm still shaking out the cobwebs. As we get closer to the ground, I hear The Producer talking to someone over the radio. He's saying "for me, for me" over and over.

At least, I *think* that's what he's saying.

And then, whirling. The helicopter whirls in one direction, but I feel like I'm on a merry-go-round careening in the opposite direction. Nothing is in sync.

We land, but no one gets out. I want to get out. I want to get away from people. I want to get away from aliens. I want to get away from objects.

What I want doesn't matter.

I hear muffled voices outside. Young men's voices. They shout "Yes, sir!" They shout "Colonel". I hear heavy feet climbing aboard. "Detainee Smith in custody," a Southern man says.

"And Doe is on the stretcher?" a deep voice says.

"Affirmative," the Southern man says.

"Follow Containment Protocol Sigma."

A man in an olive drab biohazard suit approaches. He has a syringe in his hand. It's full of green liquid. I wonder if he's about to euthanize me. As the needle goes into my neck, he offers a quip. "Welcome to Fort Meade, you freak."

'For me'. *Fort Meade*. 'For me'.

Fort Meade for me.

2

I wasn't euthanized. At least, I don't *think* I was euthanized. I woke up, so that must mean I was merely sedated. But who's to say? Maybe they killed me, and I'm now conscious in the afterlife. Or maybe I died in a traffic accident while crossing the Kennedy Bridge, and this entire trip is happening in the afterlife. In some part of the multiverse, that happened. In another part of the multiverse, I'm the bearded hippo who shits the biggest diamonds ever, and this entire trip is happening in a nightmare. In a third part of the multiverse, *you're* the bearded hippo who shits the biggest diamonds ever, and you're experiencing my story as a nightmare.

I think, therefore I...*might* be.

I look up and to my left. I find a ceiling fan. It's gray. Made of steel. Seems clean. I wish it were covered in dust. Then I would feel more at home.

Of course, in a way, I am home. The Producer kept his word, he did take me to Maryland. Fort Meade rests between Baltimore and D.C. When I lived in Maryland, I would hear it get mentioned every once in a while on the local weather report. "Your high at Fort Meade up to a balmy fifty-seven today," the mustached weather man would declare. "Your low at thirty-five."

In this room, the temperature is constant and comfortable. If I had to hazard a guess, I'd say it was sixty-six. My brother, the Mothman, first appeared in Point Pleasant, West Virginia in 1966. My father, Indrid Cold, visited the human, Woodrow Derenberger, in 1966. The Orion Ballroom ceiling is adorned with sixty-six pentagrams. Therefore, it would be quite the synchronicity if the temperature was, as I suspected, sixty-six. After feeling out of sync with the motion of the helicopter, I would find myself suddenly *in sync* with my fate. There are no coincidences! Everything aligns according to the Cosmic Plan!

I hear the rustling of polyester sheets above me. I'm in the bottom of a bunk bed. Someone else is on top. It's Doyle Ladd. I know this because I see his stunted, tanned fingers pass by as he climbs down the ladder. He's no longer wearing his scrubs, cap, and gloves. He's now in an orange jumpsuit, matching surgical mask, and handcuffs. Of course, the soldiers have also confiscated his utility belt. No more bonesaw!

He looks down at me. His eyes don't look big enough to absorb me. He shudders. Speaks. "Have you awakened?"

I nod.

"Would you like to talk about any of this?"

I shrug my shoulders. They make a fluttering noise. I notice I'm no longer wearing clothes. I notice I'm no longer wearing skin. They removed the rest of my human costume. They took away the bandages. I am a raven. I am six feet tall. Looking down, I see my belly, perforated with a half-dozen holes. I see mist in the holes. I know the mist is part of my body.

I know this in the same way that I know my eyes are full of lava. Not actual lava, of course. They're not burning. They're not even hot. They're filled with a liquid that's thick and red. They slosh around in their sockets. They never slosh out, though. I'm not sure how they stay put, given how much they slosh. Perhaps my brain exerts sufficient gravity to keep the liquid tethered to my head.

As I've been thinking, Doyle Ladd has been yammering on. Something about how our "barracks" are bugged. When I try to focus on his exact words, I catch him mid-sentence: "...so anything we say will be used against us. Yes, we must be careful what we say. Of course, you can't say much of anything. You can't even screech, with that big clamp they have over your beak. And telepathy is no good. I've tried, and all I can hear is the chatter of your appetites!"

I look down at my beak. I do notice some heavy iron manacle-sort-of-thing wrapped around it. I try to open it. I can't.

"Your reputation precedes you. They don't want you pecking at them. It's the same reason they declawed—or, should I say—de-taloned you. The humans treasure their pretty faces."

This is a lot to absorb. I only had the opportunity to use my talons once. I didn't know the penalty for using them would be so stiff. And what of my beak? I'm assuming they'll let it loose, from time to time, so I can feed. But will I have to be "a good girl" to win that privilege? I try to raise my head off the pillow, but it's too heavy. The iron manacle on my beak weighs me down. A ball and chain attached to my left foot prevents me from flying away.

I'm imprisoned and mutilated. But at least I can see the ceiling fan, off to my left. Round and round and round it goes. At least I feel some of the breeze. Each waft of air makes me feel stronger. The ordeal would be tolerable if I were alone. Even if I weren't alone, it would be tolerable if my company kept to himself.

But Doyle Ladd wants to chat.

"I suppose you want an explanation."

Surprisingly, I don't. I just want quiet. That's all I've ever wanted. A ceiling fan, a room, some food, a toilet, a book on my nightstand, penned by some obscure madperson, and a nightly walk down dark, deserted streets. There's no place like home. There's no place like home. There's no place…

"Because this barracks is bugged, I will only tell you of matters which they, who listen to us, already know. It's the least I can do. I helped them kidnap you.

"You must understand, I bear no malice toward you. The kidnapping was part of a quid pro quo. In exchange for my assistance in transporting you to the roof, the United States National Security Agency promised to assist the Kippleodian Resistance. They don't like how the Homerealmers violate American airspace at will. So, reasoning that the enemy of their enemy was their friend, they expressed interest in supporting our rebellion.

"My contact at the N.S.A. attended MothCon in disguise as

the producer of that *Virgil Falls Zoo* documentary. The N.S.A. actually made a fake Mothman documentary, and had one of their spies present himself as the producer, just to have a convincing backstory for his appearance at the convention."

The Producer wore a name tag stating he represented the Nevada Studio Alliance. *N.S.A.* I feel foolish. I should have seen this coming. His name dropping was too over-the-top. His performance lacked credibility.

No, on second thought, I'm being too hard on myself. There's no way I could have seen this coming. Maybe he was unbelievably over-the-top, but in my experience many people at conventions are over-the-top and most pass themselves off as something they're not. Conventions are performance spaces. People laugh because they think they'll look good by laughing. (Or perhaps they laugh because they want to join in with the communal experience of laughing.) By the same token, people publicly chastise unpopular foes from their perch on convention panels because they think they'll look good by doing so. (Or perhaps they chastise because they want to join in with the communal experience of chastising.)

This is the twenty-first century, after all, and no one is who they say they are. The insecure filter their photographs on Instagram. Deep fakes sculpt reality into any desired image. Can I be blamed for just giving up and accepting The Producer at face value?

Not, *exactly* at face value, of course. I didn't believe he actually knew David Lynch. Nor did I believe he was a bona fide producer. But I believed him to be a hack producer, along the lines of those kids who make movies in their backyards with iPhones and enter them into local film festivals.

In retrospect, The Producer was a genius. He led me to believe I had seen through his fraud. But his fraud was, in fact, a pseudo-fraud. I believed he'd inflated his credentials. I believed he was a UFO buff who had somehow gotten wind of my plight and wanted to help.

I shouldn't have trusted him.

And Doyle Ladd keeps on yammering: "Ordinarily, I wouldn't have assisted him in imprisoning you. But he pledged the United States' support, and we need allies. In particular, we need allies who aren't trapped, the way we are. You see, your father is a war criminal. He commanded the mission that obliterated Kipple. The *Zodiac* crew were the ones who assembled the pieces of a mile-long 'Cosmic Slingshot'. They positioned it just outside of Kipple's orbit. An asteroid was on course to narrowly miss our planet, but the Cosmic Slingshot deflected its course so that it hit us directly.

"We all died. Well, our *bodies* were dead. Your father made sure that all of our consciousnesses lived on. Right before the moment of impact, he had the *Zodiac* make use of another experimental weapon: the so-called Soul Magnet. When it was positioned over our planet, the consciousnesses of all Kippleodians were sucked up to it (like metal filings drawn up to a magnet). Then these consciousnesses were implanted into…"

Doyle Ladd finds it difficult to go on. He kicks the bed. Moans the moan of a man who has only facts, but no answers. I have never seen a Kippleodian so upset before.

"You must understand: this body is not my body. My body is dead. This body is a pile of ectoplasm. It houses the consciousness of each and every Kippleodian who lived on the planet's flatlands. The other body you saw, the pale one, going by the name Whitey Mare and Mary White, houses the consciousness of each and every Kippleodian who lived in the planet's mountains. When the Homerealmers need a guest worker, they summon the consciousness of one Kippleodian up from the ectoplasm. The minute we're finished with our job, we're sent back into the deepest recesses of this goo, into a state of suspended animation. That way, they don't have to tolerate us living in their midst. They don't want us to 'contaminate' their culture, you see.

"We're in a coma until we're called upon. Then we manifest in the ectoplasm and do our job. Then we return to the coma. They never have to see us, except when we're doing our jobs.

"They strip us of our individuality, too. All the males from the flatlands are called 'Doyle Ladd', all the females, 'Layla Dodd'. All the males from the mountains are called 'Whitey Mare', all the females 'Mary White'. These aren't Kippleodian names. They're Homerealmer names. Maybe if I stay physically manifested long enough, I'll remember my real name. I want to.

"Hopefully, this helps you understand why I collaborated with the N.S.A. We share a common enemy. Your father has invented a highly efficient method of genocide, one which simultaneously kills and enslaves. The first Cosmic Slingshot was irreparably damaged during the Kipple Massacre, but another is under construction. Soon, all those who reside in Earth's flatlands may find themselves common residents in one ectoplasmic body. Soon, those residing among Earth's mountains may find themselves common residents in another.

"So, you can understand why I was willing to play a role in your abduction. I was just doing my part to help my people. I expected to be debriefed, and then given my freedom. Instead, I'm locked up, just like you!

"I'm not even sure what I would do with my freedom. I suppose I would work with the United States to crush the Homerealm. But what would I do in any spare time afforded me? I'm not sure. Perhaps that's why I'm being held here, in this barracks, with you. Perhaps they don't want to immerse me into freedom all at once. Perhaps they want to grant me my freedom incrementally. Yes, that's quite possible."

And with that, Doyle Ladd finally shuts up. I lap up more wind from the ceiling fan. I watch it go around. I'm not happy, but I'm content. Time passes. An hour? A day? A week? I don't know. Perhaps in one universe I'm watching the ceiling fan go around for an hour and in another, it goes around for a day. In a third, it's been going around for a week. What universe am I in? What universe are you in? I don't know. Do you? All I know is that we cannot choose our own adventures. The stars fixed our fates at the moment of our births.

3

And now I'm hallucinating. I'm back in my house, in Indiana. It's a vivid hallucination. I see my dusty ceiling fan. I smell the stale laundry. I find great comfort in these sensations. There's no place like home.

Pardon me, I'm mistaken. Actually, there is *no home*.

What I mean is, even *hallucinatory* comforts are taken away from me. Just as quickly as I arrive home, the vision crumbles apart. I see a grid of square glass panes superimposed on the world. I hear them all shatter. It sounds a little like static. I'm no longer seeing a ceiling fan. I'm no longer smelling stale laundry. Reality has changed channels. I'm somewhere else. I smell a weird combination of vanilla, figs, and dandelions.

What I mean is, I'm smelling cheap perfume. It smells like my mother's purse. This is no coincidence. It's my mother's perfume.

Actually, it's my mother's perfume *and* my perfume. I'm back in the house where I grew up, in Maryland. Not Fort Meade,

Maryland, but the rural outskirts of Elkton. My mother will only allow me to use a certain type of perfume: the perfume she uses. Chantilly, I think it's called. It's marketed to middle-aged women.

I don't want to use perfume. Mom demands I use it. She's always rushing through the door unannounced, spraying that shit over me and my bed. "When you stop smelling, I'll stop spraying," she says. She mutters the words through clenched teeth.

I find it difficult to bathe. I don't like to see myself naked. Undressing is uncomfortable. Washing myself is uncomfortable. So, I smell. Getting out of bed is uncomfortable. Going to school is uncomfortable. So, quite often I pretend to be sick. I stay at home. I love my bed. That's where I feel safe.

I'm in bed now. I'm looking at a twelve-inch black and white television. It sits atop my bureau, flickering. It's the only light in my bedroom.

It's dusk, it's summertime. A thunderstorm has just cooled things down. Fireflies cling to my window screen. The breeze feels good wafting through the window. It smells fresh. Not at all like a middle-aged woman.

It's sometime in the late '80s. I'm watching a PBS miniseries called *The Power of Myth*. It features two men: Bill Moyers and Joseph Campbell. Their banter is empty, grand, and ridiculous. Campbell portrays himself as a well of knowledge. Moyers portrays himself as an eager student. They talk about the hero's journey and Jesus and Gilgamesh and Native American lore. They envy the Wisdom of the East. They roll their eyes at the Wisdom of the West. They want me to follow my bliss.

"What happens when you follow your bliss?" Moyers asks.

"You come to bliss," Campbell replies.

Moyers grins, as if he's on the receiving end of a particularly clever Zen koan.

I'm young and naive and want to think Campbell is wise, but in the back of my head I know it's all doubletalk. *My* bliss is to be left entirely alone. People at school never quite seem real. I think they may be humanikins. I want to avoid them. On the other hand, Mom seems all too real. I want her and Chantilly to go away. That would be my bliss.

But they don't go away. Mom is always checking on me, intruding, dumbing down my world, dousing me in Chantilly. If she knew I was watching Joseph Campbell she would scowl and say "You're *weird*." She wouldn't go away until I had changed the channel. Therefore, bliss is literally impossible. I know she can burst through the door at any moment.

I tried following my bliss once. Earlier that year, in the winter, I played hooky from school. Instead of catching the bus, I hid in the woods behind the house and pretended I was lost, without food. I pretended I was in the final stage of death by starvation.

The Dying Game had only one rule: I couldn't eat. In fact, I had to hide the bag lunch Mom had packed for me and pretend it didn't exist. I buried it under a pile of dried-up, frost-encrusted leaves. I buried myself under a separate pile of dried-up, frost-encrusted leaves. It was the happiest day of my life.

On the television, Campbell is talking about the concept of the Wheel of Fortune. The camera pans over a medieval drawing. It depicts Fortune as a blindfolded woman holding the Wheel. She must be a bodybuilder, because four men are grasping onto it like passengers on a no-frills Ferris wheel. The first has risen to the zenith of the Wheel. The second has fallen to its nadir. The third is industriously climbing up to replace the man at the zenith. The fourth is falling and will soon replace the man at the nadir.

The door knob wriggles. Mom bursts in, all out of breath. She looks at the TV, wrinkles her nose. "What's *that* you're watching?!" she asks.

I want to answer, but can't. I have an iron clamp over my beak. She looks over at me and shrieks. "What are you doing? What are you do—? What *are* you?" Then she howls, like she's some sort of wounded junkie. It's a scratchy, guttural wail. It scares me, and that's saying something. She's screamed at me all my life but I've never heard her go full tilt feral before. She's reaching for the bottle of Chantilly I'm forced to keep on my bureau, next to the TV. She's wielding it the way a frightened exorcist wields holy water.

The vision crumbles apart. I see a grid (this time, composed of *triangular* panes of glass) superimposed over the world. I hear the glass shatter. It sounds a lot like static. I'm no longer in that bedroom. I'm no longer smelling Chantilly. Reality has changed channels yet again. I smell…

4

…chimney smoke. The wind carries the scent into the woods, where I have buried myself in a pile of dried-up, frost-encrusted leaves. I'm playing The Dying Game. I'm playing hooky from school. I'm playing hooky from my captivity at Fort Meade, too.

Playing.

Playing.

Playing.

I seem to be an accidental time traveler. I didn't consciously make a decision to time travel, but my time travel abilities must have kicked in during these reminiscences. Subconsciously, I escaped. I could not escape, in three-dimensional space. So I escaped in time. I followed my bliss.

But bliss has its problems, too. The Dying Game is escapist fun, but like all diversions it lasts only so long. Eventually it becomes clear that it's The Dying *Game*, not actual death. No matter how still and stiff I make my body, I can't stop my mind. Dead people can't think, so any thought coursing through one's noodle makes a dent in the game's verisimilitude.

The best I can do is slow my thoughts down. I have refined a technique for doing so. The stampede of images that trample through my eyes distract me from the game, so I close them. When I do so, I'm no longer forced to consider the thousand tawdry objects in my immediate vicinity. (Chipmunks hopping through dry leaves, fleas hopping through chipmunk fur, etc.)

However, this little trick puts its own dent in the game's verisimilitude. Most corpses require the services of a mortician to close their eyes. (A fresh corpse has its eyes open.) So to play The Dying Game with closed eyes is cheating.

By now, you may have gathered that The Dying Game is quite difficult. True oblivion is always just out of reach. The best I can do is reach a state of pseudo-oblivion. (Ha! Pseudoblivion!)

And even that doesn't last long. Noise intrudes. A low-flying helicopter. I open my eyes. It's a black medevac helicopter. I know it's up to no good. Still, I admire its whirling blades. They're even prettier now than they were back in the year 2020, at The Zodiac Hotel.

2020 is the past, because I already experienced it. But it is also the future, because I'm playing hooky from school in the late '80s. The black helicopter existed in 2020 and also exists now. It looks better now than it did then. Before, its blades looked like the *ghosts* of blades as they whirled around. Now, as their blades whirl around, they shimmer with all the colors of the rainbow.

The helicopter is black but a rainbow encircles its blades.

I imagine Joseph Campbell lecturing me on the supposed symbolism of this moment. "The rainbow *encircles*. And what is a circle but the visual representation of a *cycle*? Struggle. Achievement. Decline. Fall. And then, once again, the renewed Struggle to rise up again. Youth. Adulthood. Old age. Death. And then, once again, Rebirth."

I imagine telling Campbell that I feel ambivalent, at best, about my original birth. (By which I mean, my human birth.) I imagine letting him know that this *rebirth* business, this "Nid Cold" business, this removal from my costume business, isn't any better.

But I must put away my imagination and report the latest news about the helicopter. It tilts forward. The circular rainbow dislodges itself from the blades. It descends. Rushes toward me. It's some kind of weapon. I try getting up, but I've still got the iron muzzle over my beak. This weighs me down. But I must try. I am a heroine and Joseph Campbell insists I take a journey. Giving up just won't do. So I force myself up onto my feet.

But I'm still hobbled by the ball and chain. I pick up the ball and make a go of it. The best I can do is take a few awkward, hunched-over steps. My wings get caught on branches and briars.

The circular rainbow gets closer. It stinks of sulfur. Sounds like a lovely waterfall. Existence equals nuance.

I try flapping my wings. I can't quite make them work. It takes muscle coordination to fly with wings. It requires the neck and the shoulders and the feathers to work together as a team. But my muscles aren't team players. Or, at least, they haven't yet *been taught* to be team players. An arthritic, one-winged turkey could fly faster than I can.

But I am the heroine. I can't give up.

So, I try levitating. This proves more effective. Levitation doesn't require muscular strength. It relies solely on the strength of *my mind*. My mental powers have been developing substantially. After all, the power to time travel came to me even though I'd made no effort to acquire it. So, being physically awkward will pose no barrier to my escape!

I levitate three feet off the ground and zoom toward the closest available shelter: Mom and Dad's garage. I make quick progress. I find that I can "fly", via levitation, at five times the speed I could achieve while running.

But the circular rainbow had a head start. The sulfur stench and sound of rushing water linger just behind my shoulder. There's a door that leads from the backyard to the garage. We live in the country. It's always unlocked. I grab the handle. Twist it open.

And then I hear a mechanical noise. An earthly noise. A whirring noise. The main garage door is opening. By this, I mean the door through which cars enter. And I see my father's gray Camry. It's afternoon. He's home from work. I look through the windshield. I see him.

Actually, that's mistaken. What I mean is, I *half*-see him. There's some glare on the windshield. He looks in my direction. He probably notices I'm staring at him. The best way to get the attention of a driver is to stare at them. Sooner or later, they'll notice you.

He wails. Bites his fist. Jogs out of the car. Grabs a rusty shovel. Swings it at me. Screams. "Demon, in the name of Jesus Christ I command thee begone!"

I can't plead my case. (The clamp, the beak, the lack of human vocal cords.)

And then the circular rainbow, the reeking rainbow, the rainbow that sounds like rushing water, catches up to me. It came in behind Dad's car. Wraps itself over my head. Travels down to my breasts. Carries me back off into the air.

The last thing I see is Dad falling to his knees. He's weeping and stuttering. "Th-thank you Lord J-Jesus."

I'm grateful to see him again, even if it is under such circumstances. I can't blame him for rejecting me. He didn't know it was me. He had never seen the real me before. What sort of reaction could I expect?

Besides, my father is a puppet and Jesus (perhaps the greatest of all puppeteers) pulled his strings. Made him wail and bite his fist and jog out of the car and grab the shovel and swing and scream and fall to his knees and pray.

Jesus. Giuseppe. Might they not be one and the same? Or, at the very least, two aspects of the same entity? The names are very similar.

I wonder if Dad will tell Mom about the "demon" in their garage. I wonder if he'll start renting himself out as an exorcist. I decide he'll probably do neither. He'll try to calm down and then go into the house and pretend it never happened. Maybe he'll read the Bible instead of the newspaper tonight. Maybe he'll listen to the local gospel station instead of the local country station. In time, he'll second guess himself. He'll lock the vision of the red-eyed, mist-riddled giant raven into a special compartment of his brain, the compartment in which every human locks their memories of anomalous events. He will never allow it to leave that compartment. He'll double down on Christian fundamentalism. Start going to church more often. His encounter with the anomalous will heighten his devotion to the conventional.

This is what I think about, as the circular rainbow lasso floats me toward the waiting helicopter. My parents' house is out in the country, so there's no one around to take photos of my re-capture. The helicopter doors slide open. The lasso and I float into it.

I retch from the smell of the sulfuric rainbow. The helicopter flings off into the sky, like a rubber band released by some little boy. Unlike a rubber band, though, it doesn't slow down and plop to the ground. It accelerates. Rattles. And then we're weightless. We're in orbit. The ball and chain do little to stabilize me. I still float all over the place. I throw up. My beak is still clamped shut. I'm choking.

One of the soldiers shouts at close range. "You're not getting off that easy." I must suffer even worse indignities before I'm allowed to die.

Apparently, there's a keypad on the side of my beak clamp. The soldier keys in the combination, releases it. I spit out purple bile, enough to make a small puddle. I float. My puke floats. We float in and out of each other. I look around, hoping to get some assistance. A towel, or something to wipe the puke out of my feathers. No luck. The soldiers are busy with other tasks. One of them pulls a lever labeled "Art Grav". We're no longer weightless. I plop onto the floor.

My head pounds. I curl into the fetal position. The helicopter seems to be going off in all directions at once now. Flickering red and blue lights enter through the windows. I wonder if it's the cops. (We're exceeding the speed limit.)

Of course, it's not the cops. There's no law and order to speak of. The helicopter is doing things no helicopter should be able to do. It must not really be a helicopter. I see nebulae and galaxies outside the windows, but they're all blue and red.

Sometimes they're half blue and half red. Sometimes they start as blue but end up as red.

Then, I stop seeing nebulae and galaxies. I start seeing pentagrams. Yes, sloppily drawn pentagrams, gigantic pentagrams, innumerable pentagrams glowing and floating out in space.

This isn't a helicopter. It's a spaceship. Or a dimensional ship. But everything is still labeled "Property of D.o.D." Department of Defense? If so, how did our government obtain such technology? Are they in cahoots with the Homerealm? That might explain why the N.S.A. double-crossed the Kippleodians. For all I know, the United States has already become a fully owned subsidiary of the Interdim Quatros Corporation. That would explain a lot.

But it wouldn't explain everything. Why does this rainbow make a sound like rushing water? Why does it stink like sulphur? Joseph Campbell might know the reason, if he were here. Or, at the very least, he would make up a reason that would sound reasonable.

"The rainbow sounds like rushing water because water is the realm of the spirit," Campbell would say. "In the first chapter of Genesis, we read of the Spirit of God hovering over the dark, primordial waters of the void. Water, in this sense, is associated with creation. Later on in Genesis, we read of the Lord God using water to judge humanity. Judgment! Brimstone! But then, after the destruction, what does God offer humanity? The rainbow! A truce! 'Never again will I use water to destroy the Earth.' So, you see, this foul-smelling rushing-water rainbow lasso indicates that Nid Cold has been *created* (or rather, with her removal from her human costume, *re*-created), but still faces the certainty of imminent damnation. Yet, at the same time, she can rest assured that she will *survive* her damnation, as Noah did in the flood. And as Utnapishtim did before him, in *The Epic of Gilgamesh.*"

But Joseph Campbell is dead, and I haven't yet run into his ghost. If I ever do, I'll read him the riot act. I'll tell him life is not as simple as he says it is. Sometimes a stinking rainbow that sounds like rushing water is just a stinking rainbow that sounds like rushing water. Sometimes, symbolism is forced.

But that won't help. He'll smile that sweet, mountebank smile of his and tell me to go follow my bliss. And what can you say in response to that? Nothing!

I could try to peck out his eyes with my beak. That's the daydream going through my head right now. I imagine traveling back through time and crashing the party at the Campbell/Moyers interview. Flying through the window, shattering glass, seizing my prey.

In fact, if time travel works the way it has before, I should already be in that room. I have time traveled simply by thought-traveling. Why, then, am I not time traveling? Perhaps the lasso is at fault. Yes, it makes sense. The ball and chain around my leg is there to prevent my escape via physical space. The rainbow lasso is there to prevent an escape through time.

And so my daydream falls apart.

And *my world* falls apart, by which I mean that I'm hit by yet another wave of cognitive entropy. By which I mean, the phrases drift apart from one another. Words and letters devolve even as I try to reassemble them in my head.

Cognitive entropy becomes *Cog nippy.*

Words and letters devolve become *World Off.*

And *then* (as if matters weren't bad enough), they devolve one more time. They can no longer even pretend to be words.

Cog nippy becomes *cah puh. World off* becomes *woof.* The arc of consciousness is long but bends toward nonsense, and more nonsense, and nonsense-squared.

5

When I come to, I'm stumbling. The ball and chain has been removed from my ankle, but I'm stumbling. I'm indoors. The floor is perfectly flat. There are no curbs to make me trip. No uneven sidewalks. But I'm stumbling.

I'm stumbling away from a corpse. Yes, I'm stumbling and I'm wailing. Dry heaving, too. The room stinks of the sulfuric rainbow. The room stinks of corpse rot. The room stinks, and stinks, and stinks. I am stumbling through the stink.

The corpse is on a slab. I'm in a morgue, and I'm stumbling away from the slab. The slab is gray and the room is gray and the floor is gray linoleum tile, like a cheap kitchen floor. The walls are padded. That is, padded and gray.

I'm not in a morgue. Or, at least, this room isn't *just* a morgue. It's also a padded cell. Yes, it's a padded cell with a cheap kitchen floor. The room is a unique combination of kitchen, morgue, and padded cell.

I'm wailing because there's something wrong with the corpse. The center of her body is missing. Her belly and loins have been removed. She's me. Or, rather, she's my costume. I think she's been here for a few days. Her face looks wrong. Her mouth shouldn't be drooping open. Her eyes shouldn't be gray and glassy and unfocused. She shouldn't smell bad.

I mean, there definitely have been days when I've smelled bad. When *she* has smelled bad, that is. But the smell of body odor isn't quite the same as the smell of post-mortem decay, right?

Truth be told, the *stink* (of the corpse) reminds me of my *sink* (in my kitchen, back home in Indiana.) Sometimes the dishes go unwashed for weeks. When the guilt and shame finally become unbearable, I'll lift my heavy head off my pillow and wash them. About halfway through the pile I get to the ones that have been submerged beneath the dishwater, and I gag from the stink of mold and decay.

In fact, the memory of my unwashed dishes is so intense that it should set off an excursion through time. I should be back home in Indiana, in my kitchen, lifting up the first of the dishes submerged beneath the dishwater. But I can't.

Why not? Well, there's a rainbow-colored ankle bracelet locked onto my lower leg. It must serve the same purpose as the rainbow-colored lasso from the helicopter. They took off the physical ball and chain and put on its time travel equivalent.

And while I'm on the subject of changes, my beak is no longer clamped down. I can move my head around without fighting the weight of the iron. But, as with the ball and chain, there's more to the story: I no longer seem *to have* a beak. I still have feathers. I still have my de-taloned bird claws. But that long, black raven beak? MIA.

I put my claws out in front of my face, just to make sure I'm right.

I'm right.

Confirmation of my assessment comes from a voice. Not a telepathic voice, in my head. An actual voice, coming out of speakers in the ceiling. A young man's voice. He speaks slowly, robotically. He seems to be reading a script. "Fear not! Your beak was a vestigial organ. Your species actually feeds on wind, not food. So a beak is not necessary for you to eat. It was only useful to you as a weapon."

I suppose that explains why I've always loved ceiling fans. I grazed on their wind. It may also explain why someone (codename: Giuseppe the Puppeteer) manipulated trees to make it seem like the night was a windy one. For some reason, they wanted to keep me outside.

But I can't dwell on the beginning of my journey. I must focus on my present dilemma. I have no talons. I have no beak. I have no ability to time travel. I still have my wings, but it takes a lot of work to stay aloft with them and the results are less than impressive.

All I can really do is levitate. I know, it sounds silly to dismiss the power of levitation. If—at the beginning of my journey, while I was admiring the cover of *Myth and Reality*—I had suddenly started to levitate, my life would have been upended. I would have been awestruck and fearful. I would have doubted my own sanity.

But now, levitation seems trivial. It does little to keep me safe and it's not particularly weird, in the context of all my other experiences.

Speaking of weird experiences, a motor starts to whir beneath the linoleum tile. About five feet away, a trap door opens. Something huge and mechanical rises up from the floor. It reminds me of one of those old mainframe computers from the '60s, a massive hulk of a machine. About ten feet long, four feet high, and three feet deep.

The mainframe has no gauges, no wires, no power cord, no keyboard, no punch cards, nor any slot in which one could insert a punch card. It is, however, adorned with seven circular buttons. Each emits a pale yellow light. Someone has used a magic marker to label the buttons 1-7, from left to right. The same magic marker was apparently used to scrawl "Property of D.o.D." on the machine's side.

The speakers in the ceiling crackle back to life. The young, slow, robotic male voice speaks again. "You have seen your former body on the slab. Or, at least, the parts that weren't already removed by the Homerealmers. Do you miss living in this human body? Press the button marked '1' to indicate that you don't miss it, because you see yourself first and foremost as a Homerealmer. Press the button marked '7' to indicate that you yearn, unceasingly, to return to it, because you see yourself first and foremost as a human. Press the button marked '4' if you feel ambivalent on the matter. Use the buttons in between these options to indicate nuanced feelings. For example, if you feel ambivalent, but lean ever so slightly toward seeing yourself as a Homerealmer, press 3."

The government wants to interrogate me. This isn't a surprise. I am, however, taken aback by their question. It's an odd starting point. No, on second thought, it's not so odd. They don't really care about how I see myself. How I "identify", as the kids say these days. They merely want to know where my sympathies lie. They want to know which side I'm on.

At least, that's what I *think* they want to know.

If I were being held captive by Homerealmers, I would press 1. But since I'm being held captive by humans I press 7. I tell them what they want to hear. Or, at least, what I *think* they want to hear.

A voice comes out of the speakers, but it's not the young voice I heard earlier. This time, the voice is that of an old man. "Very interesting answer. Now, let's put it to the test."

I hear a motor whirring behind me. Turning around, I see a row of three trap doors opening in the linoleum. From each one, there arises a structure. Each is about the size of a phone booth. Each is shrouded in a tarp.

Then, another motor starts whirring. This time, the noise is overhead. Part of the ceiling slides away. A metal claw descends from the hole. It reminds me of the claw you see in those bamboozling arcade games; the ones in which you try to grab a stuffed animal. It removes the tarp from the structure on the left, revealing not a phone booth, but a phone booth-sized cage. That is, a cage large enough to hold a man.

Only it doesn't hold a man. It holds a domestic turkey.

The turkey, as it turns out, has been sleeping. The sudden intrusion of light startles him awake. He's squawking and pacing and utterly freaked out. He's able to poke his neck through the bars, and he's too stupid to understand why his body can't follow. He keeps trying to squeeze through the tight opening.

The turkey's gobbling is drowned out by more whirring. Another section of ceiling slides away. Another claw descends, this time from above the middle structure. Descending, descending, then lifting the tarp, the veil. The revelation proves disturbing.

It's another cage big enough for a man, and this one actually holds a man; an emaciated, *naked* man, to be precise—a disgusting collage of knobby joints, body hair, veiny feet, pendulous balls, inchworm cock, protruding ribs, chapped lips and missing teeth.

I take him for a junky. He has that ageless quality some junkies possess. I can't tell if he's fifty years old or thirty-five and prematurely aged by hard living. He's mumbling and pacing and utterly freaked out. He points at me and laughs to himself. "So there's two of you now, eh? Fuckin' night-gaunts is what y'are. Gonna take me away to the Ghooric Zone are you?"

Over the speaker, I hear the old man chuckling. "He used to be an English teacher. He read too much Lovecraft while under the influence of crack. He came to believe the gentleman from Providence was a true seer. Hilarity ensued!"

"His tombstone proves it!" the naked man shrieks. "'I am Providence' is a pun, meant to imply that he was an instrument of divine will. Yanno? Like, God allowed him to suffer at the hands of the night-gaunts so that he could warn the rest of us about your kind!"

If memory serves me right, Lovecraft had recurrent nightmares of being abducted by hideous winged monsters called night-gaunts. I can understand why the naked man would draw a comparison between those dream creatures and real entities such as myself and S'indrid.

Over the speaker, the old man again. "The police found the erstwhile teacher in this condition, wandering around a junkyard in Pawtucket."

"Because aliens *like junk!*" the naked man says. "They feel most comfortable residing among clutter. John Keel says so in *The Mothman Prophecies.* So if I was gonna let them have it, where else was I supposed to find them?"

I find comfort in this aspect of the naked man's ravings. Maybe I had no choice but to let my house go. The filth, the clutter, are my birthright!

"Mr. Keel wrote a highly interesting book," the old man voice says, "about which there is much to discuss. But not with you, wild man. Let's move on to the guest of honor, the occupant of cage number three."

Even before the third claw finishes its descent from the ceiling, I know the guest of honor is my long-lost brother S'indrid Cold.

As soon as I see him, I wish I'd never seen him. There's something wrong with his globby red eyes. They appear less tethered to their sockets than they should be. The liquid actually oozes out a little. Or, maybe he's crying red tears. It's hard to tell. He has his eyes partially tucked under his right wing.

His left wing veers away from his breast at an unnatural angle. His feathers are tattered. The fog emanating from the holes in his belly looks more like dust than fog. He wears a ball and chain on one leg, and a rainbow ankle bracelet on the other. He's bent over, hobbled. I can't see everything, but I'm pretty sure they sawed his beak off too. Just like they sawed off mine.

The old man on the intercom giggles. "S'indrid, meet your sister. Nid, meet your brother."

How do I know, for sure, this is S'indrid? How do I know it's not some other Mothman, completely unrelated to me? Because he inserts an indignant thought into my head, that's why! *No, I don't want to mate with you. What a hideous greeting! Our father is even more wicked than I thought, if he has raised you with a taste for incest!*

I try to answer him back with telepathy. After all, I've acquired the powers of levitation and time travel. I might be able to use telepathy, if I try. But it doesn't work. I want to say: *I really don't want to sleep with you*, but my telepathic voice comes out as quiet, infantile babbles. *Ree ree doe won!* The worm in my brain is louder than any telepathic message I can muster.

I wonder if The Producer is somewhere around here. I make up a little story, in which he's watching this scene unfurl. I pretend he can hear the telepathic chatter between me and S'indrid. I pretend he's laughing at the misunderstanding. To him, my life from here on out will be one long sex farce. Like an episode of *Three's Company*, the humor will stem from misunderstanding.

And now, another whirring sound starts up. Another portion of the ceiling slides away. Down comes a soldier in a glass booth. There's a hole in the booth, through which he sticks a pistol. The booth is positioned in such a way that the soldier can shoot any of the three prisoners. He could even shoot me, if he wanted to. It's weird, seeing him up there. He looks like a ball turret gunner in a World War II bomber. He looks like a hunter in a deer stand. He looks like neither and both. He is his own creature.

The speaker crackles. I hear the old man again. "In one min-ute the soldier will shoot one of these three targets. You get to decide which one dies. Press 1 if you would like for him to kill the turkey. Press 4 if you would like him to kill the human. Press 7 if you would like for him to kill the Mothman. Please do this now."

So they want to put my loyalty to the test. They want to assess how much I value the life of a bird vs. the life of a man vs. the life of a birdman. The answer seems obvious. I press 1. The soldier's pistol sounds like a firecracker mixed with a dog growl. He's a skilled marksman, that's for sure. Shooting a caged turkey might not seem like an accomplishment, but it takes some skill to get the bullet to sail in between the steel bars. The turkey lets out a shrill, high-pitched squawk. Its guts spill out onto the linoleum. Its head keeps thumping against the bars as its nerves misfire. It looks every bit as confused in death as it did in life.

"Very good," the old man says. "Decisive, and you don't seem at all squeamish about the results. I believe you'll find the next round more challenging. In thirty seconds, the soldier will kill one of the remaining targets. Press 4 if you would like him to kill the human. Press 7 if you would like him to kill the Mothman. And, just to be clear, if you do not make a selec-tion, the soldier will kill them both."

S'indrid still thinks I'm lusting after him. He inserts the following thoughts in my head: *Stop it! Stop thinking those thoughts! I won't. Never, ever. Not even to save my life!*

I don't like being lectured for having thoughts that aren't even mine. Is that why I press 7? In one universe it is. But am I living in that universe? Maybe I press 7 because S'indrid looks old and/or sick and/or tortured, and I want to end his suffering. Maybe I press 7 because the crackhead's ugliness is easier to bear than S'indrid's ugliness. Maybe I press 7 because I want to impress my captors. Maybe I press 7 because it has always been my destiny to do so. In reality, the decision isn't made with any logical consideration of pros and cons. I make it for no particular reason. I make it because it feels right, at that moment.

I press 7 because I press 7.

From the speaker: "Marksman, please switch to the pistol with silver bullets."

The soldier puts his regular pistol back into his hip holster. Then he fetches another from his thigh holster. I don't want to be in the room during the shooting. I don't want to see another death, hear another shot, or smell more gunpowder. What I want never matters.

The deed is done in three shots. The first one catches S'indrid in his chest. He stumbles backward. His blood (an oily black and green mess) gushes forward. The second shot catches him right between his eyes, blowing up his skull. The third blows up his neck. His death throes look a lot like the turkey's. The only difference is that the turkey's *head* is thumping against the bars, but in my brother's case it's his *legs*. S'indrid doesn't have a head anymore.

6

After the ordeal in the kitchen/morgue/padded cell/shooting gallery, a trap door opens below my feet. I plunge into the bowels of Fort Meade. A giant inflatable cushion breaks my fall. The cushion is garishly adorned to resemble the American flag. It looks like a giant air mattress pilfered from a redneck orgy.

Soldiers grab me off the cushion and escort me to a conference room. It doesn't look like a legitimate conference room. What I mean is, it doesn't have a solid oak conference table. There are no screens or power point projectors. It is, in fact, tiny. A rickety card table sits in the middle. A cheap vinyl tablecloth has been draped over it. The tablecloth is adorned with images of red and white firecrackers against a blue sky. It's the sort of thing you'd buy at a dollar store for a Fourth of July picnic.

The Producer sits at the table. His name badge no longer says Nevada Studio Alliance. It says National Security Agency. There's no sign of his scooter or even a walker. I suppose that was all part of his disguise. He invites me to sit in a chair, but that doesn't look comfortable for my wings. Instead I sit on the floor, legs crossed at the ankles, and levitate until we're eye to eye.

"I was not what I appeared to be," he says. "But then again, neither were you. And so here we sit, two entities who were not what we seemed to be, now revealed for what they really are. Or, at least, *beginning* to be revealed for what we really are. There's more revealing to be done, I think you'll agree. And since you've just proven yourself loyal to humanity, there's no better time for the revealing, don't you think?"

I nod.

"Good. So, as you may have guessed I'm not really friends with David Lynch. But I *am* friends with an even greater celebrity." He reaches underneath the tablecloth and pulls out a close-up photo of the orange toad. It's his official photo, the one in which he's trying to look stern and intimidating.

"This might surprise you, but Donald is fascinated by cryptozoology in general and the Mothman in particular. He has to be careful not to talk about it too much, because some of the fundamentalists think your kind are demonic! Nevertheless, he *does* talk about it. Hell, last year he even tweeted about it! I mean, at a certain point, fuck the fundamentalists. Am I right?"

I nod.

"Exactly. They'll believe what he tells them to believe. He's gotten them to admire Ayn Rand, and she was an outright atheist! If he says cryptids are just a natural part of God's creation, they'll go along. I mean, last year, when he quoted Joe Manchin's tweet about the West Virginia Mothman Festival, and said "I go along with Joe!" neither Manchin nor Donald suffered for it. That was his way of tipping his hand, you see, letting on to donors that he was adept in consorting with gods and monsters. Many donors dabble in the occult, you know. So they admire Donald's alliances in that realm. Not to take anything away from the Navy SEALs, but creatures like you, Nid, well you're the *real* special forces.

"With that in mind, we here at the N.S.A. would like to reach an understanding with you. We'd like to forge a mutually beneficial relationship. You see, we're working with the Homerealmers. They're a powerful race, and we'd rather be with them than against them. However, we must proceed carefully. We don't want an Operation Barbarossa on our hands. Stalin was wrong to trust Hitler, and the United States, our home*land*, cannot trust the Home*realm* to act like a good ally. I'm not sure how much you've learned about their technology, but we know they possess a weapon that could destroy the Earth. We're outgunned. We need leverage. Something—or some*one*—the Homerealm values. Something—or some*one*—that will make them think twice before doublecrossing us.

"For over fifty years, your brother filled that role. We had a plan: if our intelligence sources ever got wind of a betrayal in the making, we'd send word to the Homerealmers that we had Indrid Cold's son in our custody, and that would lower the temperature. It would make them amenable to brokering a deal. You might be tempted to think S'indrid was being held hostage. But in reality he wasn't a hostage. He was, rather, *an instrument of peace*. Wouldn't you agree?"

Of course, he wasn't an "instrument of peace". He was a hostage. But I see where all this is going. Now isn't the time to raise objections. I nod.

"Good, we're on the same page. They say the key to every successful relationship is good communication, and I suppose our relationship (our patriotic, business relationship I mean) is no different. Don't you agree that open, honest communication is key?"

I nod.

"Excellent! You're so much more agreeable than your brother. But then again, his loyalties were never as clear cut as yours. For example, can you believe he refused to answer a question that came directly from Donald? I mean, can you imagine the nerve? The ingratitude? The United States provided for his every need, and yet he couldn't answer one little question. But you'll be more helpful, won't you?"

I don't want to nod, but I nod.

"Great! Now, I suppose I should preface this next question with some background information. You see, Donald is a very busy man. He's a big picture kind of guy. He has underlings who take care of all the details. So, while he's certainly the world's most knowledgeable expert on the paranormal, he's a *big picture* sort of expert.

"Case in point: although he's fascinated by the Mothman case, he's...well, I'm sure you'll understand the workload of the leader of the free world. What I mean is, he's never actually watched *The Mothman Prophecies* all the way through." The Producer giggles and twiddles his thumbs. "Nor has he read the book. Mostly, he just likes the title. He likes the idea of a creature who can tell the future.

"Now, in the book and the movie, the Mothman, himself, never tells the future. In the book and the movie, Indrid Cold is the one who does that. He calls John Keel with all sorts of prophecies, a fair number of which turn out to be false. But, because Donald has only seen the first ten minutes or so of the film, he doesn't know that. He thinks the Mothman can tell the future.

"Next Tuesday is a very important day for Donald. And, of course, he's quite anxious to tap any and all prophetic resources to determine the outcome of this election. He has the Christian prophets working overtime, and the answers they've given him are encouraging. However, he's afraid they're just telling him what he wants to hear. So one day he summoned me down to Mar-a-Lago. As we were golfing, I could tell he had something on his mind. He wasn't his usual, cheery self.

"So I asked him what was the matter, and you know what he said to me? He said: 'Do you want to know what my greatest fear is?'

"And I said, 'Donald, I cannot imagine you being afraid of anything. Fear is too strong a word. But if I can help you feel less alone with the weight of your duties, and give you a listening ear so you can share your *concerns*, I would feel honored beyond all measure.'

"And Donald had just the slightest trace of a tear in his eye, and he said to me, 'I love America so much, and my greatest fear is that she might not love me back. Go ask the Mothman: will I win reelection? Ask him if I'll win in a landslide. Ask him if fraud might prevent me from my rightful second term.

There's so much work left to be done to keep America great."

I can see where this is going.

"Here was a dear, sweet old gentleman, just asking for a favor. And your brother refused! First, he wouldn't acknowledge the question at all. Then, he answered but gave the wrong answer. He was more than obstinate. He was violent. Of course, we couldn't allow that. So, we had to teach him a lesson."

Yes, of course, a lesson spelled t-o-r-t-u-r-e. My father was wrong about S'indrid. He wasn't mad. He was noble. Too noble. He lived a noble life and died like a turkey.

"Of course, I could have fibbed and told Donald that S'indrid had given the correct answer, but it's not that easy. Donald wanted a video recording of the prophecy.

"Thankfully, you were just waiting in the wings! (No pun intended.) You, someone who lived in Indiana, the home of our wonderful Vice President Pence. Yes, we suspected you would be a good team player and answer Donald's question. However, we had to be certain. That's why we gave you the loyalty test.

"But enough chit-chat. Why don't we just go ahead and record your prophecy now? That way, we can lead you to your room and let you get some rest. There's a ceiling fan in there, and a couple of box fans, too. I understand you find wind refreshing."

I nod.

The Producer reaches under the card table. Pulls out a small digital camera and tripod. "Now, Donald probably wants to think of you as the Mothman, not the Mothwoman. After all, the movie was called *The Moth*man *Prophecies*. No one has ever heard of a Moth*woman*. Besides, the only visible difference between you and your brother is that he is, er, I mean *was* just a hair bigger than you. So, when we shoot this, you don't mind if I call you 'the Mothman', right?"

I shake my head.

The Producer grimaces. "No, you don't mind or no, you don't want to be called 'The Mothman'? Knock on the table once, if you mean you don't mind being called a male, and twice if you do mind."

I knock once.

The Producer heaves a sigh of relief. Smiles. "Oh boy! Good! So as soon as I finish setting this up we'll get started! I know you've been through a lot today, but if you're as much of a trooper as I think you are, you'll nail it in one take!"

As The Producer readies his camera, I realize I've reached the zenith of emptiness (I mean none of what I say). I've reached the zenith of ridiculousness (the President of the United States wants the Mothman's election prediction). I've reached the zenith of grandeur. (I've been thrust into an historical moment!)

The Producer yells "Action!" I look into the camera, see the ominous red light. We're recording.

"This is N.S.A. Tape Q4723309WDHGZNG. Interview with the Mothman. Subject: 2020 Presidential Election. Because the Mothman lacks the ability to speak, he will respond to my questions as follows: one knock on the table will indicate a 'yes', and two knocks will indicate a 'no'.

"So, without any further ado, let's get started in earnest. First, I'd like you to confirm your identity. You are, indeed, the Mothman? Not just *a* Mothman, but *the* very same Mothman who appeared in Point Pleasant, West Virginia in 1966, and whose story was dramatized in a major motion picture starring Richard Gere?"

I knock once.

"Good. And as you peer into the future, do you see President Donald Trump defeating the socialist, Joe Biden?"

Part of me wants to be mischievous and knock twice. But the room with fans sounds too good to pass up. So, I knock once.

"Will it be a landslide?"

This time, I pause before answering. I put my right wing up to my forehead, as if I'm using the powers of my mind to suss out the truth. I hold the posture for thirty seconds, then give the card table a good hard knock.

"And if it appears, for a time, that the president has lost, will that be a false result?"

To mix things up, I knock quickly. I want to make the impression that the answer is so clear it takes no time to see it.

"I see. And will that false result be due to massive voter fraud?"

Time to pause again. I give the camera a thousand yard stare, as though I'm looking beyond the camera, into eternity, for the answer. Then I knock once.

"Thank you, that concludes the interview."

The red light turns off. The Producer grins. "What a good girl you are! You catch on quick." He winks. "Now, if you'll excuse me, I need to prepare this little movie for a private screening at the White House. We may need to do another such video soon. Heavy is the head that wears the crown. Our leader needs reassurance, from time to time. But that will be all I need from you for now. The soldiers will show you to your quarters."

I have betrayed my brother. I have betrayed my country. By aligning myself with humans, I have betrayed my *species*. And for what? A room not all that different from the one I had in college. The N.S.A. prison looks like a dormitory.

I even have a neighbor. The naked Lovecraftian crackhead lives right next door. He still hasn't put on clothes. The soldiers don't seem in any particular hurry to get clothes on him. Perhaps he always walks around naked.

He stops me right before I open the door to my new digs. Chats me up. Seems nervous.

"I must say, little lady, I had you all wrong. You're no night-gaunt! Why you're a sweet little nightin*gale* who thought enough of me to save my life when it would've been easier to save your brother's. I don't care how you look, I know you're a human, a human *woman* deep down inside. I'm real grateful, um, young lady." He puts his hand on my shoulder. Squeezes it. Traces his finger over it and up my neck.

I try to ignore him, as I've tried to ignore all the other creepy dudes I've encountered in my life. I lie down on the bed and watch the ceiling fan, hoping it will calm me down. It doesn't. I know I'll have to watch that crackhead. I know better than to think he's genuinely attracted to me. They're putting him up to it. They want us to…

I leap up from bed to lock the door.

The door has no lock.

About the Author

Nicole Cushing is the Bram Stoker Award®-winning author of *Mr. Suicide* and a two-time nominee for the Shirley Jackson Award.

Various reviewers have described her work as "brutal," "cerebral," "transgressive," "taboo," "groundbreaking," and "mind-bending."

Rue Morgue magazine recently included Nicole in its list of 13 Wicked Women to Watch, praising her as "an intense and uncompromising literary voice." She has also garnered praise from Jack Ketchum, Thomas Ligotti, and Poppy Z. Brite (aka, Billy Martin).

Nicole lives and works in Indiana.